# *PRELUDE*
# *TO*
# *STARS*

by
G. David Nordley

# PRELUDE
# TO
# STARS

*Brief Candle*
Press

Previous versions of these stories were originally published as follows:
"Burdens" *Artemis*, January 2001
"The Fire and the Wind" *Analog Science Fiction/Science Fact*, July/August 2003
"Out of the Quiet Years" *Asimov's Science Fiction Magazine*, October 2004
"Alice's Asteroid," *Asimov's Science Fiction Magazine*, October 2005
"Mustardseed," *Asimov's Science Fiction Magazine*, August 1999
"Haumea" *Extreme Planets* (anthology), February 2014
"The Protean Solution," *Tomorrow*, June 1994
"This Old Rock," *Analog Science Fiction/Science Fact*, April 1997

All other material is original to this work and is printed with perssion of the author and publisher.

Cover design: Brief Candle Press

First Brief Candle Press edition published 2015
www.briefcandlepress.com

ISBN: 978-1-942319-08-5

# DEDICATION

To Dr. Sherman W. Schultz (1922-2012)
Who gave to Macalester College students throughout the latter half of the 20th Century the gift of reaching for the reachable stars.

# ACKNOWLEDGEMENTS

My thanks to members of the Whensday People writers group, for their gift of time as first readers of many of these stories. Thanks also go to editors Gardner Dozois, Sheila Williams, Stan Schmidt, Algis Budrys, and David Conyers, David Kernot, and Jeff Harris for purchasing these stories originally. Thanks especially to Deb Houdek Rule for getting started the project of making my backlist available in print and electronic format.

# PREFACE

**P**relude to Stars covers my stories that take place within the solar system with the exceptions of the Hartigan O'Reilly mysteries, the Mars stories and the Venus stories. I hope to add another novella to the O'Reilly tales and have them published as a separate book. I have something similar in mind for the Venus Terraforming stories. The Mars Stories are already in *After the Vikings*.

Many years ago now, I wrote a lunar independence novel, which has yet to find a publisher, and featured the career of Sally Duluth, a weight-lifting, lunar-born flight attendant on the Earth-Moon passenger run who rises to the captaincy of her spacecraft during the turmoil of the independence struggle and plays a key role in the resolution. You'll meet her here in *Burdens*, and briefly in *The Fire and the Wind*, and *Haumea*.

Sally is the base character of the common background into which, more or less, these stories fit (sometimes with a bit of a retcon shoehorn). They mostly take place in the latter half of the 21st century as space transportation technology develops from chemical rockets and mass-drivers to high-power electric propulsion and finally the mass-beam riders that presage interstellar exploration. They range from the Earth and Moon out to Haumea, the next dwarf planet beyond Pluto.

Following the stories are "Story Notes" with some background information on each story.

G. David Nordley, Feb. 2015

# TABLE OF CONTENTS

# BURDENS

Emilio Fuentes looked at his orange juice in disgust. No doubt excellent juice, it was less appetizing for his wishing he could have something else in it—but with competition this weekend, he knew better than that. Bran muffins, juice, and cold, lean rump would have to do. There could be no letting up until after the Olympics.

His concentration on his innards was broken by a crash at a nearby table. A short, chunky Anglo woman with short blond hair and a big chest had made a fool of herself by falling off a chair. She looked vaguely familiar as she tottered to her feet, making apologies. With Latin gallantry he got up to assist her, and she gratefully took his hand.

Which was when he got the first of what were to be many surprises. It was not the hand of a woman as he knew them; it was large, its fingers were strong and thick with muscle; it felt much like his own. Perhaps, he thought, she was used to walking on crutches or using a wheelchair—that would explain her strength and unsteadiness.

"Thanks," she told him, as he helped her unsteadily to her chair. "I'm new here and afraid I'm not very used to this." A very bad case of jet lag, then?

A discreet glance down the neck of her loose blouse revealed both less and more than expected there as well. A suspicion dawned.

"It is nothing, *señorita*. I have just come to the Orkneys myself, for the weight lifting open. My name is Emilio Fuentes."

"The Argentine farmer who became the South American 52-60 champion! What good fortune to meet you." He found his hand in a grip of iron, confirming his suspicions. He winced, not so much from the grip but from the politically correct title of his weight lifting class; it signified men who weighed 52 kilos were in open competition with women who weighed 60. Yes, the numbers were a rough match, but, but . . . even in his own mind he could not find words for the sense of humiliation and frustration with this ill-considered experiment of the Olympic gods.

"Oh!" she noticed. "Sorry. I keep saying sorry today. I'm Sally Duluth. From Coriolis. Farside . . . "

"I know. The Moon woman." He held back another groan; what did politeness cost? Her inclusion in the trials was a travesty, a circus, a sideshow in what he and others had struggled to bring weight lifting back from its reputation for stealth drugs and gene doping to the status of sport. But she should not share the burden of her exploitation, and, for all he knew, on her planet, among her own sex, she was a perfectly respectable lifter.

Perhaps he could talk her out of trying it here. "Would you join me, señorita? An orange juice perhaps?"

"But yes, I'd be honored. This is very good luck, running into someone so soon." She hesitated, however, eyeing the distance between the two tables.

Emilio smiled. "Perhaps I should join you?"

"No. I'll do it . . . Maybe with a little help?" She did have a very winning smile.

"My pleasure." He got up and offered his hand to assist her to his table.

"They forgot to turn on the acceleration warning sign on this spaceship," she joked.

He laughed.

They talked shop for a while and he found out that she was a serious lifter, but still an amateur, on a leave of absence from a job, of all things, as a purser on a lunar ferry. So she didn't even have lunar gravity to work against, most of the time!

And she was totally ignorant of the culture of terrestrial lifting, who could do what and so forth, knowing only what was on the sports pages. He ingratiated himself by displaying his knowledge, thinking it could do no harm.

She took him to another world. Her parents were French and *Canadienne* and operated a restaurant at the maglev spacecraft terminal at Coriolis, Farside. Her name, she explained, had come by the way of the St. Lawrence Seaway; her patronymic grandfather had been found a century ago on a hospital doorstep in Duluth, Minnesota, and as an adult had chosen that name over that of one of several foster families.

He'd been a merchant seaman, engineer, and ended up in Montreal after a stint as master of an ore freighter. Her mother's family was from Carcassonne, for as long as the records went back. They had gone to Luna as engineers on the maglev launch ramp project and, in the face of considerable criticism, had decided to start a family right there; Sally was only the eighth person to have been born on the Moon.

Emilio, himself, had been born on a farm west of Sarmiento, south of Lago Musters to a family that traced its roots to Catalunya. People tended to focus on the farm, forgetting his sometime civil engineering career. " . . . so my family came not so far from Carcassonne; perhaps we are related?"

That broke the ice. They chatted for about an hour in a futile search for common ancestors, but it finally came time to face the issue. No doubt she was the best they had on the Moon or she wouldn't be here, but . . . "*Señorita*, forgive me, but you are a woman, training in low gravity—if even that. You are here on Earth to challenge the best on this world in an Olympic games tune up, and you cannot even lift your *own* weight in this gravity! If I did not see you here before me, I would think it incredible."

She sighed. "Doesn't seem like such a good idea right now, does it?" Then she looked him in the eye, not a woman at all. "Have you ever seen anyone in our class snatch half a metric ton?"

"Hah," he snorted and tried to do the math in his head. "That's about eighty kilos here. You'll need to do that just to get in the competition." But the way she looked . . . "You think you can do that?"

She nodded, cold-eyed.

Emilio knew that look of determination and began to wonder. He shook his head; from the Moon or not, she was probably as good a bluffer as any of them. At this level it was half psychology. There would be no talking her out of this. A few more pleasantries and he said goodbye.

★ ✵ ★

Come the weekend, in dreary, pelting October skies, Emilio visited the ancient cathedral in Kirkwall, its dark, heavy stone vault and massive leaning red stone pillars a remnant of the days when Christianity was still more or less unified. Its Gothic and baroque elaborations of architecture and theology came later; remarkable edifices, both—and both clearly inventions. He thought of human beings spreading to other worlds, natural and artificial, each with their own gravity, their own atmospheres, and their own ways of being strong. Let it go, he thought. Why try to make the branches of the tree of humanity grow back into it trunk?

Yet we retain common themes, he thought. The cathedral with its long crypt-lined hall was a marvel of a then-modern age compared to the perfectly intact five-thousand-year-old earth-covered stone room that he had visited earlier that day, built on essentially the same plan. The Olympics themselves were to that cairn as we are to Caesar, he thought.

Kirkwall was a good place, he reflected, to contemplate ancientness, to get in touch with what the Olympic games meant, and to remotivate himself. Four hours before he would strive to send his iron weights toward the heavens, he sent his prayers before them as he did light isometric exercises, quietly testing one set of muscles against another.

It was the dark of boreal evening when he left the cathedral. As he told his rental Ford to unlock itself, he happened to look up at the ruined bishop's palace, with its ancient arches struggling to hold themselves up against eternity. Below them was Duluth, standing without apparent difficulty by her car, looking southeast. The full moon was rising beneath the clouds. She happened to look his way and caught his eye. He smiled and waved as he got in his car and drove off. Tomorrow, he would make her lose her dream, destroy herself, or both. He shook his head; men should not compete against women in such a way. Yet, the pride of Argentina was at stake and he would have to destroy her.

The championships had brought Kirkwall a new gymnasium, now the pride of the old town. A strange place for such a championship some would say, but, Emilio thought, it was evident from all the huge stones in most unnatural positions that lifting had gone on in the Orkneys for a long time.

The competition followed the new Olympic format. A day of snatches, a day of clean and jerk, those with the top ten totals advance to the elimination, which selects the final five. A day of rest and then the finals. Weights went up from an agreed minimum at 2.5 kg intervals. You got three tries at each weight, could pass at any time, and in the case of a tie, the one with fewer attempts at the highest weight ranks higher.

Ivana Rudenko went first; tall for this class, she seemed too thin to be competitive, but she handled the first lift with no apparent problem. The two-class handicap given the women was a compromise with biology and tradition. Most lifters he knew felt it unfair to both large women and small men.

There were exceptions: Olga Svertnostikova had a fourth place finish this year in the 60 kg open category (she weighed 75 kg). No woman had come close to him, Skoda, Illyman or Broeking at 52 kg. But most of the top ten finishes for women were below 60 kg, and those made such a news splash that his friends kidded him about his cojones. The only thing worse about competing against women, he told himself, was not competing at all.

He passed the first round and dismissed the second with ease—a mere warm-up. Safely in the final five, he watched on the monitor behind the stage, as Duluth went for her first lift, a snatch at 70 kg. It would take 72.5 to get Oman Illyman, the Turk, off the bubble. Oman was steady—a good bet for third and would take an occasional meet when someone else screwed up.

A snatch should be a clean, smooth movement taking the barbell from the floor to overhead in one smooth, explosive movement. The Moon woman was all over the place with the barbell, staggering and undulating like a belly dancer, but incredibly not dropping it, and somehow steadying it over her head for the required three seconds by brute force. Her form was laughable, her reactions must be all wrong for this gravity, he thought. Yes, it counted; the lights went on. But In his mind, he couldn't dignify it by the words "clean lift."

Who did she have with her? He glanced to see who was watching from the side of the stage. The slim, gray haired woman with the knee wrap must be her trainer, he thought. The coach? There he was. George Balding, a nice enough former lifter when *seco*, but his pickled brains were no threat to anyone. No match for Humberto Alvarez, the former Argentine national coach in his corner.

"*Señorita*," he called as she huffed by, understandably mad at herself.

She smiled.

He shook his head. "I begin to believe you are strong, but, *madre de Dios*, I hope you can prove your point without dropping the load on anyone, or yourself! You must get those legs out pronto! It goes fast down here."

That got him the cold stare and: "Thanks for the advice, señor Fuentes."

He finished second as usual, by five kilograms, to Skoda. Sally managed 82.5, but so did Illyman, who had fewer misses and advanced.

The clean and jerk was much the same story, though the pause at collar bone level made the Moon woman's clumsiness less obvious. In the final, Skoda hit 215 total, Emilio did 210 and Illyman finished third at 197.5. Duluth, at 180, had a top ten finish in her first try, and had shown Emilio the strength to do much better, if her form came around.

★ ❋ ★

In London, it was Skoda, Fuentes, Illyman. The Scot, Broeking, was fourth. Sally Duluth had moved up to sixth.

★ ❋ ★

Three weeks later in Salzburg, the Moon woman's mechanics had improved, and her ability to power the barbell around laterally was, to Emilio's experienced eye, unbelievable. She was strong enough to make the final five this time, so on the final round it was Emilio, Skoda, Broeking, Duluth, and Illyman. The Anglo press was all over Duluth; a top five would let her into the Olympics. The Argentine press was paying as much attention to her as to Emilio, which irritated him. The ones who did talk to him hit him with that old saw about the locker room and he then said some things he shouldn't have. Some *puta* translated them for the Anglo's edification, and "cold" no longer described the looks he got from Duluth.

Professionally, this was fine. He intended to force her to destroy herself; it would not do to like her. But he could not help a certain admiration colored by an inescapable attraction. Anyway, he wanted to reserve the really bad feelings for Skoda. He would endure pain to beat Skoda. He would give up years of his life to beat Skoda.

On the first round of the finals Skoda pretended to have trouble on the clean and jerk at 95 kg. Emilio knew better and passed, but Duluth took the bait and lifted with him, and at 100, and at 105. Emilio could tell her knee wrapping was no precautionary measure and so could Skoda, but Duluth, madder and more determined each round, kept going.

Emilio got in at 105, hoping Skoda would wear himself out playing games, but it went on through 107.5 Duluth was limping now. This was crazy, a month before the games, he thought.

He was up first at 110, but the right side or the barbell went up faster than the left, he couldn't recover easily, felt a twinge in his back, and dropped it rather than rip something.

Illyman had gone out at 105 and Broeking had two misses at 102.5, so it was essentially the woman and the two of them. "That woman is from some other planet!" Broeking grumbled as he went by Emilio, perhaps not realizing what he was saying.

But Skoda was grinning as he went to the stage, "A game for men, no?" he growled, loud enough for Duluth to hear. Skoda almost swaggered to the weights. Emilio smiled to himself. So it is *castellenos* that are supposed to have macho problems? He had been lifting against Skoda for five years, and could sense the overconfidence. Not a good attitude at this weight, Emilio thought. It helped to be a little mad, scared and desperate.

It was less a surprise to Emilio than it was to Skoda when the barbell slipped from Skoda's hands.

The Moon woman was next, and Emilio could see in her face that combination of emotions that made for a supreme effort. He wanted to tell her it wasn't worth it, not now.

But that was not for a competitor to say in a competition. She stomped by, trying to punish her limp. Her stance at the barbell favored that leg, Emilio could tell. She bent over, puffed, and then lifted, and screamed, not only from effort, but at least some in pain. Dizzily she rotated almost a half circle, but did not drop. With that incredible lateral strength of hers, she steadied the weight over her head, one knee locked under her, the other obviously not bearing much weight, and she held. The lights went on. The crowd went insane.

Duluth threw the weight down, raised her arms over her head, then limped badly back from the stage.

"*Señorita*," he risked, "your knee. It isn't . . . "

"I'll survive," she snapped.

Emilio had two minutes to take the stage, but he turned to Humberto Alvarez, instead.

"Papa, I'm not going on. My back is killing me."

Humberto nodded. "You realize that Skoda has given you an opening, don't you? You want him badly."

"*El Diablo, sí!* But not now. I want to get him at the Olympics, when it counts. And do you want to see Sally Duluth lift again today? If I must destroy a woman, I will do it only for the honor of Argentina."

Humberto smiled. "*Madre mía, no!*", then looked Emilio in the eye. "They will be hard on you now, the Argentine press, but I think today you have risen above that."

Emilio spat. "Papa. Will you have a word with that *norteamericano* coach of hers?"

The buzzer signaled that his time was up. Duluth had won for the first time on Earth, and over world-class competition. The noise was incredible. The press mobbed her. A couple of Argentine reporters came over to him later, almost as an afterthought, and asked if his back would be better for the Olympics; he assured them it would be.

★ ※ ★

At the train station the next day, Emilio spotted a woman walking toward him in a casually elegant long blue dress and a loose white short-sleeved top. The skirt hid whatever appliance she wore on her knee, but he caught the stiff-legged limp, realized the dress made her look taller than she was, and knew it was Duluth long before he could see her face. It would have been easy to move away, but while he contemplated that she got close enough to recognize him. They stared silently at each other, a long, awkward silence.

"Well," Emilio said at last, "you do not run from me, so perhaps you will talk to me."

"Perhaps."

He shrugged "It is difficult, at this level, to be friends. It is much more difficult for me to regard a woman as a colleague."

"At least you are honest about it."

He gave her a wry smile. "I am headed for Barcelona."

"And I for Carcassonne."

"Your people?"

"They have their own vacation plans. We'll meet again in Quito in two weeks."

Emilio smiled. "So high it is close to your world as we poor Earthlings can manage." In a controversial move to garner records, the Ecuadorian Olympic committee had moved the weight lifting competition and some other field events to a venue at a 4500-meter altitude resort.

She shook her head. "As far. At the time of the competition, the Moon will be on the other side of the Earth."

"I meant in the gravity. A little closer to Lunar values, but not much. The altitude reduces gravity by seven tenths of a percent and centrifugal force reduces gravity by about three tenths of a percent over near-polar latitudes, such as at Kirkwall, or my home in San Lucas."

Sally laughed. "Gravity again. I handled Kirkwall well enough."

"Yes, *señorita*, but at the Olympic venue, we get an extra kilogram, which could be enough to get one into the next two point five kilogram bracket.

She looked at him strangely as if she realized for the first time that he had a mind. "Okay, you know your stuff."

"I am a civil engineer when I am not lifting, as you would see in my biography. Do you think I plough my family's fields? There are machines to do that."

"Sorry." She stood silent for a while, looking around at the station's kitschy decorations.

"Is your back better?" she asked, after a while.

He grunted. "If you would be a professional, you must learn not ask such questions." He smiled to take the sting out of the words. "Unless you have a lie detector. It is in my interest for you to be deceived about the state of my health, so I might lie to you. Of course, anticipating that you would assume I lie, and therefore assume the opposite of what I say, I might tell the truth and thus steer you away from it."

She laughed. The train arrived and they boarded together. He had a private compartment reserved, and invited her to join him. They rolled out of the station with her sitting across from him, her eyes glued to the window and whistling the theme from "The Sound of Music."

Emilio sighed; the women in his life were generally the darker, smoldering type. Sally Duluth seemed to have a terminal case of cheerfulness; he wondered where she found the pure, vicious hate one needed to push a body just over its limits.

They sat silently as the Alps went by.

"Do you like pain?" he asked, thinking he could compete with

French farmland for her attention.

Her head snapped around and she stared at him.

He stared back. Ah, sparks!

"That's an interesting question; the pain itself, no. But I suppose, without the pain, I would not get as much of a high from a good lift." She looked out the window again for a while.

He said nothing, and she finally turned back. "I think, too, I like being able to handle it, overcome it, not let it control me; I like being *able* to sacrifice my body for what my mind decides is important."

"The ecstasy of martyrdom."

"Perhaps, though I've never thought of it that way. It's just very, very important to everyone that I succeed. More important than my pain."

"Oh. And what is this that is so important you martyr yourself for it?"

She thought for a while. "You've never been to the Moon."

Emilio laughed. "My trainer would sooner send me to hell! Perhaps he would let me visit Jupiter, where the gravity is *higher* than it is on Earth. That is the conventional wisdom, at any rate. It is why everyone is so interested in you, *señorita* Duluth. It is the 'man bites dog' news story."

She shook her head. "I've been a news story since before I was born. People told my parents I would never be able to go to Earth. Or if I did, I would have to be in a wheel chair all the time. In my childhood, tourists would talk about me. 'Poor little Sally, cut off from her human heritage because her parents wanted to perform a cruel experiment with human life.' There was a lot of propaganda against people living on the Moon permanently. There were efforts to limit people's time on the Moon to one year, for their own good. "

"Propaganda?"

"They were afraid if people lived there, they would become a separate species, or take over the resources and steal the investment Earth people made in the Moon. But they didn't want to sound like imperialists, so they made up a big health issue."

Emilio raised an eyebrow. "It seems they were right about taking over."

Duluth frowned. "Earth got its investment back a million times over. Cislunar Republic companies don't charge any more for stuff made on the Moon than before the election. Less, in fact; some of the middlemen got cut out. We're not freaks; we're just people."

Emilio considered this. The mental picture of Moon people he had grown up with was one of weak people, dependent on Earth for almost everything, arrogant intellectually, a small morally dissolute minority that had stolen the heritage of "all mankind" for their own use. Sally Duluth certainly didn't fit the weak image. Of course, he realized, she worked very hard to *not* fit that image.

"I see. So when you lift, *señorita*, you already have a whole world on your shoulders. The weights, they must be nothing."

"Is Argentina any less heavy? And even though it breaks your back, that burden, would you give it up?"

He shook his head.

There was another part of the image of Moon people that intrigued Emilio as well, the morally dissolute part. Everyone knew that news broadcasts from the Moon had to be electronically altered to paint digital tops on casually bare-chested lunar citizens. The thought that *señorita* Duluth might be casual about *her* chest, and maybe other things as well, inflamed Emilio's mind, mixed in with thoughts of conquest and a bit of a Don Giovanni self image. Training, he knew, raised the testosterone levels in female athletes and it was likely this, more than his Latin charm, that explained the number of his successes. Still, needs are needs.

No, he told himself, you do not know this woman; she is a competitor and might even hurt you. He felt his back twinge.

She looked into his eyes as if she knew exactly what he was thinking.

He cleared his throat. "I understand, that, uh, on the Moon, things, uh, relationships, are a little more casual, perhaps."

"You sound a bit conflicted about that. I thought Argentina was a pretty modern place."

"Yes and no. In Argentina, when people are sinful, they are forgiven, but that casual couplings are still sinful is not much disputed." He laughed. "The Moon seems to have forgotten about sin."

She laughed. "You want me, but if I give myself to you, you'll think I'm a whore or something?"

"And, *señorita* Duluth, as I understand from lunar culture, you would have no particular emotional attachment or love for me. It would just be an amusement for you. I would not necessarily become your master or even your boyfriend."

She giggled, eyes twinkling. "Then it would be perfectly safe, and it *is* a long train ride. And while you are not my boyfriend, you can at least call me Sally."

Up to this point, they had not touched each other. But he felt like he was carrying a Scottish caber between his legs and sensed that she, in her way, was every bit as inflamed.

They reached for each other simultaneously, their hands meeting in the middle. They stood, embraced carefully and kissed. She reached for the upper rail to steady them against the lurching train, exposing her midriff. He slipped a hand under and discovered her athletic bra.

She laughed. "My worst moment in one gravity was the first time I looked at myself in a mirror." She let go for long enough to pull her top over her head, followed by the bra which she held away from her at arms length with two fingers as if it were something loathsome. "I know we evolved here and that is the natural form of a woman, but I was still horrified. I got a couple of these *toute suite*."

She dropped it and had his T-shirt over his head in an instant, revealing his back brace. He shrugged and did the same with her skirt, which showed her right knee encased in plastic.

"You lie down on the bench," she said as she eased her panties down around the appliance and slipped out of her sandals. "I'll straddle you, with my leg off the edge, okay?"

It was okay, more for the release of the tension between them it represented than for his fairly ordinary physical release. It was hard to tell how much of a release she got, and, of course, one did not ask. She seemed satisfied, and lay on top of him for a long time, purring like a kitten between soft, feathery kisses. You are a fool, Emilio told himself when it was over.

As the train approached Carcassonne, Emilio went with Sally to the door. "The next time we meet, *señorita*, we cannot be lovers, we cannot even be friends."

She frowned. "I know. You will try to destroy me. I will try to destroy you, and myself as well." She gave him a poke in the groin. "But there will be an after."

He shook his head. "You must get that out of your head. No after. Only the games. From now on, *only the games*."

The train came to a halt and she stepped out onto the platform and limped off without a look back.

Emilio watched her as long as he could. Fool, he told himself. This is why men and women should not compete against each other. This is why!

✳ ✳ ✳

All Ecuador and much of the rest of the world seemed to be in Quito's new half million-person stadium, standing as the athletes of the nation marched in to a new Olympic militaire. Argentina was around the oval and in place on the infield by the time the *Republica del Espacio Cislunerio* banner marched into the stadium, and Emilio was with Humberto just on the curb of the track as they marched in.

There were just three of them. The white-haired lady trainer; George Alvarez, Humberto's grandson, on leave from his engineering job on Lunar L1 Station to be Sally's new coach; and Sally herself, carrying the silver-on-black Cislunar Republic banner. On the first day they had met, Sally had described it; silver circle in the center for Luna, the diagonal stripe of stars, silver against black and black against silver, symbolizing the fifty-three stations, which were now part of the republic. She held the flag out in one hand, defiantly obliterating assumptions of "luny atrophy." But Emilio, knowing what to look for, could see the stiff-leggedness in her gait. She would have an artificial knee by the time she was forty, he thought.

When their eyes met, he nodded to her and she gave him a thumbs-up with her free hand.

He nodded gravely to her. Whatever had happened between them had to be put aside.

He was even more stern as Skoda, walking haughtily alone even among his team, stalked by. He would call on his hatred of that man later, but for now, he had to think, to plan. He looked at his own blue, white and gold Argentine banner. Friendships and enmity would have to be set aside this week. He had a higher duty.

The weight lifters had come three weeks ago, and were now fully acclimatized. Emilio and Skoda had met one more time before the games, in Bogotá. Skoda had won easily, Emilio not pushing him over ninety kilograms on the snatch. To the disappointment of the press, and the great relief of anyone in the know, Sally Duluth had sat that one out. But now it was serious.

The Games came down to a repeat of Salzburg; at least Skoda played it that way. The last five were the same, with Illyman moved up a notch to fourth. By the draw, Sally was first this time. She passed at 80 kg on the snatch while Emilio and Skoda picked up some easy insurance.

Sally's knee had seen an unavoidable week of hard training and the preliminary competition. Emilio had heard that her cartilage was gone, and that it was bone against bone for her, with a nerve in between. If it were anything but the Olympics, she would be in surgery.

They all passed at 85 kg. 87.5 kg. Championship territory. Now someone would have to go. Rudenko dropped it halfway up; she was clearly out of her depth. Broeking made it, barely, on his third attempt. Illyman put his chip on the board with a puff, a grunt, and a solid hold on his first try. He looked grim, but was in. Sally passed to 90, as did Skoda. We are insane, thought Emilio, but he passed as well.

Sally screamed again snatching 90 kg, but this time her form was perfect.

Emilio and Skoda both made 90 on the first try, Illyman on the second. Nobody made 92.5

"Hey, señorita," Emilio called, derisively. This was no time for niceties; an Argentine gold medal was at issue. Psychological pressure was part of the competition.

"Down, boy," she shot back, giving as good as she got. A woman yes, but what a woman!

"How's it going?" Emilio was serious now. He hadn't liked the sound of that last lift, and he didn't know if George had heard it. He wore that loony flag on his sleeve the same way the Argentine banner graced the front of Emilio's tunic.

She looked at the floor. "They say we females have a higher toleration for pain. So maybe I've got an advantage."

He thought about Skoda, Skoda's ego, and his own ambition. Normally one would give a competitor nothing, but from what he heard, she was not going to beat him today.

"If you've got one lift left in you," he said, "wait until it counts." The Argentine coach would kill him for saying that, but that worthy wasn't around just now. Emilio's confidence was supreme; he was going to win. But who would be third?

"I hear you," she said.

The clean and jerk would decide the overall. The three of them sat out 110 on the clean and jerk, record territory for the class not too many years ago. And again at 112.5, as the Turk disposed of Broeking. George held Sally out at 112.5 kg and there was a murmur in the crowd. Emilio thought again about that silver and black flag on George's sleeve and wondered just how much pressure he'd put on himself by speaking to Sally. She might indeed have one good lift left in her. Emilio stepped up to the 115 kg barbell and had less of a problem than he made it look.

Skoda swaggered up to the bar. He had beaten Emilio easily in Bogotá. Humberto looked at Emilio and nodded. Salzburg all over again. Skoda got things a little sideways, lost his grip and dropped the bar. More buzzing from the audience.

Then surprisingly, the Turk made it. If altitude and the equator were worth a kilogram, Emilio thought, how many kilograms was the Olympics worth? His own words had been "wait until it counts." He had not expected so much passion in the placid, self effacing Illyman—forgetting that without passion he would not be here at all.

Skoda, serious now, threw the bar up as if it were a toy, and stomped away.

At 117.5 kg, Sally Duluth passed again! The crowd buzzed and was dead silent. Humberto looked at Emilio sharply. His eyes said, *Do you have the guts of a woman?* Emilio passed.

Skoda passed. Illyman passed. They would fight it out in 120 kg territory. An honest fifty-two kilogram man, Emilio had cleaned and jerked 120 kg once, in practice.

Sally stepped up to it. Emilio watched her concentrate, blow the thin air into her lungs, squat and wrap her hands around the steel. He remembered that first handshake. Her stance was odd. She was favoring the left knee by putting the right leg slightly forward. How would she ever get its center of gravity over her?

She started screaming before the bar was off the ground, a scream of defiance meant to block out the pain. Then it was up, on her collarbone, canted slightly right. She wobbled, but somehow kept her balance, moving the barbell back and forth as if at will. She bounced, breathing deeply and then with another shout she threw her legs out and pushed her arms up under it. Slowly they straightened. Her face was a mad grimace of triumph. Slowly, painfully, she got her legs straightened and under it. Three green lights. She threw the bar down and pumped her fists in the air.

George was on her in an instant, and the crowd was cheering wildly. Good for her. But *Dios*, what did *he* have to do now?

Emilio's time was starting, but the judge put up his hand to let the commotion over Sally die down. Emilio put Sally out of his mind. He left a little bit of Skoda in. Hate was the spice in his emotional brew. Someone yelled in Spanish about letting a woman beat him. It didn't matter. He would not let Skoda beat him. Skoda, Argentina, and the bar filled his mind.

Emilio had mastered the ability to step back from his self-conjured emotional cauldron and go through a mental checklist of what he had to do. Feet exactly right. Hands talced, grip right. Rhythm. Huff and puff and hate and NOW, with everything he could muster, the barbell came off the floor slowly as if glued to it. Damn Skoda! Faster now, it kept coming up almost as if it were his will instead of his muscles pulling it. He writhed under it like a limbo dancer and used his legs to bring it up the rest of the way. Halfway. He was going to do it, his adrenaline was running riot. The rest, he knew, was more grace and timing than brute strength. He bounced just a little, then, while the bar was going up he threw himself under it before it could fall. Then he could use his legs. Piece of cake.

The South American crowd went crazy. Skoda was being pressed, not by one but by three competitors. He arrogantly passed. So did the Turk, who apparently though he might have just one left in him.

So they went to 122.5 kg. It was 60-68 weight class territory, they were 52-60's, and all things must come to an end.

On one leg and two notches over what any woman her weight had done before, Sally collapsed under 122.5 kg, only just avoiding having it fall on her. George helped her up, and going off the stage she would not even pretend to put weight on the left leg. She was done.

She looked at him as they passed by. "Get the bastard!" she told him, through tears.

Emilio had never cleaned 120 kg before in competition. Now he had done that, just barely and was looking at 122.5 kg. He saw Argentine flags in the auditorium. How many kilograms was an Olympics worth? It was time to hurt something, time to show them he could walk into the flames. He threw some self-contempt into his witch's brew of emotion.

His back gave as he pushed it up to his collarbone, too late to stop him. The pain screamed, but he was already vertical. His arms, balance and determination got him through the jerk. Three green lights.

In agony, he stepped out of the way as the bar fell. *What had he done to himself?* He opened his mouth to scream, but his ability to think in the midst of emotional tumult asserted itself. Now was not the time to let Skoda know that he had destroyed himself. He turned his scream a pain into a growl of triumph and pumped his arms, then turned slowly as if in contempt instead of pain. Humberto, observant, protected him from well-wishers as he moved gingerly off the stage. A supportive belt eased his agony, and he stood to watch the rest of the competition as if he were still in it.

There were no more miracles in Illyman. 122.5 kg would not even leave the mat for him. Skoda had eliminated his competition, and the only thing between him and his gold medal was that 122.5 kg on the floor. He had done that before, in competition. He was the best.

But he didn't quite get under it at the end of the jerk. He started to topple forward, and dropped it just before the lights came on. Passing so much, Emilio thought, he had forgotten how heavy it was.

No matter. He had two more tries. He went back to collect himself. Sally and the Turk had gone back to their locker rooms. But Emilio Fuentes stayed there and stared at him.

Skoda frowned, looking at him.

Despite incredible agony in his back, he bent over and up as if flexing for another attempt and grinned as if to say, I have one more in me. Then he passed his turn at 122.5, conceding nothing.

Time was running out and Skoda was back on stage. He pranced. He jumped. He blew. And then he pounced on the bar and barked once as he pulled it off the floor onto his chest. But ever so slightly, he was going backwards. He tripped. The bar dropped. The crowd buzzed.

With no other competitors at this weight, the clock started again. Skoda's coach was grim, and talked to him in words of one syllable. Fuentes stared and smiled. Skoda's bravado was gone; for the first time he realized he could fail. He was better than all of them, but here now, in this one test he could fail.

All business, all concentration, Skoda stepped to the bar put his hands just right and lifted. It wouldn't come. He tried harder, angry now. It came up a few centimeters, then slipped from his hands. He stared down at it.

That tableau held for the several seconds it took Emilio to grasp what had happened. Then he walked forward to grasp Skoda's hand, history and sportsmanship banishing enmity.

But Skoda turned away and walked off, either not seeing or not acknowledging the gesture. Perhaps, Emilio considered, Skoda was in pain.

As the crowd thundered, Emilio walked slowly over to his trainer. He had to hang on long enough to give his blood sample, and then he could get in his brace and get the injections that would let him attend the medal ceremony.

✷ ✾ ✷

Emilio, numb and giddy, found Illyman at the door to the clinic. He gestured with his head to it.

Emilio nodded, and knocked. "Sally?"

The door opened and Sally emerged, her leg in a brace, looking dejected; she clearly did not know yet what had transpired.

"We should go now, yes?" Illyman said with a twinkle in his eye.

"We? Oman you . . . "

He shrugged. "I always finish third, do I not? Why should the Olympics be different?"Her mouth dropped open. "Skoda?"

"Skoda beat himself, he had more attempts at 115 kg." Illyman grinned. "My little Moon flower, you are the first woman to win an Olympic medal in a physical competition with men, the first person born on another planet to compete, let alone win a medal, and wonders of Allah you have the silver medal; now let us go get it."

"Oh!" Her expression of shock turned into a grin. "Then she turned to Emilio.

"You won the gold?"

He nodded.

She smiled as bright as the sun. "Congratulations!" She reached out tentatively toward him.

He took her in his arms, but quickly whispered "Careful, the back."

She was gentle then and her kiss utterly, intoxicatingly feminine. His back hurt much less.

They marched to the platform, Oman's hand below Sally's supporting her. Emilio walked very straight. I've broken a vertebra, he thought. I will ignore it for another twenty minutes.

"*Señorita*, will you forgive me for doubting you about half a ton?"

"If you'll forgive me for being so ornery."

"That is a lot of mass she moves around," the Turk observed.

Sally laughed, "Precisely, Oman. Your little Earth weights are every bit as heavy down here as mine up there, but much easier to move around than what I'm used to."

"The difference between inertial mass and weight!" Emilio said. "Of course!"

"Emilio, Oman, the Lunar open is in six months. How about it? I'll get you a discount on Cislunar Spacelines."

If she could do this? He would will his back to be ready. And he would tell his trainer where to go. "I would not miss it for the world, any world, señorita. Or you. But I will come to beat you again."

"And I will destroy myself again to beat you."

Illyman looked at the two of them. "I come too, with you two destroyed, maybe I finish first!"

They all broke up.

Emilio was still grinning when the Argentine national anthem started playing and the tears came to him as well.

# STORY NOTES

How much gravity do people need to live more or less normal lives, including having children? There are many opinions, but data only on zero gravity, which is problematic in the long term, and the one-g that we are used to. As I write, the Space Studies Institute (SSI) is trying to put up a rotating space station with different gravity levels to find out. I wish them luck.

In this story Sally Duluth's parents, determined to prove that the Moon could be a self-sufficient home for human beings, went ahead, ignored the advice, and had Sally. She's short, perhaps from her mother's side, or perhaps from lack of stress on the weight-bearing bones of her body. But, she is absolutely determined to prove that being born on the Moon is no handicap. She doesn't just exercise regularly, she pushes herself as far as she can, and perhaps even overshoots a bit. Weight lifters don't need hypergravity 24-7 to develop bones and muscles suitable for a planet of twice Earth's pull; a few minutes under load a couple hours a day seems to do the trick.

At the time this story was written, women's weightlifting had been dropped as an Olympic sport. It has since been reinstated, but things change, and perhaps in some future Olympiad, the sports gods will experiment with open competition. If you would like an image to go with Sally Duluth, look up Tara Nott, the 2000 Olympics 48 kg women's gold medallist. She could "snatch," or lift overhead in one motion, just over twice her body weight.

Originally, in an as yet unsold novel written over twenty years ago, I had Sally competing in the 2032 Olympics at the age of 20, anticipating a rapid expansion into space based on single stage to orbit concepts like ROTON and the DCX. This obviously didn't happen, and we are now looking at perhaps the 2052 Olympics for Sally's silver medal, if we're lucky. She is the foundation of my semi-consistent future history, which I must push now much further downstream. It will, of course, inevitably be bypassed by real history; while one can do reasonably well at anticipating various technologies and events that can happen in the future, the order and timing of these things is contingent and chaotic. I take solace in the fact that while Martians didn't invade the Earth in 1899, people still read *H. G. Wells' War of the Worlds*.

GDN January 2015

# THE MOON HOUSE

"When now?" Betsy McKay asked, looking up into the clear blue Appalachian evening sky. There'd been another delay.

"If you ask me, never!" old Ned Hochkins answered. "Damned nonsense, dropping houses from the Moon as if this were Oz or something."

But the half moon, a day or two short of first quarter, smiled to Betsy. The Moon and the sky were Betsy's friends, her solace when Ma and Dad would fight over the scraps of another bad day. She missed Dad, despite all that. He'd been gentle and huggable when he wasn't mad but he was gone four years now; his last argument had been with a man who had a gun. Some days it seemed like a century, some days like last week.

"You're out here, too, Ned," Ma said, gentle humor in her voice. He looked away and adjusted the straps on his overalls.

"Well they're late, Nellie, and I'm going," he declared and started walking back to his tent. Almost everyone was in tents, after the fire. "It's just as well; they'd likely miss the field and splatter the whole mess like a cow pie on what's left of the town."

"They're late," Dicky, said. Betsy's eight-year-old brother pointed at his watch. "Three minutes."

"Mr. Wu said the schedule wasn't real tight," Betsy said. "They sometimes have to move a little to avoid space junk. The Moon people are all still here."

All five of them stood along the street side of Willie Jones' fallow field, the one where they used to grow tobacco until it became illegal back in '27 when Betsy was eight. She remembered because she had just started to baby-sit Dicky that year after Ma gave up her writing and went to work down at the gas station after Daddy got himself killed. Jones' field was the biggest clear spot around Gottville. It smelled of wet hay now; the rain had finally come in earnest, after the fire, of course.

Betsy spied a lanky, black-haired man in the gray lunar service uniform, "Hey! Mr. Wu!" Mr. Wu was her hero, everything that tall, dark and handsome was supposed to be. She wished she weren't so skinny—after all, she was officially a woman now, so something ought to start changing outside as well as inside. It wasn't quite fair.

He looked up and waved, but then hurried over to the truck with the antennas on it, talking to the little card in his hand.

On impulse, Betsy ran after him. He wouldn't let her down. He couldn't.

"Mr. Wu?"

He turned and sighed. "Betsy . . . "

"Is everything all right?" she asked, but a look at his face told her it wasn't.

"No. There's been another diversion." His voice was tight, as if he were angry but trying not to show it.

Betsy didn't like that word, "diversion."

"The houses went somewhere else?"

Mr. Wu nodded slowly. "It was the U.N.'s decision, not ours."

"Then we should go home?"

He looked very pained and put a hand on her shoulder. "Maybe next time, okay?"

She flinched away, tears in her eyes, then turned and fled back to Dicky.

★ ✳ ★

Instead of going back to their tents, Betsy and Dicky went home. James Street was gravel track winding into fire-scarred hills, barely wide enough for two cars to squeeze by. The last rain had taken most of the burnt smell away.

1238 was a few charred timbers and a fireplace—all that was left of the little frame house her great-great grandfather had built two hundred years ago. They'd saved his picture, though—the one that hung over the fireplace mantle.

"Not much left," Dicky said for the thousandth time.

Betsy picked her way through the mud and ashes to what used to be her room and looked beyond the hump of rubble that marked the south wall to where the grove of maples used to rustle and her swing used to swing. Blackened stumps now. "I think we should rebuild the old house, just like it was, if we get the money."

"Why use money for that? We gotta hire some bulldozers and scrape it flat. Sell the land, if it's worth anything. Start fresh somewhere else. That's what Dad would have done."

"It was Mom's house, Dicky, and grandpa's."

"Yeah. Well it's gone now. And that lying Moon man hasn't got us another like he said he would."

Even the memory of a crush, she thought, deserved some loyalty. "Don't call him that, it wasn't his fault."

"Yeah, sure. Let's go, I'll bet dinner's ready. It's getting chilly and I'm hungry. "

Betsy took one more look at the ashes, then said, "Okay." She took her little brother's hand and they started down the road.

"Sis,"

"Uh-huh."

"If I close my eyes at night I can imagine there'd been no fire and I'm in my own bed and Dad's reading a story to me. Do you think if we imagine hard enough, it will come true? Just like nothing happened?"

Betsy shook her head. "Imagination can makes things come true that never happened before, but it can't make things happen again."

"Why not?"

"I don't know," Betsy said. "Maybe that imagination gets all used up."

★ ❋ ★

They had a surprise when they got to their tent. Ma had managed to make some fresh bread in the microwave, and Mr. Wu had come to dinner. Betsy's heart jumped to her throat for a moment, then she put it back down again. He had failed her, failed everyone.

"I thought you'd be gone," Betsy said, coolly, when he greeted her.

He looked very serious. "We still have work to do. Someone decided that a plantation in Myanmar had a greater need for housing, and after them, a Chinese army base in Tibet. But we'll keep trying. I made a promise."

"You shouldn't make promises someone else has to keep," Dicky said.

"Dicky!" Ma said.

Mr. Wu raised a hand. "He's got a point. In theory, we're there under a U.N. charter, but we're basically pioneers and business people. When we make a promise, that's different than the U.N. making a promise. At least that's how most of us feel. We make the houses, we make the re-entry shields, we run the launch track . . . "

"How does that work?" Dicky blurted, his hostility forgotten. "Tell me how it works!"

Mr. Wu smiled. "It's just a railroad that rides on magnets instead of wheels. We send one car at a time. They just go faster and faster until they run out of track—but by then they're going too fast for the Moon's gravity to hold them down, so they just fly right on off."

"But they have to use rockets to come back, right?"

"Nope. The maglev spaceships can land just like they take off; it's like landing on an aircraft carrier."

"Where do you get the wood for the houses?"

Mr. Wu laughed. "It's a kind of artificial wood—more like fiberglass really. Robotic mining machines gather lunar basalt for a factory that melts it with concentrated sunlight, and draws the melt into fibers. The factories weave those into sheets and paste the sheets together with a synthetic resin. The robot factory does just about everything, though we have a couple people watch over it. Could I have another roll?"

Betsy's hand got to the roll plate before her mother's. She almost, but not quite, tipped a roll into Mr. Wu's coffee, but he got the plate steadied in time. His eyes twinkled at her.

He was just another salesman, she told herself, getting everyone's hopes up, selling the Moon.

Ma cleared her throat. "When they make stuff on the Moon, it doesn't make a lot of pollution on the Earth, and doesn't use energy here either," Ma said. "And it doesn't cost hardly anything to drop lunar stuff down to Earth wherever people want so I guess everyone wants it." She sighed. "We'll just have to wait until someone thinks we're important enough."

"That'll be the day," Dicky said with exaggerated sarcasm.

Mr. Wu shook his head. "I think you're important enough."

"But what can you *do*?" Betsy asked.

He looked her in the eyes, then. Seriously, the way adults look at each other and with a just enough of a hint of irritation that Betsy simultaneously realized he was taking her seriously and that she had maybe stepped over some kind of line a little.

There was a time she might have shrunk back and covered her face, but, heart pounding, she stared right back at him. In the silence, they could hear the tent flap in the evening breeze.

His face softened a bit and there was a hint of a smile. "Look, I have to keep quiet about this, so not a word out of this room, okay?"

Everyone nodded gravely.

"I had a little chat with Lisa Reynolds—she's the Far Side administrator. Uh, what are you all doing in a couple of days, uh Saturday?"

In spite of herself, Betsy began to hope a little.

Ma gestured around the tent at the cots and the tables and the boxes. "Rearranging things a little. Getting ready for the memorial service Sunday. Why, are you rearranging things, too, Sam?"

Mr. Wu nodded then looked at Betsy with a hint of a smile. "But no promises this time."

Betsy looked up into those dark eyes and toyed in her mind with the idea of daring to call Mr. Wu 'Sam'—in front of Ma.

"Aren't things real heavy for you here?" Dicky asked. "Six times as heavy? How can you even walk?"

Mr. Wu shrugged. "When we carry heavy things on the Moon, we carry six times as much. When we jump, we jump much higher. That way, our bones and our muscles are ready to come here if we have to—and we get more done up there. Exercise becomes a habit; on the Moon; I've played moonball three or four times a week for forty years, since I was two. But, yes, we work harder here just moving around, and get tired more quickly at first." He grinned again. "And hungry

Betsy saw him look at Ma. She grinned back.

"Will you have some more chicken, Sam?" Ma asked, still smiling. This wasn't fair, Betsy thought. Ma was at least three years older than Mr. Wu.

★ ✳ ★

By Saturday night, word had gotten around that there would be another attempt, and everyone was at the field again, even Ned. The blackened stubble was floodlit and someone had brought a big yellow forklift over from Cartertown. Mr. Wu and his gray-uniformed lunar people were all around, shooing people away from the field.

The whine of a fan car broke the night, and everyone looked around, trying to spot it.

"There!" Dicky said, pointing across the field. But Betsy couldn't see it for the spotlights.

Then it dropped into the light in the middle of the field and hovered as if it was going to set down just there. It had a big U.N. on its side, and it rotated around so everyone could see it. Then it skidded sideways to the edge of the field, as if its pilot had second thoughts about setting down 'just there,' and settled into the stubble.

Its door popped up and a man jumped from the door and strode toward Mr. Wu in the same angry way that Daddy used to walk when he was going to argue with someone.

"Mr. Wu has a gun," Dicky said.

"No he doesn't," Betsy said. "That's his telephone."

They couldn't hear what was being said, but the U.N. man was angry and waving his arms. Mr. Wu was impassive. Then he pointed up toward the sky.

As if on cue, the loudest noise Betsy had ever heard shook the valley. And then, right away again.

The U.N. man's hands dropped. Spotlights rose to the sky, off to the east.

"Wind's coming from the east," someone said. "Right on target, I'd guess."

"Damn," Ned said. "I was kind of hoping it would land on the U.N. car."

Everyone laughed—living in tents wasn't fun, and the Moon's offer of houses the day after the big fire had made everyone's news service. But the U.N. headquarters had delayed and delayed.

The laughter faded as the spotlights found their target.

"Wow!" Dicky shouted.

It was the biggest parachute Betsy had ever seen, and hanging under it was a big cone on top of a huge curved dish, all black and gray, looking for all the world like the first Apollo spaceship to come back from the Moon, but this was much, much bigger. Mr. Wu said it was a hundred feet across.

It came in stately, like an old mare walking up to a water trough on a hot day. Every now and then, a flame would shoot off to the side from the top of the cone sending sparks in to the night sky, and the crowd would go "oooh" and "ahhh." Rockets, Mr. Wu had told them, to keep it on target.

It got closer and closer and then just kind-of settled into the field with a barely audible thump that nevertheless shook the ground more than the sonic boom had shaken it.

Everything sat that way for a while.

"Betsy, I have something to show you."

She spun around and there was Mr. Wu. Betsy looked up at him, wide-eyed.

"Well, come on," he said.

He took her by the hand and they walked down together through the stubble and into the spotlights right in front of everyone. A U.N. man in a coat and tie joined them.

"If you would excuse me, uh, do you think this is wise? We need to make a few announcements, talk to the media, and try to recover as much as we can in light of the misunderstanding . . . Damn it Wu, listen to me. You work for us."

Mr. Wu turned to the man, not looking to Betsy at all like the man was a boss of his. "I have something to do first. I'm sure you can think of something to say to the media, but I imagine the pictures will be quite sufficient." Then he turned away without waiting for an answer and began marching toward the spacecraft, quickly enough that Betsy had to break into a run to keep up.

They reached the heat shield, which was a black, foamy kind of thing, and even warmer than the Indian summer air. It smelled like a blacktop road at noon in July.

Mr. Wu pressed a button. There was a sharp crack and the sides of the cone split right in front of Betsy and slowly fell away, wrinkling and billowing on the way down like a tissue in the breeze.

"Moonglass cloth—I'm sure you'll find use for it. You can cut up the heat shield too, for sheds or walks or whatever, but be sure you anchor it—it's reasonably rigid, but it's about half the weight of balsa wood.

"There," he said as the last curtain of moonglass cloth drifted to the stubble of the field, revealing several characters above the door that looked like Chinese to Betsy, but right beside the door was a sign in what looked like wood. And there was a name, in English, and an address.

"That's our house!" Dicky yelled from the edge of the heat shield. "McKay, 1238 James Street!"

"We gotta house!" Betsy squealed and jumped into Mr. Wu's arms and wrapped her legs around him in a very unladylike way. She didn't care, she was crying with joy.

But when all the joy-crying was done, and all the good-byes said, Betsy realized that the Moon house, nice as it was, would never replace in her heart the home her great-grandfather had built. The Gottville of old trees and cabins that she'd grown up in was gone, and as the seasons turned she became more and more certain that she wouldn't live there long.

No, she took as many science courses as she could at school. And on clear nights, she would go down to Jones field, look up at the Moon, remember a dark-eyed man who kept his promise and began to think that home is where the heart is.

# STORY NOTES:

"The Moon House" was "sold," but never actually published (or paid for) nor was there any communications or release. There was simply a great silence. The parties involved shall remain nameless. One very short story is a small concern in the slow death of a publication and the dreams of the people who staffed it; I hope they have moved on to better circumstances. But enough time has passed, the contract was unfulfilled, and now here the story is.

What good is the Moon, should we actually reach and stay there? Once we build a launch track, proposed by Arthur C. Clarke many years ago, the transportation cost of sending things made there to anywhere on Earth becomes minimal. In the world of mid-21st century manufacturing with robotic printers, robotic mining machines, laser sintering, 24-7 solar energy for two weeks and advanced energy storage technology, lunar manufacturing of "stuff" may not only be economically feasible, it could become dominant. An additional advantage, common with all space manufacturing, would be that any pollution attendant to making stuff up there would represent pollution off-loaded from Earth's increasingly fragile environment. This story was written before Hurricane Katrina and the sad story of an inadequate response, especially in the aftermath. Much of that had to do with the logistics of getting stuff to the survivors. Imagine if houses, blankets, furniture, and so many other things could have simply dropped down to them from the Moon?

G. David Nordley, January 2015

# THE FIRE AND THE WIND

In the dead, dark stillness outside, the temperature continued down below 200 K. The high-tech tent provided some protection, but it was designed to have more thermal input than the body heat of six huddled people. There was no more fuel for chemical heaters and the small electric heat pump was silent, every erg of battery power long since drained. The only energy left powered the bodies and minds of the survivors. Each, in his or her own way, concentrated on one thought: endure, endure. Only one of them felt betrayed.

I'd just turned thirty and gotten tired of lunar geology. We knew where the ice was. We knew where the carbon was. Not here, in any useful quantities. The real action was Mars and beyond, or in to Mercury, but for that I needed some space time. So I'd figured a four-year stint and a few training missions with the CLR Space Service would punch those tickets.

Class work, of course, came before the missions.

"In space, you think of oxygen as a friend; you can't live without it. But it can be your worst enemy. You may think you can't get enough of a good thing, then a spark and you're toast."

Our lecturer, Captain Avia Martinez, had our full attention. There was a dark authority in her voice and a gravitas to her bearing that made me forget she was under 160 cm tall. Her English was careful and her accent mainly North American, though with the ineradicable tendency to pronounce her "i" a beat longer than a native would.

We all knew her story; she'd been a combat nurse in the Mexican army during the 2038 insurrection, a purser's mate on the first Cislunar passenger line, a heroine of the Lunar independence movement and more than once since on various rescue missions as the fledgling republic took over from the U.N. space authority. She was also a close friend of the legendary Captain Sally Duluth, CLR President Lisa Reynolds, and defense minister George Samios—about as high up as there is room to go in the fledgling Cislunar Republic pantheon. For the last year, Martinez had been responsible for search and rescue over most of known space—we were lucky to have her.

A hand went up; Zander Yurovich, our beefy class skeptic. That was followed by oh-not-again groans among some of the other students, which he cheerily ignored.

A somewhat forced smile flickered across the captain's face and she nodded to him.

"Computers tell you if problem," he stated. "I am electronics expert, I know this."

The other ten of us sat in an embarrassed silence deep enough to hear the whisper of air moving through the ventilation ducts. That made me think of safety and lunar society; there was no need for the ventilation to be noisy enough to hear, other than that *not* hearing it would be a warning. You grow up a little paranoid on the Moon.

I smiled to myself; side by side he and Captain Martinez were an almost comical contrast: she small, intense, dark eyed, buff and the exemplar of lithe—he pink, blond, and bloated.

"In the seven emergency calls since the founding of the service," Captain Martinez answered. "The target spacecraft or spacesuit computer was damaged or down completely and the people inside were often shielded from their own ship. Things can happen *pronto*, too fast for you to stop to ask a computer. Inside, you can glance at your wrist, maybe. You must *know* this! Generally, 0.1 bar oxygen is too little, 0.6 bar is too much."

"The *Lucky Leo* . . . " someone said and stopped as Captain Martinez held up a hand. She ran a tight class; you were expected to keep your mouth shut until you held the floor. *Especially* while she held the floor. But the name of the spacecraft was enough; there were nods and murmurs in the class.

She nodded. "*Sí*, the *Lucky Leo*. Interior view please, after salvage."

The holo stage behind the captain became a larger than life view of the inside of a spacecraft command deck. Clean, bare metal.

"This was a debris strike to start with," she said, "one that hit the emergency suit hook-up oxygen line. Unfortunately, a redundant safety valve upstream of the distribution valve jammed open. It probably hadn't been exercised since installation. Once they got the entrance and exit hole plugged, the oxygen partial pressure probably hit one bar.

"The fire started in the airlock controls and flashed through the cabin in about seventy seconds, incinerating the temporary patches. That kept the cabin from exploding, but everything combustible in any way was turned to ash and vapor and blew out the holes. What you see is bulk aluminum and titanium coated with their oxides; everything else—plastics, composites, thin wires, and, of course, anything organic was gone in seconds."

I stared at the sterile shell. Five people had been in there. Somehow, that was even more unsettling than a charred corpse. I imagined being simply erased in an instant.

"That is probably a good place to end this session. Keep that image in mind. Now, I have the standby scramble ship duty selections for those of you who have qualified. "Jones, Levine, and Ghandhari go with Lt. Rae on CLR-20. Baklanova, Petersen, and Kiwidinok, go with Captain Reynolds on CLR-23, and Yurovich, Kent, and Yu will be on call with me on CLR-18. Have your kits on board by 1800."

That woke me up. Being "on call" meant the chance for a real mission. It also meant the captain thought my course work to date meant I wouldn't be a liability. I wasn't surprised at Kristine Kent, a cool and competent South Africa refugee raised in London, but Yurovich was another matter. His constant questions and haphazard English had him down as the class clown to a lot of people. But his scores must have been a lot better than that indicated, or he wouldn't have been here.

✦ ✳ ✦

Zander was at the CLR-18 when I brought my travel kit that evening. He gestured to the spacecraft hanging from its fore and aft hard points.

"Looking like movie ship," he said. "Round and smooth. Real spaceships look like some soccer balls and sausages in erectors set."

I grunted. "Zander, the aeroshell is so it can use Earth's atmosphere to change course, if needed."

He shrugged. "*Da,* I know this. Still look strange."

Compared to the usual Cislunar ferry, it did. The nose was wedged for minimum drag and the long, thick, stumpy "wings" that held the launch track suspension magnets were fully enclosed and had real control surfaces. Its orbital maneuvering pods were high on the rear, another aeronautical contingency adaptation.

A climbing pole thrust five meters down from an open circular hatch in the belly, forward of the main engine bay. Zander gave me an "after you" gesture, so I slung my kit over my shoulder and pulled myself up. Zander didn't bother with his shoulder strap; he jumped almost halfway, grabbed the pole with one hand and thrust his bulk up, popping up through the hatch like a breaching whale.

"We get called tonight," he said. "I know. I have a date tomorrow."

I smiled and shook my head. Zander's future universe was always a dark one. But the CLR rescue service was only getting about two missions a year. While nothing was absolutely safe, space travel was getting there. The few missions that did occur got so much publicity that it obscured the fact that hardly anything ever happened; but the Republic looked on the rescue service as a reservoir of high performance spacecraft and crews for any contingency.

"You see. They train us, no? So they create something and not tell us is not real. But we know and we play." He grinned and slammed me on the back with a huge hand. "Just like is real, yes?"

"Sure, Zander," I said. "Just like is real."

"Hey, maybe we go to Saemahahn? You'd like that?"

I sighed. My oriental surname and a slight epicanthial fold were the second curse of Abraham Yu, the first being "Hey, you." I played dumb. "Why?"

"Why? New Korea at L4!"

"Zander, my folks are mostly New England Yankees, almost back to 1640. The great-great grandad I got my surname from came from Hawaii on a returning missionary ship; he was Chinese, not Korean, and not 100 percent of that."

"Oh." Zander shrugged. "Good food at Saemahahn, anyway."

"Well, they would have that. Let's get this stuff stowed."

We followed the pole up to the control deck. The cabin layout was compact and simple, a tube seven meters long and six meters wide. The lower deck was for storage or passengers and the upper deck for crew. The control deck was about three meters long and consisted of two rows of three swivel chairs. Video display panels covered the walls over the chairs, but those were backup. Helmet visor displays were now the primary interface.

The captain's cabin was in the odd rounded space in the nose of the pressure hull just aft of the attitude control cluster. The door was open, so, out of curiosity, I stuck my head in. A maximum of two meters long, it held a folding single bunk that left room for a very small group of people to meet privately, a microgalley in the extreme front, and a microhead in the corner across from the bunk.

It seemed roomier than our virtual trainer and it took me a moment to realize why. The bunk was folded up and there were no personal effects whatsoever. There were no bolt-down furnishings, no items in the aerogel cabinet, no rug and no wall decorations. This had been Captain Martinez' ship for over two years, and there was nothing of her to be seen.

Spartan? Her demeanor in class would be consistent with that.

Or maybe it was psychological—in a crunch, the ship was expendable and she didn't want to have an emotional investment in it. That would be consistent with it having no name.

"Is problem?"

"No, Zander, no problem. Our captain likes things simple, it seems."

"*Da.* I think she has bruised soul, almost like Russian."

"Maybe."

We went aft to the crew quarters. Three tiny compartments, two meters wide only at floor level, formed a U at the rear of the cabin. Each compartment had two swing-down bunks, but two compartment doors were locked, leaving me with only one choice.

"You room with me?" Zander said.

Rooming with Kristine would be much more pleasant. She was the most beautiful woman I'd ever seen, and one of the smartest. But that was a fantasy; I hardly knew her well enough to suggest it, and, besides, the odds were that we'd never leave port. I agreed to be agreeable and tossed my kit into the bin at the tail of the lower bunk in the open compartment.

"*Nyet.* You take upper bunk."

"Hey, Zander . . . "

"Look at me, *Da*? Main rocket in ship's belly; what if they not take time to wake us up before they pull two gravities."

I visualized Zander falling down on me from the top bunk at two gravities, smiled and retrieved my kit. "There is no avoiding all inconveniences in human affairs," I told him.

"Kung Fu Tse?" Zander asked.

I groaned. "Adams, Zander. John Adams. One of my fatherland's early leaders."

"Oh."

We met Kristine on our way out. She wore immaculate white coveralls relieved by a small Cislunar flag. The coveralls opened at the neck just enough to show that her skin-tight white shipsuit was fastened all the way to her throat. The effect was high Victorian in pants and left me as curious as I imagined any teenager might have been as to what lay beneath. This in a culture that had long ago discarded swimsuits as excess mass.

"We've taken the last two bunks, it appears," I said grinning like an idiot. Someone a little more on top of the situation might have said, 'but I will be happy to make other arrangements.' But being me, I just stood there dumb-faced.

That gave me time to notice that she wasn't carrying a kit.

She smiled charmingly and said in a bell-like voice with her Mary Poppins accent, "I've already made my arrangements, thank you very much. I returned to add today's lecture to my spare comcomp." She displayed a data wand. "A nuisance, but it has to be done in person. The ship is well shielded here, have you noticed?"

"We can go to Mars, if needed," Zander said.

Kristine laughed melodiously. "Yes, Alexander, we could, though I'd think we'd grow quite bored with each other's company in the months that would take."

I sighed. I wouldn't be that much of a bother to her. My last romantic liaison had been with a lady astronomer who had been cheerfully sleeping with two other guys as well. Then she left all of us for a berth on the Ceres expedition. Though she'd constantly told me to develop other relationships, keeping up with one third of her appetite had been about my limit. Nonetheless, this mysterious lady in white was now standing in front of me and my heart rate was elevated.

Hormones overcame fear of embarrassment; I had to say something . . .

"Kristine, given that we're not likely to get to know each other that way, perhaps we could have dinner at Duluth's some night." I sounded like a goddamn idiot.

She laughed and touched my arm lightly. It burned where she touched.

"Sorry, but I'm not the dating type, am I? Moreover, I must study every night until this course is over. Someone's life might depend on it—perhaps yours. But thank you for the thought." She tossed her head toward one of the other compartments and flashed a gigawatt smile. "Please excuse me for a moment."

She turned to one of the other compartments, opened the door and slipped in with the grace of a fawn, leaving only the scent of a fresh spring breeze.

While the door was open I caught a brief glimpse of two signed portraits in her compartment: one was of a blond boy of about five with a bright smile in a school uniform white shirt and blue shorts, the other was of a lunar icon, but the inscription on the photo didn't say "to Kristine," it said "to Avia."

Zander frowned. "Admiral Samios? She knows Admiral Samios?"

I read English faster than Zander. "It was inscribed to Captain Martinez; it looks like our captain is rooming with Kristine."

Zander looked toward the captain's stateroom toward the bow. "But . . . "

"I like to leave the forward room free for meetings, or as a surgery, if needed." Captain Martinez appeared at the door, looking very serious. "Do you have everything you need aboard? Yes?" she asked.

Zander shrugged. "*Da . . . Nyet.* One never has everything."

"Hmmm. You are learning, maybe. Well, what you have will have to do, because we are going somewhere. We must get ready for launch, *pronto!*"

*That* was why she was here in person. No sooner had she said it, than I heard the clang of the port's macrowaldos attach themselves to the hull, ready to lay the CLR-18 on the launch track like a round in a rifle. I turned to scramble for my seat, and bumped into Zander who stood there like a block of Siberian permafrost.

"We go where?"

"Zander," I said quietly. "Move."

"We go where?!" he said more loudly.

"Ensign Yurovich, you have five seconds to take your position, or go out the hatch," Captain Martinez said almost as quietly as I had, but the words seemed to echo off the hull.

Zander scuttled back into the main cabin, looked up at his station on the raised platform on the left side, looked down the exit pole, hesitated, and then with a grim expression pulled himself up to his acceleration seat.

"Ensign Yu . . . " Kristine said.

I'd been frozen watching Zander's personal drama and was now blocking the passageway myself. "Uh, sorry."

I jumped for my seat and began to strap in and run through my checks. The ship was entirely computer controlled, with five redundant nodes, each fully capable of running the ship, but the captain, last out of the passageway, had somehow settled in and called out "Command ready" before any of us. I couldn't see her; her station was in front of mine, and the back of her seat blocked my view.

My lights were all green. I reached up, flipped open my locker and did a visual on the various environmental packages; black for vacuum, gray for lunar surface, red for Mars, and in the spare slot, there was a white package. White?

"Station 3, ready," Kristine sang out.

The telltales on all my packages were green. I checked my straps.

"Station 2, ready."

"What's the white package for?" Zander called out?

"Yurovich . . . " The captain's voice held the hint of some extreme doom for Zander unless he responded quickly.

"*Da*, it has a green light whatever it is."

The ship settled into the launch cradle with a couple of thumps.

"Station 4 ready," Zander finally said.

"CLR-18 ready," Captain Martinez said.

"Okay, is exercise over now?" Zander asked.

The CLR-18 leapt forward and my seat pushed my reluctant body along with it. The seat swung toward vertical as the g built up to the track standard of 30 meters per second squared and felt the slight rocking motion as the ships magnets lifted it off the cradle. Three-g was bracing—eighteen times my usual weight, but like most lunies, I'd been pretty good about maintaining my high g certification.

We had pills for calcium loss, but pills can't exercise for you and no matter how much I tossed hundred-kilo medicine balls around, my arms still felt like lead when I lifted them out in front of my body.

I glanced across the passageway. Kristine was doing what I was doing, but Zander looked grim and seemed to endure the acceleration rather than play with it. I selected 'side view,' and watched track supports whip by with increasing frequency as the distant gray hills majestically glided aft. My weight began to fall away as Ft. McHenry came into view, silently chuckling at the irony of its name as I did each time I passed this maintenance outpost on the rim of Congreve Crater.

Across the passageway, Zander lay flat, pale and breathing heavily. Only his eyes moved.

"What is so funny?" he wanted to know.

"Just the name of the maintenance base."

Kristine looked over as well. "Well?"@ (well – Well?)

"I would like to know, too," Captain Martinez said sharply from in front of me.

I realized that I was the only one of U.S. ancestry in our crew. "History. It goes back to the War of 1812. The British bombarded Fort McHenry, near Baltimore, with Congreve rockets. It didn't fall, so they bypassed it and sacked Washington. But they didn't stay with a hostile force at their rear. The whole thing was kind of pointless, but it provided that "rocket's red glare" phrase in the U.S. national anthem."

"Glare wastes energy. Only time rocket's glare red is in an emergency," Zander said. "1812. Napoleon. U.S. on wrong side of war. Russian view, of course."

From the Russian perspective, I realized, my ancestors had been on the wrong side of a world war. I thought of another irony—playing Tchaikovsky's 1812 overture on U.S. Independence Day.

Kristine laughed. "The British view as well, but I think I get the point. Congreve and Ft. McHenry were on opposite sides of the Napoleonic wars, but are now together on the Moon. I suppose it's as hard with nations as it is with people, but one must, eventually, let go of such things, mustn't one?"

"An irony, indeed," Captain Martinez said. "Now, if any of you have any business to clean up back on the Moon, it is the time to do it. Our ETR is ten days."

A chill went down my spine and the small cabin was suddenly silent. They tell you when you sign up that we are primarily a search and rescue service, but that we are also part of what passes for the Cislunar Republic's military. Things hadn't entirely calmed down between the CLR and Earth's International Space Authority—particularly over the issue of self-determination for the population of the big L1 manufacturing complex. The United Nations had yet to formally recognize the new Lunar government and only a handful of member nations had done so. Some wanted to "reclaim" what they felt was partly their property.

"What happens now?" Zander asked. "Where do we go?"

"Ensign Yurovich, simply tell whoever you talked to that you haven't been briefed yet, but you'll be back in ten days. Please make it sound routine."

Another silence. I had questions of my own, but it was clear they wouldn't be welcome just now. Kristine was already quietly talking to someone on her board. What had I planned to do in the next ten days? Dad and Mom were on Mars . . . I'd just broken up with Cynthia . . . Rolf Petersen might be going out as well . . . Cousin Todd would be in his office. I touched-in the code. He was busy, but his phone took my message.

Zander was saying something in Russian and getting increasingly agitated, finally ending his call with a *"Do svidanya!"* that echoed through the main cabin.

"Bah! Mother asks too many questions I cannot now answer."

I struggled, with limited success, to keep a straight face. However, Kristine, whom Zander could not see, grinned from ear to ear, doubled over, and then clamped her hand over her mouth so all that escaped was a faint lady-like cough.

"Are you all done?" Captain Martinez asked.

"Yes," I said.

The others nodded.

The captain floated out from her station into the middle of the passageway. "We are on total radio silence as of now. No calls until I lift it. Settle in and then join me up front and I will tell you what this is about."

✶ ✳ ✶

The core of a CLR service spacecraft is a pressure cylinder five meters in diameter; the epimenage[1] of magnets, heat shield, stub wings including fuel tanks, and a small external cargo area are built around that. The upper half of the cylinder is taken up with life support equipment, mission gear, and a small air lock. The command deck is

---

[1] Epimenage (Epi + menage, Lat+Fr) "outer household" is an aviation term referring to all the things attached to the fuselage of an aircraft, here applied to an aerospacecraft.

the lower middle of the cylinder, with the "staterooms" and a head at either end. If spun on its axis at eight rpm, a CLR/SS can generate almost a lunar gravity for a passenger seated on one of the heads. It's comfortable enough as long as one doesn't move quickly in a radial direction, though the force of gravity on my feet was noticeably greater than that on my head. It makes it far more convenient and quicker than trying to do one's business in the zero gravity mode.

I was the last one into the tiny stateroom and I squeezed into the open space around the table next to Zander. The tabletop was active, but displayed what looked like a featureless white plane.

"Antarctica, Abraham," Zander said, looking utterly miserable. "We go to Antarctica!"

The white kit in my locker. I looked at Captain Martinez.

She nodded. "The Hemstead expedition has had an emergency."

The Hemstead Expedition, a half-dozen people trying to cross the continent on the surface during the Antarctic night for the first time.

"What kind of emergency?" Kristine asked, suddenly looking very concerned.

"Their two vehicles are trapped, simultaneously, in a crevasse—a freak accident, they say." Captain Martinez sighed. "I say that in this day and age, properly equipped, you don't have those kinds of accidents. Anyway, they lost almost all their fuel. They've huddled up to wait for help. We will happen to be in the best position to rescue, when it is announced."

"Is UK expedition, yes?" Zander asked.

"Commonwealth, staged from Australia. But two of the six are lunar citizens—Sam and Sue Reynolds. The Brits called us, ostensibly to show what we can do and make some political hay for their recognition policy."

Zander groaned. "So we go get killed maybe rescuing President Reynolds' British friends."

The British world had supported Lunar independence long before anyone else, and maintained good relations, while most other countries kept the Republic at arm's length, dealing through the UN-chartered, International Space Authority, the ISA. Sam Reynolds was a distant cousin of Lunar President Lisa Reynolds, which probably did have something to do with him and his wife taking on such a risky mission. Then something else Captain Martinez had said earlier suddenly came to mind: 'We *will* be in the best positions . . . when it is announced.'

"They want us to rescue them, as opposed to someone on Earth?" I asked.

She nodded.

"But they would be risking lives to arrange that, wouldn't they?" Kristine looked puzzled.

The captain nodded again. "The British, they did not arrange the accident, but someone else, maybe *they* did. The expedition crossed a dry part of Antarctica, here," she pointed to a gray area that expanded into a mountainscape on the table display. Lunar mountains are desolate, yes, but they seem like warm, sunny hills compared to that.

She looked at us as if she were searching for something, testing us. "The rest is something you must never tell anyone. There is a large, *secret* base in Antarctica—well hidden, but we have space-based surveillance data. We think it is a weapons research lab, operated by the ISA. The Hemstead expedition path was plotted to go near it."

Kristine looked at Captain Martinez. "A UN base making weapons to use against *us*?"

I bit my lip to keep silent. George Samios was probably cooking up something in a similar off-limits area near Perry Crater at the lunar North Pole. It was not something I was supposed to know, but I'd never taken the rumor very seriously, until that moment.

Captain Martinez shrugged. "The ISA operates under a UN charter, but it funds itself by special member contributions and pass-through duties at L1. In theory, the Security Council could revoke or amend the charter, but the Chinese have vetoed every move in that direction."

There had been a lot of unhappiness over Cislunar independence. Some people had lost the opportunity to skim something off the burgeoning flow of goods and materials from the Moon. Others had lost power and influence, and didn't know how to let go.

"Until the U.N. does assert control, Mr. Barman, the ISA administrator, is a law unto himself and can not be stopped." Captain Martinez tapped her foot, and there was fire in her eyes, as if there were something personal in this for her. "The Secretary General can issue orders, I think, but without budget power over Mr. Barman, the latter can simply smile, say 'yes sir' and continue doing what he is doing."

"Oh no you don't," Zander said. "The Reynolds are spies, then, yes? But Alexander Mikhail Yurovich is not spy. Is not going to spend rest of life in Earth prison. *Nyet!*"

Kristine's face was white. "Avia, pardon me, Captain, my ex is on that expedition. Timothy Lynn Richardson."

The captain shut her eyes for a moment. "A complication. But this is okay, I think. You will rescue your ex-husband. We can publicize that to draw attention away from other ideas."

"You don't understand. It was less than amicable, I'm afraid. Sorry to be such a nuisance."

The picture of the little boy in the cabin . . . a son? She'd never mentioned anything, no childcare, no school reports. Maybe too young for school. I started to adjust my fantasy life; she was beautiful, I wanted her, but was I ready to be an instant father?

"Bad luck," I said.

"Both adventurers," Zander said. "Are only so many. Eventually paths cross. Bad omen."

Captain Martinez was silent for a moment. "I am the reason this ship was chosen, not you. You three are only *el sorteo*; there was no time to pick crews. Ensign Kent, I am not sure how hostility will play, maybe . . . no. You will be professional and he will be in too much shock to cause trouble, I think."

"Is no problem. We abort, they send someone else. I, Alexander Mikhail Yurovich, will insist on this."

He was making an idiot out of himself. "Enough, Zander," I said. "We have a mission."

"Thank you, Ensign Yu. Yes, we have a mission," Captain Martinez said. "We are going to land and serve as a temporary shelter for the expedition members until other arrangements can be made once the Antarctic day begins. While doing that, we are to see that certain robotic equipment the Reynolds brought with them vanishes."

Zander threw up his arms, wobbling a bit from the Coriolis force as he did so. "Why do they not get rid of those things themselves?"

"Because they are currently surviving off the power supplies of that equipment."

"I suppose then it really wouldn't do for them to be rescued by anyone else, would it?" Kristine added.

"*Sí*. We need to do a speed-up burn as soon as we round the lunar horizon, in about six minutes. Now, stations everyone, *pronto*."

We slid out of the wardroom and filed out the door to the command deck

"We hit atmosphere hard, then?" Zander said, once we were ready.

"Seven gravities," Captain Martinez answered.

Zander pursed his lips, nodded, and said nothing more at all.

The speed up burn was routine, a fraction of a kilometer per second. The Apollo 13 mission had done a similar, smaller burn over sixty years ago, I recalled. Our 30 by 40 array of high pressure kilonewton microthrusters, barely ten centimeters deep, would have looked like magic to those old astronauts and they would be surprised to see us getting 3 km/s exhaust velocity out of Moon-produced chemicals, but they'd recognize the principle immediately. Fuel and oxidizer burned under pressure and released through an expansion nozzle.

I wondered what James Lovell would have thought of the Moon today.

✶ ✾ ✶

We turned in for a solid, drug-assisted ten hours of sleep after the speed-up burn. It might be the last good sleep we'd get until we were rescued ourselves. On rising, three of us gathered in the wardroom for breakfast.

"Missing Zander, aren't we?" Kristine said.

"He's checking out the cold weather gear," I told her.

She laughed good-naturedly. It sounded like church bells to me. "I suppose he thinks that because he's Russian, he's an expert in the area. Well, he was born on the Moon just like you and to the best of my knowledge has never been to earth let alone spent a day in the snow, has he?"

"He is having a hard time dealing with this," Captain Martinez agreed. "Ensign Yurovich may have gambled on not ever having to actually do something."

"Gambled?" Kristine asked.

Captain Martinez pursed her lips, then said, "Punching the ticket."

I knew what she meant. A service record opens doors, and usually involves no real danger. Zander had barely passed the entrance requirements six months ago. He had not spent much time in the gym since that I'd seen, and now by the luck of the draw, he was going to spend a week or so weighing six times what he was used to weighing. Courtesy of medicine, his bones would be strong enough, but muscles? That was an open question. I'd spent a couple of hours on the Coriolis Crater city's centrifugal track the previous week, and while I'd stayed upright, it had not been an enjoyable test. Only two hours, and I rated myself in much better shape than Zander.

On the other hand, Kristine and Captain Martinez were Earth-born and both looked to be in excellent condition. The captain had served with, and trained with, Luna's legendary Olympic weight-lifting medallist, Sally Duluth. I had no doubt she was stronger than me. I really had no basis for judging Kristine's physical ability other than her looks; and she made such a point of being quite proper and lady-like, thank you, that I could hardly imagine her doing anything grossly physical. But there seemed to be not an ounce of fat on her one-and-a-half meter frame.

A roar and a string of Russian broke my thoughts. A moment later, Zander barged into the wardroom, naked to the waist, carrying his Antarctic gear. In the minuscule gravity, waves of fat rolled up and down his torso in an almost cartoonish slow motion. There was nothing comic about his demeanor, though.

"Captain, we have more big problems. Boots are too tight."

"Ensign, they are almost identical to our vacuum boots."

"*Da*, that is problem! Vacuum boots need be tight, keep body from bloating. Insulation no problem, vacuum is great insulator. But snow and ice and wind are not like vacuum; they carry heat away very efficient. Blood needs room to flow to keep feet warm. Snow boots should be . . . *bolshoi* . . . big. Big enough so feet can move and keep warm. Other clothing too; sealed but loose."

Kristine chuckled and placed a hand daintily on Zander's big pink forearm. "I know where you were born, Zander Michailivich . . . "

"I was born Lunograd, so what? I have my grandfather's journals and I ask many questions about Siberia. He told me how to live there, should I ever have to. Tight boots are not good."

"Zander," I said, "the suits have almost certainly been checked out to far worse conditions than what we'll encounter . . . "

Captain Martinez held up a hand and looked very thoughtful. "I am a little sorry for radio silence now. I think I would like to check on the origin of this gear. To the best of my knowledge, we have no arctic simulation rooms on the Moon as yet."

"I have solution, to boot problem, anyway."

"We are still going to do the mission, Zander," Captain Martinez said, surprisingly gently.

"*Da,* not that solution. What we do is I give my boots to Abraham; he gives his to Kristine, she give her boots to captain. That way there are three of us with roomy boots and not-frozen feet."

"But what about you, Zander?" I asked.

He looked miserable. "One does not need boots when flat on back. But if I do, I use spacesuit boots from Mars kit. I take pressure liner out and replace with crumpled paper. My grandfather did crumpled paper in Siberia. Worked fine. Only good use for Pravda, he said."

Captain Martinez said, "Hmm. CLR-18, what is the insulation factor of crumpled newspaper, as compared to, say, aerogel?"

Zander was impressed enough with the difference to change his plans to aerogel.

It was Kristine who now looked concerned. "If Zander is right about needing to flop around in oversize boots, and the kit makers were wrong, one suspects that there may be other things wrong on this mission, doesn't one?"

Captain Martinez shut her eyes for a moment, then opened them. "This is not risk free. The time to atmosphere entry is eighty minutes. Put the arctic gear on now; that will save us trying to do it in heavy gravity. We'll do what you suggest, Ensign Yurovich; there is some fast drying aerogel in the medical locker."

After hours of idleness, we were suddenly very busy doing everything we didn't want to be doing once Earth's gravity took over. Kristine went for the head and Captain Martinez slipped into their cabin.

I looked at the instructions for putting on the arctic gear and began to follow them, then stopped. Kristine had been ahead of me on that one—while there were arrangements for taking a piss while in the gear, one would rather not.

The ship began to lower its cabin temperature, mercifully. Even loose and open, the cold weather gear was very effective at keeping me warm.

"Atmosphere entry in ten minutes."

The announcement was punctuated by a couple bangs of attitude control thrust and the abrupt cessation of any weight at all.

Where did the time go? I quickly grabbed and stowed the gear I was checking and strapped myself in. A glance at Zander showed him rigid and stoic, expecting the worst. I wasn't sure of myself either. Exercising under weights or in a centrifuge for an hour or so was not like the continuous real thing and I knew it. Our lunar mythology was founded on Moon-born Sally Duluth going down to earth and winning a silver medal at the '36 Olympics; that's how we thought of ourselves; tougher and smarter than they were, despite the low gravity. But the personal reality, I knew, was going to be very different.

"Atmosphere entry."

It began with a hiss that gradually became noticeable over the general hum of the ship's equipment. Weight snuck up on me like Christmas as the hiss built up to a roar. It was very even, not jerky like you see in some films, just weight and more weight. A full Earth gravity, then three, then five, then seven; I couldn't lift my arm at seven, though I could lift my fingers easily enough.

Zander moaned, very softly. There was a slight burnt smell in the cabin, from who knows what. The weight backed off fairly quickly, five . . . three . . . one.

"When do we get down to one?" Zander asked, stopping in mid sentence as he realized we were already at one gravity, gliding like a stone at terminal velocity with the force of the wind of passage beneath us equal to our weight.

"Our target has been acquired," the ship announced.

That would be the stranded expedition.

"Stand by for retrothrust in ten seconds, nine, eight . . . one."

Boom, rush, and roar assaulted our ears from below and I was slammed into my seat. Two gravities. My display showed the ice below us lit by the flame of our descent. It seemed coming up far too fast, but slowed at the last. Acceleration melted away until we were hovering.

"We have an anomaly. The landing gear will not deploy. Probably due to ice."

"Hover lower," Captain Martinez said, sounding cool and professional as our fuel reserves blasted away. "Maybe we can steam it loose."

"There is some risk."

I could feel the risk. We were rocking and skidding back and forth as the ship tried to stay in the same place balanced on a column of fire, its backwash reflecting off the ice.

"Accepted. Lower."

The rocking, scudding, and buffeting increased. The gear stayed up.

"I'll never be able to climb out the top," Zander said.

I looked up, way up. The top air lock, our only way out if the bottom was blocked, was above the plus-Z level and would be a very difficult climb, up and down.

"Belly view," I said to my display. Maybe we could put the lower hatch over some kind of crater, or depression . . . I was rewarded by a sheet of ice that looked very flat and unrelieved. Then one of the ship's jerks showed something else.

"Captain, we're carving a trench with our exhaust," I said. "If we can put the hatch over it . . . "

"Got it, Yu. Manual control."

Captain Martinez moved the ship forward slowly, then yawed and cut thrust simultaneously. We thumped hard, lights and power went off as we skidded for a second in total darkness with a screech that sounded like the ship was being torn apart, that subsided to an occasional rocking motion. Kristine let out something between a gasp and a sob. The slipstream noise that had been with us since entry continued, moaning like a cat in pain. Were we somehow still moving? I had a nightmarish vision of us smoothly sliding across the ice toward some huge chasm; a crevasse, I remembered, was what huge chasms in the icecap were called.

I tried raising my arms. It didn't feel any different than in the centrifuge; strength would not be an issue for me, but endurance remained to be seen.

My screen came back on. The main cabin looked like a huge dark cave, lit by our screens. Still, no one said anything.

The awful slipstream noise continued; we continued to move along at twenty-one meters per second and nobody seemed to be the slightest bit concerned. Was I dreaming this? Had the impact done something to my brain? I shivered.

I rotated my couch to the sitting position manually. The ship was on power-1; photonics only, probably for fear of sparks. Our atmospheric velocity was twenty-three meters per second in the minus-y direction. The numbers varied up and down, but I felt no acceleration: busted sensor, I thought. But then there was the constant slipstream noise in my ears.

"Down," Captain Martinez said. "Is everyone okay?"

"Elephant sits on me," Zander said. "Okay except for that."

"No worries here," Kristine chimed.

I could contain myself no longer. "Doesn't any one else hear that noise?" I asked. "It sounds like we're still moving through the atmosphere and that's what atmospheric velocity sensors are indicating, though they might be broken. Are we sliding across the ice cap? Is it that smooth?"

Kristine laughed.

"Is wind," Zander said. "Air moves by us. Relativity."

The air was moving by us. It began to sink in now; outside would not be the simple, benign, perfectly insulating vacuum I had grown up with. Outside would mean swimming in a current of freezing gas, ready to suck every last joule from my body.

"Ship, any damage?" Captain Martinez asked.

"There is a probability of some dents in the outer hull," the ship replied. "Several minus-z sensor heads, while still connected, are likely to be out of alignment. The plus-z thruster ports are blocked and all the lower thruster port doors were sheared off in the skid. High speed atmospheric maneuvers should not be attempted until this is repaired."

I glanced at the fuel state on my board; we had about 2 km/s free space delta-v left, enough to reach orbit on the Moon—but about 8 km/s too little to reach orbit here. Moreover, we would have to use much of it in our fuel cells to maintain power and warmth. No point in worrying about high speed atmospheric maneuvers—we were going nowhere.

"Our radiators are at minimum and there is still difficulty in maintaining cabin temperature above freezing," the ship reported.

"Keep the head and sleeping compartments above freezing," Captain Martinez said. "We'll have to live with what you can do for the rest. I think we can risk cabin lights now."

The lights came on, but it was not the familiar cabin. Here and there sparkled white patches; the very moisture in the air had condensed on certain surfaces. My shivering increased, as though my protective clothing were not doing its job. Suddenly, I wanted out of this, very badly.

"We should be within a few hundred meters of the stranded party," the captain said. "But there's no signal. Let us all try standing up. Remember, we are the rescuers."

I swung my legs over and stood up easily enough; it was just like the centrifuge. No, it was a little different: no rotation, no vibration. In the centrifuge there was always a slight sense of motion. Here, it felt very solid. Standing, balancing, I found, took much less energy.

Captain Martinez walked to the center of the cabin, moving as if she were born to it, which, of course, she was. Kristine stood easily as well.

Zander had rotated his couch to face the center of the cabin, and sat, face grim, with both hands on the arm rests. Then, with a mighty groan, he heaved himself vertical and nodded gravely.

"Open the bottom hatch," the captain commanded.

It retracted easily enough, and revealed a few centimeters below, a sheet of solid, glistening ice. The captain put a foot on it, gingerly, but it was an awkward posture; if the ice gave way, she'd lose her balance.

She motioned to Kristine. "Come here. Hold onto my hand."

Thus freed from fear of falling, she stomped on the ice. Nothing happened. She stomped again, much harder, several times.

There had to be a hollow nearby, I thought. Even if we'd missed the trench, the engines had been still firing when we hit. "Maybe if we run the engines for a few seconds . . . "

"CLR-18, what do you think?" the captain asked.

A few minor clanks ensued. "A cold gas test indicates that some of the array nozzles may be blocked with ice. This may not be a problem; however, caution is warranted."

"*Sí.* We will not risk it. We need to get under the ship and clear a way."

The captain stomped once more on the ice, to no effect, and backed away from the opening.

"Captain?"

"Yes, Ensign Kent?"

"One of us could exit the air lock, rappel down the side of the ship, find the trench, go under the ship and survey the situation from the outside."

"Robot work," Zander said.

"Our robots aren't much good in one gravity with frozen joints," the captain replied. "Are you volunteering, Kent? We should both go, for the buddy system."

Zander tottered over to the hatch and looked down. "Any lights on bottom of ship?" he asked.

Captain Martinez nodded. "Yes?"

"Ice is very clear. If we turn off light inside, and turn on light outside, maybe we see something."

"Do it," the captain said.

The inside lights went off, and as our eyes adapted, an eerie glow came up from the ice below the hatch. We could, as Zander thought, see the glow of our outside lights through the ice.

"Not very blue," Zander said. "Ice thin. Axe in kit."

"I'll get mine," Kristine said and scampered back to her station, moving quickly and easily.

The two earth-born women, I thought, would easily surpass Zander and me in physical prowess. Or would they? Zander perhaps, but I had done my exercises. Despite what I felt like, I should be, just from male muscle mass, the strongest of the crew. No, I wasn't the athlete that either Kristine or Captain Martinez were, but this might be a situation where sheer size mattered.

Kristine came back with an ice axe and began chipping away. Soon, a pile of ice chips began to accumulate. I found a plastic bag and a brush in the galley, and brought them over. There was only room for one person in the work area, but, when she took a rest, I moved in and swept up. We developed a rhythm, Kristine chipping away for a minute or so with me sweeping after. Chip, sweep.

"Do you want to have a go with the axe for a while?" she asked me after a kilosecond or so of this.

I nodded and moved into position and picked up the axe. While it was harder to lift in the Earth's gravity, it felt light—easier to move around than something of similar weight would have been on the Moon. I raised it and swung the point at the ice, aiming to widen the hole Kristine had dug. My arm and the axe fell with breathtaking speed, I missed where I was aiming at and the axe tore itself from my grip and landed in the bottom of the hole.

"Keep your head steady and your arm straight," Kristine said when the laughter died down.

I did this and was rewarded with a satisfactory crack and splinter of ice with my next blow. At first, the work was all in lifting the axe, but as I gained confidence in hitting my target, I started to push it down a little as well. I began to work up a sweat, and, for the first time since landing, was not a bit chilly.

"Did you hear that?" the captain asked. "Strike that way again."

I swung the axe again, hard, on the side of the minus-y side of the hole and it hit with a satisfying "thunk." I hit on the other side and the sound was more like a clink.

"Move over," the captain said, and she took the axe. Kneeling on the edge of the hatch on minus-y side, she tapped on the hollow-sounding area. Then she measured her distance, took a swing and got the thunk. She nodded and motioned us to back away a bit. Now she lifted the axe high over her head and with a slight "oof" brought it down with blinding speed. Boom, crack, and we were through. Almost immediately, a bitter cold draft swirled up from the hole.

Be careful what you wish for, I thought, as I shuddered and rezipped my parka.

The captain stuck her head through the hole and looked. Then she stood up and faced us. "There are people dying out in that. Widen the hole so you can crawl through into the trench melted by the rockets, then get your axes and cut a stairway—I do not think the lift will work in this cold. I will try again to locate any survivors."

In another hour, we had something resembling a ramp into the trench. The CLR 18 had surged back and forth against the wind as its belly jets cut the ice, so the trench was in the direction of the wind. It looked about two meters deep at its deepest point, a little upwind of where we'd hacked through from the hatch. With the ship blocking the top of the trench, it became a Venturi tube, and the biting, freezing wind ran through under the ship even faster than above it. The one advantage to this was that it quickly blew away the debris of our chopping. Finally, the moment of truth came.

"Please, ladies first," Kristine said, saving me from a perhaps unwise effort at gallantry.

"Rope," Zander said. "Or you blow away."

Kristine looked at him, nodded, and tied a line around her waist. The hard part was finding a place in the cabin to anchor it. Finally, we tied a knot, stuck it through the wardroom door, and closed the door on it.

Kristine pulled her facemask down, grabbed the edge of the hatch with both hands, then slid into the trench and was promptly carried away, the rope running freely out the hatch.

It would, I thought, probably tear out the wardroom door when Kristine's mass fetched up against its knot at that velocity. I braced myself against the hatch edge, grabbed the hissing line with my gloves and tried to brake it.

My right glove burst into flame and I let out an involuntary yipe, let the line go, and batted out the flame against my belly. But the speed of the line had slowed. Holding on to his couch seat, Zander stomped on the rope; it smoked alarmingly, then went taut. I went back to it and pulled and pulled. In a couple of minutes, Kristine was back with us.

"Don't stand on ceremony," she called to me over the whine of the wind. She was probably smiling, but behind the cold mask, who could tell?

I checked my right glove. One of the layers had burned away, but the rest seemed intact. I could replace it later. I flopped onto my belly and let myself slide down, hand under hand, into the maelstrom. Knowing what to expect, I was able to gain my feet and hold position by leaning into it.

Kristine and I managed to work for about an hour, with me far more tired than she by the end. Zander had to sit most of the time, but could occasionally hand us things like pitons and ropes. We found we could work more easily if we tapped pitons into the ice upwind, and anchored ourselves with ropes against its incessant current.

The steps we tried to cut seemed slippery and unsatisfactory whatever we did. Finally, we resorted to a combination of rope and step, and in this way were able to get back into the ship using both hands and feet.

When we got back in, the cabin—now down to about minus 3 Celsius—felt positively balmy. I ached everywhere; after an hour's work I felt more tired than I'd ever felt after a session in the centrifuge. Fluid ran out of my nose freely, ignoring my feeble efforts to snuffle it back in. The outer layer of my parka felt like sandpaper when I wiped it off.

"You know where we are now," Zander said, sitting heavily on his seat, and panting from his minor exertions. "On Moon, you wait two minutes in air lock, then walk out and do your work. Here, takes half day to just get out of ship. Still do nothing."

At least my feet had not frozen. I thanked Zander for that.

★ ❄ ★

Captain Martinez had had no luck in detecting a signal from the stranded explorers and now sat before us looking very serious.

"We had a good fix before we landed; they should be within this hundred meter circle." She pointed to a circle on the map displayed in the table screen. "We are here." She indicated a point. "In principle, we need only to march in this direction for half a kilometer and they should be in sight."

Zander groaned. "In this weather, may as well be other side of planet. They dead, likely."

The captain closed her eyes, and opened them. "Likely. But not certain, and, we still need to recover the spy machines. Kent, you and Ensign Yu will make the first trek. It would be better if I could go; I am stronger and more rested, but I have to stay with the ship for security reasons. Despite the way things are out there, we may not be the only people or things about. Are you up to it? People's lives are at stake."

I was dead tired, my muscles in pain all over, and just getting warm again.

"Energy. Stimulants," Zander said. "They can do enough better with fuel to be worth the time to eat. Food is heat."

The captain pursed her lips. "Yes, Kent, Yu, energy bars for both of you. I'm going to save the emergency stimulants for later, but cocoa should be useful."

I jammed three meals worth of bars into myself, and Kristine did as well. The cocoa I washed them down with warmed my insides. If I ignored my muscles, I felt ready to go again.

★ ❄ ★

We added backpacks, belly packs, and hand torches over our parkas. The extra weight bothered me less than I would have thought.

Our target area was upwind and to the right, but we went out the rear of the trench, letting the wind blow us up the slope. Once out of the tube, it was less fierce, and it took no effort to stand upright on the ice. The Antarctic night was not totally dark. The stars and my home world, with its crescent at an odd angle to the horizon, cast light enough for our night vision goggles to give us a sense of the icescape, an expanse of little dune-like ridges pale as the Milky Way, separated by deep stygian shadows that could hide anything. The stars looked as bright as I'd ever seen them from the Moon's surface; Eta Carinae was spectacular and the Magellanic clouds were high above me. The southern cross was upside down, but still only halfway to the horizon.

Kristine touched me. "Homesick?"

"Yeah."

"Shouldn't we get to work?"

I nodded. The heads-up display in my goggles indicated our target was toward where half of Orion and Sirius lay above the horizon. We started trudging in that direction, with the radar built into our torches scanning ahead of us, looking for crevasses. Half a kilometer—only five football fields—but it seemed much longer.

We were not too uncomfortable; well-protected from the wind the sound chilled us more than the wind did. Finally, we reached the center of the target area. I scanned 360 degrees all around us, but even with infrared amplification at maximum, I couldn't see anything.

"Look, moving lights."

I looked where the dark shadow that was Kristine's arm pointed. Far away—much too far to be from the lost expedition—tiny feeble glows bobbed and winked in and out.

"Stars on the horizon? Some refraction effect?" I hazarded.

"Not bloody likely."

"Do we risk a flare?"

"They know we here!" Zander's voice said in my helmet. "News that we were coming is out and CLR-18 was big flare itself. Nothing to lose. But need to find expedition, fast!"

"Ensign Yurovich is right," the captain said. "Use a flare. Besides, it will be useful to know if there is any report of it."

"We have news?"

"Line of sight to the Moon, Yurovich. When President Reynolds announced our rescue effort, just an hour ago, Mr. Barman called her and told her it was appreciated but unnecessary, and that the UN had its own resources nearby that could be sent. The look on his face when she told him we were already on the ice was something to behold. Anyway, if your moving lights represent a public effort, they will acknowledge seeing your flare, I think; if covert, they will maintain their silence. Ensign Kent, the flare."

Kristine took a long skinny object from the side of her belly pack. She broke off a paper tube, which the incessant wind quickly took away, and stuck the spike this uncovered into the ice, slanting it well into the wind. We backed off and the rocket lit off with a poof, jetting upwind.

"Look down—you don't want to be blinded," she said.

It was hard not to watch the rocket's progress, but I lowered my eyes to scan around the alien landscape. In a few seconds, it was lit up bright as day. I spun around slowly, as Kristine, ten meters away, did too. Nothing. The flare was quickly blown far downwind.

"Inertial guidance says they have to be there. Could they have dug in deep enough to hide from us?"

Kristine pointed her goggles directly down at the ice and nodded. "They might have done. Let me chance another flare."

Just as the light of the second flare faded off to nothing, I caught a glint. I aimed the radar in its direction, and got a bright metal return in a linear ice feature about fifty meters away. "Over there! A marker of some kind."

By adjusting the radar frequency, I saw that the bright return sat over the ghost image of a small crevasse or a depression of sorts in the ice. "I think there's a hole or open crevasse below."

★ ✻ ★

It was visible on infrared when we got there, but just barely. Two of their sledges formed the roof of their shelter, now covered with blown snow, and the third was wedged flat in the crack below it. On that narrow sledge, they'd erected a four-person tent.

They'd left a pitoned rope hanging over the edge, which lay across some footholds hacked into the slanted ice wall of the crevasse. Kristine hung on to the rope with one hand while she laboriously dug snow out to get down to them. I tried that when I followed her and found that I had nowhere near the endurance of strength that she had. Indeed, after six hours in full gravity—four hours more than I'd ever spent in my life before—I became quickly fatigued and had to rest often, though I had no problem with simple strength after I did.

They were unconscious when we reached them—six huddled together in a tent meant for four, hypothermic but not frozen solid—or in rigor mortis, yet. Among them were three roughly spherical objects about the size of soccer balls with four jointed legs folded under them. The tops had been removed and alligator-clip wires ran from them to a small, boxy thermionic heat pump that wasn't putting out anything anymore.

Kristine started digging through her kit immediately while I reported in.

"Captain Martinez, we've found them and they're in bad shape. Vitals on the way in as soon as we can risk exposing them. Kristine is deploying our emergency heaters, but they'll only be good for a few hours. We need power. Is there any way we can get a line here from the ship?"

"We have three kilometers of conducting cable on board, but it is in a top locker. The door actuator motors are frozen. The door is structural, held in with pins when closed; it cannot be opened without moving those pins and the pin motors are frozen, too. Is there anything in your kit you might use?"

I took my packs off and rummaged through the stuff, hoping to see something of use. Some of it seemed clearly useless; an ultralight titanium solar oven concentrator, for instance—great for when the Sun rose in a month or so. A square meter or so of photovoltaic cells, too, rolled up in a tube. Smart fiber emergency blankets—the expedition members had already deployed their own.

"I don't want to hurry you," the captain said, "but the approaching infrared sources are maintaining radio silence. They are on vehicles, too. I would guess an ETA of five hours. The people approaching aren't announcing themselves. The UN has announced a relief operation, but it's not due here until tomorrow. When I asked about the approaching sources, they said we might have an instrument problem. It is not an instrument problem."

"The satellites would pick them up."

"The ISA is the only organization doing polar surveillance just now; they control the data. We'll remedy that in a couple of hours. A covert group would not necessarily be concerned with casualties and may not want any witnesses to their existence. They could pass off their early arrival as bureaucratic confusion, maybe. But I am not sure we wish to count on that."

The air in the tent felt noticeably warmer now. One of the expedition members groaned, the first sign of life from any of them.

"I've put sensor patches on all of them now," Kristine said. "Medical telemetry on the way."

I thought about telemetry and communications as I helped Kristine untangle the people. One woman, just coming back to awareness, started shaking uncontrollably. The heaters were helping, but it was still frigid in the tent. We had all the power we could need just 500 meters away.

Communications; the ship had a communications laser, tight beam. I had a flexible photovoltaic panel, and Kristine would have one in her kit as well. "Captain, how much power can you put on us with the communications laser?"

"About ten kilowatts continuous, less absorption by the atmosphere and blowing snow. Do you want us to try to heat you with it?"

"No, we have field photovoltaic arrays in our kits. There's no sun, but maybe you can make one for us."

There was a delay on the other end.

"We can't point the comm laser at you yet; its actuators are frozen, too, but Ensign Yurovich is working on it. You should proceed with your plan as if he succeeds, I think."

"Roger that."

I looked around the cluttered tent for something resembling an extension cord. There were about two meters of wire between the robot power supplies and their thermionic heat pump. I disconnected the heat pump, punched a small hole through the tent with my knife and pushed the end of the cord through.

"Kristine, I have to go outside for a few minutes."

"No way. As I have to stay with the people, that would violate the buddy system. Our heaters will hold us for a while."

I pointed at the spy robots. "If we recharge the robots, they'll be able to go back and forth between the ship and here better than we can. These people's lives may depend on it. Ours may depend on those being far away when these mysterious infrared sources get here."

Kristine stared at one of the unconscious explorers, lips pursed, eyes narrowed. I'm terrible at reading expressions accurately, a liability made worse by a vivid imagination. The nametag read: Richardson. "Less than amicable . . . " Kristine had said. I don't know what he'd done to her in their past life together, but I imagined she wouldn't be totally devastated if circumstances allowed saving only five of the six lives in our hands.

"It has to be done soon or we may *all* die," I added.

"Sorry. It's just all a bunch of macho games, isn't it? Covert operations, control, deception—those things all belong to the previous century, but here we are taking these ridiculous risks. Well, scream if you break a leg out there, will you?"

"Right."

As I exited the double flap entrance of the tent, I hesitated. Should I really leave Kristine alone with Richardson? That, I decided, was an uncharitable thought. Besides, I had enough worries of my own. I pushed my way out through the flaps and pulled myself up the ice stairs.

The wind, if anything, had picked up. It found some open crack in my right sleeve and sent a chill up my arm. The sledge roof creaked ominously as I crawled over it on my belly, but held. I had to use my axe to fish the plug end of the cord up from the tent roof below. It took several tries, but with the axe in my right hand, I was finally able to tease the cord up high enough to grab it with my left.

I rested for a minute and started to get cold. Not here, I told myself. Keep moving.

I had to lift my mask and hold the cord in my teeth while I fished the solar cells out of my pack. I then had to take my big over mittens off to unsnap them. The thin material of the gloves underneath may have done well in vacuum, or still air, but the icy wind sucked heat from them. I would have to endure it.

Then I discovered two things, one of which I should have checked below. The arrays didn't want to unroll in the cold wind and the prongs on the plug on the cord didn't match the plug on the arrays. I decided to tackle the second problem first. The cord had a standard Australian plug while the arrays, like everything on the Moon, had a North American standard outlet.

"Zander, will the expedition equipment take 110 volt a.c.?"

"*Da,* converters will provide proper d.c. voltage from any a.c. input up to a kilovolt at any frequency from fifty hertz to a kilohertz. Batteries take longer to charge maybe; less max current with 110. Working on laser."

"Roger that." I looked at the array. The cord emerged from a small box that was probably an inverter—a shame lose to power by going from direct to alternating and then again going back to direct. The plug was frozen hard and my hands were getting that way fast. I jammed them into my parka pockets and discovered my universal tool; it had needle pliers jaws on it. If I'd been inside, I'd probably have tried taking the plug apart. As it was, the clock was ticking.

Brute force time, I applied the pliers to a slanted plug prong, twisting. The plug casing shattered, leaving the bare prongs still, thank providence, attached to their wires. Holding them with the needle end of the pliers, I shoved each prong into one of the North American socket's parallel slots. There was enough friction to hold them there.

Now I had to replace the damaged insulation somehow. Here my studying the content of my kit back on the CLR-18 paid off. There was a package of wipes in my parka's right front pocket. I got them out, wrapped several around the connection, then twisted a last one into a short length of cord, with which I tied everything in place. That would have to do; my fingers were so numb by this time that I couldn't get my mittens back on.

"Damn! Can't get gloves on, fingers too cold."

"Get hands under parka, down in waistband, in crotch," Zander said.

That, I realized, was an excellent idea. I did this quickly, freezing my groin in the process, but the fingers started to warm. As they did, they hurt like hell. I groaned.

"Fingers hurt, yes? Good. Not lose them. Now shut eyes."

Why that? I wondered. Oh . . .

The world exploded in light, dazzling me before I complied with Zander's direction. I lay there bent over in a near fetal position, hands hurting, blinded with purple spots in front of my eyes and shivering uncontrollably and getting wet.

Wet? I opened my eyes again, gradually. The light of the comm laser was a deep red, I knew, but it was so bright I saw it as white; my yellow parka was a deep orange, however. The snow on top of the sledges was beginning to melt. My ersatz insulation job! The tissue would get soaked and it would short.

My hands felt usable again. Forcing myself to move deliberately, I got my gloves on again and lifted the cord above the melting snow. The array was unrolling now, of its own accord.

"Good show, Zander. What did you do?"

"Microwaves go through boron fiber hull, warm actuators."

"We used the CLR-18's spare radar unit *and* the laser," Captain Martinez added.

I propped the array up on the marker and looped the cord around the top to hold the array to the marker in the wind, and hold the connection out of the wet. "Thanks, it worked."

I had to lean on the bottom to keep it from flapping away, however. Tape. Again, I needed some tape, or the equivalent. My med kit.

I took my hands out of my mittens again; the combination of biting wind and hot light felt weird, but by blocking most of the wind with my body while keeping my hands in the light, I was able to open the med kit and find the tape. I didn't do a pretty job; just looped the tape around the bottom until it ran out. The result flapped and vibrated, but seemed like it would hold for long enough. The telltales told me it was pumping out power. Repacking the med kit took a ridiculous amount of time, but I thought I might need it again. Finally, I got myself back down the crude rope and step arrangement and in through the double flap arrangement.

The stench almost drove me out again. Our emergency heaters, combined with modern insulating fabric, sheltered us from the most of the wind, and the heat of seven human bodies—six unwashed for over a week—had brought the small space up over room temperature and driven from refrigerated hiding every noxious odor known. Clearly, in the last days, some of the expedition members had not been able to use even what primitive toilet facilities they had—which I suspect were overflowing.

Almost reluctantly I pulled off my mittens, hood, facemask, and nodded to Kristine.

"Two hours, Abe. You were out there two bloody hours and you look like death warmed over."

"Sorry. We have power?"

A spark crackled and a wiry, sandy-haired man lifted his head up from the robots he was working on and smiled. "We have power. I'm Sam Reynolds."

I stuck out a defrosted hand. "Abe Yu. I see Kristine has taken care of you."

She shot me a look of pure fury.

"Kristine Kent? Small world, or rather small universe, I fear," Reynolds said as he shook my hand, firmly enough for someone near death's door only a couple of hours ago. Kristine had apparently not introduced herself, at least not fully.

There was something in the way he said that which spoke of mixed feelings for his rescuer.

Kristine sighed. "You have heard a lot about me, I suppose. It was not my choice to be here, you know."

"Understood. We've heard a lot about you and the Moon," Reynolds added, a bit wryly. "There's always another side."

Oh, crap, I thought. What they'd heard, they'd heard from her ex, of course. He'd had weeks to unload. "Less than amicable" was what we'd heard from Kristine.

"Nothing personal toward the Moon, I'm sure, other than that I live on it."

Reynolds grunted. "Abe, my wife, Sue Reynolds, is over in the corner. She'd give you a hug but she's not feeling well just yet."

The woman put her head up. "Oh, I'll be right in a few minutes."

She didn't look like it—and she put her head back down very quickly.

"I'm working on Richardson now," Kristine said. "He might not make it. We need to start I-Vs on the other three."

I thought about the implications of "He might not make it." Whether or not she had murder in her heart, it could get quite tense if her ex didn't make it while under Kristine's care. Sam Reynolds, eying the robots with a smile on his face and wolfing down an energy bar, seemed to get stronger by the moment. I figured I could leave that part of the mission to him for the time being.

"Kristine, I'm lousy at sticking needles into people. Why don't I relieve you with Richardson?"

One look from her and I realized my effort to be diplomatic about the situation had failed completely.

"On the other hand, we all do what we have to, I suppose."

"Right. My kit's over there." She gestured to the pile of bags in the corner of the tent. The yellow box was open on top.

I fished out my emergency medical kit again, thankful that I'd taken the time to repack it properly. Its I-V module was about half the size of a deck of cards, but had what was needed. Kristine's would be identical. Two I-Vs, three patients—I would have to do some kind of triage.

"I can give you a hand," Reynolds said. "I feel strong enough."

Another kind of triage. If we didn't get the spy robots powered up and out of here soon, we'd all likely get killed.

He seemed to understand what I was thinking and shook his head. "There's nothing to be done with these until their batteries charge."

I nodded. "Okay, thanks."

Two men and a woman were still unconscious. They were on their backs, and covered. The readouts from the sensors Kristine had attached showed their body temperatures were still depressed about five degrees Celsius. One of the men had a heartbeat that seemed way too slow, and seemed to have stopped breathing except for irregular gasps almost a minute apart. The woman was breathing more rapidly than the other man, but both seemed stable for the moment. The guy that was gasping would be first.

He didn't respond to the stab of the needle and his blood was as blue as I'd ever seen. His core temp was down to 29.7 C. A microanalyzer built into the needle module sent the data to the ship's computer. It told me to give him D5NS, so I found the dehydrated tablets, put them in the I-V bag and handed the bag to Reynolds, who crushed them, ran sterilized water in through a filter/heater collar, hooked it up to the needle and hung the bag from the roof of the tent with tape.

While he did this, I turned to the woman simply because she was nearest; the condition of the last two was essentially the same as far as I could tell. I bared the arm, wrapped the elastic around it and looked for a vein. She moaned when I slid the needle in. I got almost no blood out of the woman—must have missed the vein. An alarm started beeping—the telltale on the last member. I made an instant decision to finish what I was doing. I had to try somewhere else; the vein was visible enough, so I tried a little ways up the arm from where I tried the first time. This time, the telltale in the smart needle indicated I was in.

I turned the hookup over to Reynolds, then stepped awkwardly over him and the woman to the next person. As there was nowhere to kneel and scarcely a place to put my feet, I bent over the man, Simmons. He'd stopped breathing, though there was still a weak heartbeat. His core temp was right at 30 C; too low.

"Ms. Reynolds, move over," I said, touching her shoulder. She groaned and shifted her body further into the tent wall; the whole tent wobbled and my first I-V pulled free from the roof and landed on its patient.

"Got it," Sam Reynolds said.

I knelt down, got the breathing tube in the man's mouth and started breathing for him.

"You!" a new voice said, weak but still filled with hostility. "Stay away from me, you bloody bitch." Kristine's ex had come around.

"I didn't plan to be here" she said. "For now, just pretend you don't know me. I'm going to give you some glucose. Just relax. It will all be over soon enough."

"Bloody well better be."

"I'm trying to save your life."

"Which wouldn't have been in danger if it weren't for your little spy mission here, would it?"

"I didn't make the bloody crevasse, you idiot!" Kristine had definite tears in her eyes now.

"Abe, do we have another IV, anywhere?"

I looked up, "No."

I turned my attention back to Simmons and got his breathing going again, then asked, "Sam, do you guys have another I-V kit in here? In your medical supplies?"

He shook his head and pointed down, reminding us that the sledge on which the crowded tent was perched lay jammed in the crevasse where much of their supplies had tumbled. "There was an ice bridge thick enough to defeat the radar, but flimsy enough to give way with the weight of two sledges. Unlucky."

"Yeah," I said. "Unlucky." I looked at Simmons—he was breathing on his own again, but it looked marginal. "Kristine, how's it going?"

I looked over. She wiped her eyes with her sleeve.

"Is yours still breathing, Kristine?"

"Just barely. I think he's fading." Her voice was cold and professional.

Hatred of a formerly loved one, I thought, must lie over love like this icecap, accumulated over eons of coldness hiding what was there before. Sear the covering away, and there it is, again, in its most elemental form.

"Captain Martinez," I said.

"Go ahead," her voice echoed from my helmet speaker and Kristine's.

"We may lose a couple of people. We need more medical supplies here, somehow, quickly. Two I-V's and a defibrillator at least."

There was a silence of several seconds. There was a fair amount of noise in the tent now, but I could still hear the wind over it, stronger than ever. "Then I will bring them. Ensign Yurovich will take command of the CLR-18."

That, I realized, was a momentous decision for her. She might have sent Zander, but he clearly wasn't up to it physically. He could talk to the ship's computer just fine, though.

"You'll be able to see the beacon on radar . . . " I said

"I can follow the laser beam, I think. Martinez out."

I felt like an idiot. There would be a brilliant highway of scattered light leading right to us.

She arrived in fifteen minutes, towing a pallet that turned out to contain everything she could think of—additional rations as well as medical supplies. And she was in time. An hour after she arrived, our patients were apparently out of danger and Sue Reynolds had recovered enough strength to assist in caring for the others.

I had just started to think we'd get out of this unscathed when Zander called.

"Code C, Captain Martinez."

Captain Martinez held up her hand. "Radio silence. Our visitors are almost here." She turned to Sam Reynolds "How are the robots?"

"One percent. Actually, that's fairly good; they were designed for thirty days. They could go ten kilometers on what they've absorbed so far."

"Not far enough, is it?" Kristine said.

Captain Martinez looked at her for a moment then shook her head. "Easy, Kristine. Throwing them down the crevasse is not good enough; they have too much metal and would be too easy to find in the ice, I think, though it might delay their recovery. We will send them to the ship; that's CLR property. They shouldn't search it."

I had a bad feeling about that. "Officially they aren't even there. That gives them freedom of action and gives the ISA deniability."

Captain Martinez closed her eyes. "I was once very close to someone in the ISA. They are not all banditos; many think they are doing what is right for all humanity."

"Do we bet our lives that's right for this particular group?" Sue Reynolds asked.

Captain Martinez didn't answer immediately. In the silence that followed one of the emergency heaters gave out with a sputter and the wind noise and flapping tent fabric made it very clear to us that clocks were still ticking.

"No. But to send the robots to the ship . . . it is our best hope, I think. But it must be now, *pronto!*"

Sam immediately started disconnecting leads. I grabbed a tool and began reattaching the housings.

"Code B," Zander called out from the ship.

We didn't need to be told what that meant. I started putting in every other screw.

"Richardson's gone," Kristine said, tonelessly. "Heart stopped."

"Defibrillator?" I asked. How could that have happened? He'd been talking just a minute ago, not sensibly to be sure, but talking.

"In here? How could we clear? He's gone now, anyway." Kristine sobbed.

We were all silent for several seconds. Deep down she must have still cared, I thought. There must have been a happy time for them once with dreams of lifetime together.

"What about everyone else?" Captain Martinez asked.

"Conscious or resting with stable signs," I said.

"We're all right," Sam Reynolds said. "Sue and I can take care of things. Do what you have to do."

Captain Martinez stood up; she was probably the only one who could do so in the cramped tent. "*Sí*. Yu, come with me." She hesitated a moment. "Ensign Kent, deal with it later. We need you, too, now. Suit up and join us as soon as you can."

She stared at the captain for a moment, then wordlessly started getting her gear together.

We lugged the robots out and sent them on their way, the steel tips on their spidery legs making short work of the rudimentary ice steps that I'd had to negotiate so carefully. I was about to go in when Captain Martinez pointed at the solar array and the laser illuminating it.

"Remember how difficult this was for you to find? I think it should be even more difficult for them. Do not ask any questions, as I want the listeners to believe the lies I will tell." She put a gloved hand in front of her mouth and looked at us. We nodded.

"I will now break radio silence. Ensign Yurovich, we have recharged the batteries on one of the motorized toboggans, but would like a little more power, so keep the laser on us as we move south to prepare location A."

Captain Martinez pulled the tape away from the array, unplugged it, and began walking south with it over her head. "Keep the laser on us, Ensign."

After an initial hesitation, the comm laser beam started following her. I quickly zipped up my parka and pulled down my face protection as the warmth of the beam left me. Then I grabbed the marker tripod and disassembled it. We had the location in our inertial guidance units. No one else needed to find us just yet.

About fifty meters beyond the crevasse, Captain Martinez rolled up the array and stopped, but told Zander to " . . . keep the beam on the array as we go south."

He catches on quickly, I thought. With barely a hiccup, the bright sunny spot on the snow kept heading south at the speed of Captain Martinez' walk. It would be so bright in the infrared, I realized that observers would have a hard time distinguishing any objects in the beam—or whether there were any in it at all.

Captain Martinez walked back toward my position, a dark shadow silhouetted by the retreating laser beam spot. When she arrived, she took a cylindrical object from her pocket and, holding it like a telescope, carefully sighted some object in the sky through it. A pulse of violet light stabbed upward, so short I could almost see it as a pulse instead of a beam. A narrow beam data burst to a relay satellite, I surmised.

Almost simultaneously Zander said "Code A."

"Down," Captain Martinez whispered.

We scrambled down, but instead of going inside, Captain Martinez took her ice axe and began chipping a ledge in the ice. "We need to keep a lookout."

She stepped up onto the ledge she had just cut.

I followed, having to crouch a little to keep my helmet just high enough over the edge of the crevasse to see. She'd cut the ledge for her own height. What I could see of the ship was the area on top just beneath the bright origin of the comm beam, and a slight glow from below from the open hatch, I presumed. The rest merged into the blackness of the polar night.

"I have cargo. Am securing." The hatch glow faded into night.

"He seems to be moving around now," I whispered to the captain.

Captain Martinez nodded. "He will be disassembling the spy

robots, hiding their components in various places."

"Can he get all that done?" I worried—Zander could barely move.

"Look at ship's telemetry, channel A."

The ship's atmosphere read 1.1 bars, $O_2$ 80%. "Captain," I said, "He's flooded the hull with oxygen, to stimulate himself. That's dangerous."

She nodded gravely but said nothing.

"Does he have time?"

The captain shook her head. "Listen."

The whine of turbines had become noticeable above the constant gale. I flipped my visor up and scanned in the direction of the noise with my infrared binoculars, but saw nothing.

"They are near the ship," Captain Martinez said. "The wind disguises the direction of the sound."

Of course. I turned to the ship and scanned the edge of the pool of light thrown by the comm laser. I caught the slightest hint of motion and saw a gray shadow emerge from the cold black. It looked a bit like a tortoise on tank treads. It was followed by another and then another; they were huge, half as large as the CLR 18 itself.

I flipped my goggles down and noted the inside pressure was down to 0.85 bar, ambient for this altitude. Perhaps Zander had finished his chore, or came to his senses about the danger.

Black shadows detached themselves from the newly arrived vehicles and headed into the trench that lay under the ventral port. I knew better than to suggest that we try to do anything; we were virtually weaponless and only three of us were in shape for any physical activity.

The telemetry from the ship vanished; I looked at the captain.

"Interference; they're swamping the carrier wave." She took out her hand-held device again, sighted through it, turned away to another location in the sky, and spoke rapidly, though I couldn't hear what she said over the wind.

One of the ice vehicles started moving, heading south toward where the patch of light from the com laser was now focused.

"It won't work," I said. "When they find we aren't there, they'll interrogate Zander."

"Maybe he will tell them we must have left the beam somewhere along the route. He would not know then."

"They'll get it out of the ship's memory."

"No, that would be much too hard. The ship would wipe it first. Ensign Yurovich is a clever person."

I was looking at Captain Martinez when she gasped. At first I thought she'd been hit with a bullet but then her facemask was lit up with a strange bluish light. I turned around. The CLR-18 had split open and was gushing flame.

"Zander . . . "

Captain Martinez pulled me down. "The propellants, they are hypergolic. When the flame reaches the tanks it may . . . "

The boom arrived right on cue. Then the wind halted eerily and a white snow started falling on us that was somehow different. I took a mitten and glove off to feel it; it didn't melt, but crumbled into a fine white powder. "Titanium oxide," I guessed out loud. Much of the ship's exterior had been made of titanium.

The whine of turbines announced that our visitors were on the move again. We waited for five minutes and poked our heads up. The upper half of the ship was gone and what was left looked like the rib cage of some alien monster skeleton bathed in red light from numerous fires still in progress. A scan with the binoculars was futile; the visitors had vanished into the gloom, or got caught in the explosion. I hoped for the latter; if only Zander had been able to take them with him!

"I know it doesn't look good," I said. "But we have to see if . . . if there's anything left."

"They may be waiting for us to show ourselves," the captain said.

We said nothing for what might have been a minute.

"We must risk it, anyway," she said at last. "Wait here, I will tell what has happened and what we will do."

✦ ✳ ✦

Kristine came out. "Oh my god," she said when she saw the wreck. "He's not likely to have survived that, is he?"

"No, it is not likely. But even if it is the worst, the flight recorder should have survived. We will see what they did and then we will see that everyone knows."

"If we make it out of here alive," I replied.

"Even if not," the captain replied, the ice in her voice somehow on fire.

We stepped out of the crevasse and pressed toward the embers. Though the wind had resumed it seemed less menacing now, a minor problem compared to the disaster that had occurred. Zander had brought it on himself, I told myself. Not exercising so he needed the extra oxygen. Now he was dead and we were not much better off; without the resources of the ship, we would soon be in the same state as the people we came to rescue. None of us spoke a word of that, however. Whatever he had done, we would have to find what remained of our comrade.

When we got there, the remains of the ship's hull jutted up over us like some ribs of a turtle skeleton on its back, burnt away from the belly down. We walked in through a crack in the shell to where we'd been meeting and donning our Antarctic survival gear just a couple of hours ago. The equipment was gone to cinders and there were just longerons covered with white titanium oxide ash to show where our stations had been.

The least damaged area was at the bottom near the door. Near that were three blackened human skeletons, any of which might have been Zander. The wind whistling through the wreckage seemed to call my name with his voice. "Yu, Yu . . . " I shivered.

What remained of a titanium rib fell with a snap and landed with a boom, just missing us. I had never believed in ghosts, but then, for a moment, I felt doubt.

"We should go down into the trench," the captain shouted. "The data recorder is behind a panel near the hatch. It is sheltered now under there; the wind has changed direction. We can talk there."

Wordlessly, we walked out of the burned out shell the way we came. The trench was littered with debris of all kinds—some intact, some little more than ash, and everything between, all trapped in ice melted from the fire. But when we got underneath the wreck, what amazed me was that the underside or the ship appeared untouched and the ice unmelted.

Kristine tapped the refractory foam that covered the bottom of what had been the CLR-18. "The atmospheric insulation works in both directions, apparently."

"I am at a loss," Captain Martinez said as she recovered the flight data record. "I suspect they were about to discover the spy robots and he managed to destroy all the evidence to save us, at the cost of his own life. You do not know what blesses you until it is gone."

"Poor Yurovich. He knew the chance he was taking by using hyperbaric oxygen," Kristine added. "He put the mission ahead of himself after all, then. We shall all miss him."

I nodded, but felt uneasy. Self sacrifice and taking chances had not been in the character of the Zander I knew. He had been smart as a whip and always looked for ways around difficulties. Then I remembered the change in the pressure reading in the ship¬—from over pressure to ambient. I also remembered the big engine bay door lying in the trench, covered with the same insulation Kristine had just tapped.

"No, no, he would find some way out of that," I said, looking around wildly. "Maybe he had left the ship before the explosion."

"Ensign Yu . . . " the captain started, then stopped.

I heard that faint voice calling through the wind again, but this time it sounded even more like the wind. "Yu, Yu. Help me."

"Do you hear that too? Do you hear that?" I yelled at the top of my voice. "Zander! It's us. They've gone away. You can come out now!"

"Here. Panel is too heavy." His voice was faint, but we all heard it as the wind relented for a moment. A landing gear door panel, probably scraped off in our crash landing!

"Zander, it's probably frozen in. Don't waste your strength. Keep talking, we'll find you.  Sing something."

"*Ochi chier-nue . . .* "

Kristine giggled, on the edge of hysterical relief.  "He likes you, captain dark eyes."

"*Qué?*"

More giggles from Kristine; "Keep singing!  I want to hear Moscow Nights next."

Zander kept singing and as we moved toward the south end of the trench, his voice became clearer.  I searched for the engine bay door, found it among debris of all kinds and started walking toward it, but since I still didn't trust myself to run in a full Earth gravity, Captain Martinez and Kristine beat me to it.  They pulled on the panel and the ice cracked with a bang, releasing it.  They turned the panel over.  There, resting on a bed of aerogel, was Zander.

With a groan, he sat up.  "Concert over.  I hid because not sure how they would question me.  I thought ship would defend itself."

"They tried to burn their way into something with a cutting torch, I think.  They did not know about the oxygen."

"*Da*, I am sorry."

"You did what you could.  Can you walk?  Camp is about half a kilometer away."

Zander was quiet for a while, then held out his arms.  "I walk or die."

We took turns helping him up the incline at the end of the trench and, through the dark and the blowing snow, struggled toward camp, trusting the captain's inertial compass for the direction; our eyes were useless.  Despite our gear an unceasing head wind began to rob us of body heat.  162 kelvins outside—I thought of Zander's feet in ordinary space boots self insulated by a layer of aerogel.  My feet moved freely in warm air, thanks to his knowledge of arctic survival.  But his might be frozen to blocks of ice.  Stoically, he said nothing and continued to step, step, and step.

When I heard the sound of the turbines of the unidentified snow vehicle's return, I was almost relieved.  It would all be over soon, one way or another, and I wasn't sure how much I cared how.

"Drop to the ice," Captain Martinez ordered.

We complied without protest.  It was good to lie down, despite the cold.  I felt infinitely tired.

"Ensign Yu, stay alert," she said.

I looked over at her and she was on her back, pointing her communications device at the stars again, almost directly overhead.

"They find us soon," Zander said.  "Despite our coldness, our bodies shine too hot in infrared."

"Just hang on for a little while," the captain said.  There was tension in her voice, but, strangely, I thought, hope.

They were upwind of us, and it was surprising how quickly the blowing snow piled up against our bodies. Maybe, they would not find us.

*"Lunar spies, stay down, spread your arms and legs!"*

Whatever boom box they were using put out enough power to hurt my ears. The wind was no match for it. It had its emotional effect as well. Resistance against something that loud simply felt futile. There was something I needed to know, before. This would be my last chance. "Kristine, I am sorry if I seem not relevant, but the split between you and your former husband. Was there a political aspect to it?"

"That matters? No, not really. After we got past the romance, I just didn't want to be so, so dominated, so bloody owned. He wasn't going to change, so I had to make a decision. It wasn't his fault, I'm the one that changed, and he was very hurt, angry. I broke his arm the last time he tried to have his way with me. He got our little boy."

"What? You have no child on the records."

"I put as much distance between us as I could. When I emigrated to the CLR, and the independence movement came, he started making anti-lunar noises. Custody was a weapon against me. But Ricky was difficult in school, a bother. Then Ricky died in an accident boating with his father on Loch Lomond the next year. So that resolved itself, didn't it?"

"You must think he . . . "

"He could have," Captain Martinez broke in. "We think he sabotaged the expedition; he was going have the ISA base rescue them. But I think they had no intention of doing so."

"The bloody . . . I've no need to apologize then, do I?"

She had killed him. Killed him and mourned him. Love or hate? I thought. Love and hate.

*"Martinez, we want the flight record of your ship. Stand up slowly with it in your hand."*

The ice six inches from my right mitten exploded into a shower of chips just as the crack of the projectile thrower reached us. 106 decibels apparently weren't enough to make them secure in their power over us.

Slowly, Captain Martinez got up, leaving the tubular comm unit in the snow under her. It was about three feet from me.

"Have courage, my friends" she said, *"vaya con Dios."* She looked first at me, looked down briefly. Then she started walking toward her fate.

They weren't, I thought, likely to leave witnesses to this. There was something I needed to say, and had not had the courage to say it so far, but . . . "Kristine, this is a lousy time, but I don't want to die without saying this. I, I've had . . . I think you're someone I'd like to be with. I wish we had time."

"Abraham, you're right. It's a bloody lousy time."

She let me feel like the idiot I was for several seconds, then added, "But thanks for the thought, I know it was well meant and sincere. For whatever it is worth, fate has now linked our names together for eternity, hasn't it? I wish you well, but as a friend."

"I had to say something."

"Of course you did. Centuries ago, when the dikes of Holland burst and saltwater flooded the polders, the trees, dying from the salt water at their roots, blossomed and sent their pollen into the wind. Life never gives up, does it?"

"*Nyet*," Zander added. "It does not. There are only three of them in each vehicle. All three from nearest vehicle are with captain. Kristine, if Abraham and I distract them, draw their lights, can you run in darkness to steal it?"

A second spotlight from the second vehicle stabbed on us, centered directly on Kristine.

"They are hearing every bloody word we say, aren't they?"

"*Da*. A bug." Zander turned his head to Kristine with a grunt. "A tiny one, like flea. Maybe it jumps from your ex-husband to you."

Kristine shuddered. "From out of death's heart . . . Well, he won't be shedding any more bugs, will he?" She sighed. "I think this whole scene is getting a bit boring. I'll be some time, as the man said."

She got up, gracefully as always, and started trotting away from the empty vehicle, a spotlight full on her.

"Kristine!" I yelled.

"Ensign, get dow . . . " The captain's voice cut off with a sudden crack.

There were three sharp reports, and Kristine went down. Ice exploded next to Zander and me. "Kristine . . . " I sobbed softly.

"I obey orders," Zander said. "I stay down." Then he started crawling like a seal away from me. The spotlight on us followed him as ice exploded all around him as he inched and flopped along in random directions to nowhere in particular. I heard men laughing.

But I was left in the dark. I could think of only one thing to try—the captain's communicator. She suspected a bug, I realized, and had said nothing to us that it could relay. But she'd been talking to someone up there. Somewhere overhead. I looked up and saw a streak—even in the urgency of the moment, I realized that it must be a meteor and wondered. Then I took a deep breath, lunged for the communicator and grabbed it. When I did, I saw the ship's record disk under it; Captain Martinez had been playing for time—with her life. Hurry, I thought. I rolled to my back and looked up through the communication device and scanned around overhead. Suddenly, I saw a bright icon displayed among the stars. But I couldn't find a transmission button, or anything with my gloves. It might be voice activated I thought.

The spotlight came back to me—I could have thrown the communicator down, but I'm stubborn. Expecting a bullet at any moment, I started talking.

"Whoever's up there, Captain Martinez has been captured, Ensign Kent and maybe Ensign Yurovich have been shot, and I'm next. If you can, help, please help. If not, tell people what happened. I'm . . ."

The device exploded in my glove, its shrapnel digging pits out of my visor. I rolled over as fast as I could. I got hit hard in my backpack, like a kick.

A brilliant flickering light, much bluer than the spotlight, washed over the snow around me. A distant crackling sound reached my ears. I rolled over again and discovered my legs were still working. Far overhead, a rocket seemed to be descending right on top of us.

The spotlight winked out. I heard a loud clank, whir, a bang and a roar; a missile leaped from one of the vehicles toward the sky, and then another.

They were met by thin violet beams that hurt my eyes despite their dimness and the visor. The missiles exploded almost instantly. Then one of the beams lanced down and touched the ice in front of the nearest vehicle, creating an instant cloud of steam. When it dissipated, the vehicles were heading away at what was likely their best speed.

I struggled to my feet. Kristine lay on the ice about twenty meters away, the captain about fifty. In a triage decision that hurt as much as any I've ever made, I went for the captain; I'd seen what happened to Kristine.

I found I could run in one gravity; the pounding on my knees was incredible, but I did not collapse. When I got there, the captain was unconscious, but breathing. Her visor was shattered and there was an ugly bruise on her forehead, but she was breathing. They seemed to have just missed her. Okay, I could run for Kristine.

The roar of the descending spacecraft, a black angular shape with about the same cross section as the CLR-18, but longer and much meaner-looking, drowned out the wind with its belly jets. Its gear snapped down without any problems. I stumbled and turned my attention back to what I was doing. My back hurt like hell, burning and freezing at the same time. I tried to ignore it, but I slowed despite myself, trying to run in Earth gravity with a full set of arctic gear on against a twenty-meter-per-second wind on little food and without any sleep for about forty hours.

My shadow doubled in front of me. I blinked and it stayed double. I looked up. Another rocket was descending. What was this, I wondered, a lunar invasion of Earth?

Kristine was just ahead of me, and in the glare of the descending rockets, I could see blood on the snow.

I collapsed beside her on my knees and gasped for air, hardly able to think.

"Abe . . . "

She was conscious

"Take it easy. Where?"

"Severed spine," she gasped. "A leg wound, too, I think, but I can't feel that, can I? Silly how little it hurts for so much damage."

"They can fix that."

"If I don't bloody bleed to death first. The leg, Abe. Stop the bleeding."

"Yeah." I got my pack off and found my med kit had been blown to bits. I worked hers off as gently as I could, fearful of the damage I might do, found the kit and got my gloves off. The frigid wind froze my hands almost instantly; I tried to shelter them and ignore it as I cut away the layers of cloth where the hole and the blood were, just above her knee. It was a mess; she'd probably lose the leg. Stop the bleeding, somehow. I jammed gauze in the hole and wrapped tape around to hold it tight, making a bloody, sticky mess. But it held. Now for the wound in the back.

"Abe, about us. Yours doesn't sound like such a bad idea right now. Sorry."

I squeezed her mitten, a totally inadequate gesture, but all that time and prudence permitted. She returned the squeeze, briefly and closed her eyes.

"Kristine . . . I've got to turn you over now," I said.

There was no answer.

Biting my lip, I eased her over.

The wound in her back was a crater. White bone shone through the shredded parka, backpack, and meat frozen as if in a supermarket. I thought part of her spine was gone.

Four black-clad people surrounded us. Stretchers, tarps, and plastic boxes appeared as if by magic.

"Ensign, Yu, we've got her now." It was a woman, short, with a wisp of blond hair showing behind her visor. "Just take it easy, very easy, lean forward into my arms and don't move any more than you have to."

I wondered what the hell my back looked like. I kind of keeled over more than leaned, but she caught me and picked me up as effortlessly as if I'd been a child and spread me out on a stretcher.

Then I fainted.

The roar of rockets and acceleration awakened me. Someone's hand took my hand as soon as my eyes opened. A firm, strong hand.

"We don't have enough fuel to make orbit; we're just hopping to the British station on the coast."

I think I nodded. Things got very fuzzy after that; I fell into a deep sleep. I dreamed Kristine had slipped into my bunk, lay on top of me and began to make love to me, but Zander interrupted us to ask why we were going to Antarctica, so Kristine pushed herself up to answer him and broke in half, making a huge mess of blood and bone chips and intestinal matter, which began to float around the small cubical getting on everything.

I opened my eyes and started to scream; but I was on a clean bunkroom, wrapped in sheets and strapped down, in free fall. Then acceleration hit and I passed out again.

The official story is that the CLR-20 rescued us as well as the explorers. The media never mentioned the other long, black ship, which is just as well because the U.N. would have had a righteous fit about a nuclear powered CLR ship operating in the Earth's atmosphere.

So I must have come up with all that in a delirium. When I met CLR Commodore Sally Duluth officially, at Shepard City on the celebration of the fourth anniversary of the founding of CLR Service, she seemed to be meeting me for the first time—but there was a twinkle in her eye to match the one in the dark eyes of Captain Martinez.

Zander met us there; he lives in Shepard city now, teaching history and playing golf. He is just as big, but, I think, noticeably firmer, and noticeably quieter.

After the speeches and the ceremonies, Zander and I went out alone into the vacuum. Earth hung high in the sky with Antarctica tilted toward us. It was clear down there today, and I was able to find the Antarctic Peninsula and from that, the mountains. West of there, the bodies of Kristine Kent and her former husband lie in a crevasse, far too deep for anyone but those of us who were there to know that they did not die accidentally. Kristine deserved better; she deserves a place in a hall of heroes of the Republic, someday. But the lie preserves the peace, for now.

Zander placed his hand, all the more bear-like for the vacuum glove, on my shoulder. There was no need for words.

# STORY NOTES:

Changes in political administration can happen peacefully—or not so peacefully, even in this current enlightened age. The political background is complex. Once a United Nations operation takes hold, it can take on a life of its own. Did you know that United States troops in South Korea still serve under the blue United Nations flag?

In this scenario, the International Space Authority, set up to keep the U.S., Russia, and China following the same basic astronautical rules of space, modeled after the laws of the sea recognized by most countries, has become itself a power center, with corrupt bureaucrats taking a cut of all Earth-Moon trade to fund the operation, and themselves. Residents of Cislunar space—administratively from just above Clarke orbit to just beyond the Moon's orbit—eventually had enough of it, and managed to get through an autonomy resolution that established a government that finally demanded full independence and freedom from the ISA bureaucracy.

There was some blow-back, a siege of the L1 space colony and manufacturing center, followed by a period of near cold war between the Earth and the new Cislunar Republic. The Earth is vastly more populous and wealthy, but people at the bottom of a gravity well tend to avoid throwing stones; so I've imagined a period of tension and competition short of war.

Going it alone, the Cislunar Republic (CLR) needed to establish its own version of a space-going "coast guard," rescuing astronauts in distress, catching contraband runners, and generally showing the black and silver flag where needed. If you have that kind of service, you'll need a training organization and facility. This is all spanking new of course, staffed by some of the pilots and crewmembers who used fly shuttles between Low Earth Orbit (LEO) and the Moon, and decided to cast their lot with the new republic. Sally Duluth was the purser on the shuttlecraft *Mani* when autonomy began; Avia Martinez was one of the flight attendants working for her.

At some point, necessity trumps fear, and some of CLR ships are equipped with a nuclear propulsion system able to get their ships down to the Earth and back again. We don't specify the technology here; there are several possibilities, one being an aneutronic proton-boron reaction. A thorium-based nuclear-thermal system with a higher-temperature primary heat exchanger might be another possibility. Such a spacecraft would use compressed air flowing through a secondary heat exchanger as reaction mass in an atmosphere, and switch to a primary heat exchange system using liquid hydrogen as a moderator, coolant and propellant for extraterrestrial operations.

G. David Nordley, January 2015

# OUT OF THE QUIET YEARS

## 0.4 MILLIGAUSS

I watched the surface magnetometer telemetry average with growing anxiety. It was up ten times the average of the last five years, or the last five days for that matter, and it was growing too fast. But there was no backing out for me now. I could hear Captain Sin in the background.

" . . . so the party's over, Amalthea; old Jove's magnetic field is coming back for real this time. We've got to pull you out of there, *now*, and we're coming to do it. Our ETA over Mount Barnard is three two seven point twenty-three hundred. End."

Lu Sin pirouetted away from the comm panel to face me and floated in front of our spacecraft's bubble nose, a spare, severe woman whose light complexion and short straight silver hair made a stark contrast with the great orange-yellow globe behind her. She had a reputation for never making mistakes, and for being a very private person. She was senior.

Not knowing why Jupiter's magnetic field turned off hadn't put science in a very good position to predict when and how fast it would come back on again. Like volcanoes, magnetic fields are a result of the 'weather' of a planet's heart—chaotic, sensitive, unpredictable. Geologists can show you where even Earth's field has faded off and come back in the reverse direction more than once. The quiet years might have been decades, centuries, or millennia. They turned out to be seven years, three months and twenty-two days. The end, of course, had caught everyone by surprise.

The comm panel finally came to life: Callisto orbit to Amalthea and back is about a dozen seconds, if you're a photon. A stout, iron-haired, crew-cut, thick-mustached man appeared in the screen. I did a double take. Was it him?

"Open. No problem with evacuation here, *Billybrown*, we're seeing the highest field readings in five years and protons to match. Some of us still have ideas about becoming parents. Just make sure you have brakes on that bus! End."

I stared at the blank screen. It could be him, but I wasn't sure. The man I remembered had a full black beard and was still athletically thin. I'd never seen my father's chin. This man was a robust walrus type—but . . .

"We are locked onto the power beam," the ship reported. When the gauss first started climbing eight hours ago, the bureaucrats wanted to talk it over, but we'd pretty much insisted on going, and the Callisto Equilateral port manager, Chunny Kim, was sticking his neck out for us. Technically, it wasn't up to him to allocate the resources we represented, but this situation wouldn't wait; the event had caught Amalthea without deep space transport. The lock-on meant that no one at Callisto Equilateral had pulled the plug on us. It was commit time.

We didn't consider a robotic mission. It wasn't going to be cut and dried and since Callisto was being evacuated, too, it would have to be controlled from Himalia. There was over a minute of lightspeed delay between there and Amalthea—too much. So we have a crew—two for redundancy.

Lu Sin stared at me. "Are you still sure you want to do this?"

"Lives are at stake."

"And careers. We'll look pretty silly if the field fades again."

The rise has been steady all over the planet, not the flickering thing you get from a loose plasmoid off the solar wind. No, Jupiter means it this time. We're already starting to see trapped particle energy increases.

"Are we ready?" she asked.

I just nodded. I had a personal reason for going on the rescue mission, but Lu Sin had no close friends anywhere, as far anyone knew. I supposed this was just part of her concept of duty. Altruism and, duty.

This was a new phase in my life: I suppose at thirty-six, I was finally growing up.

Lu Sin nodded back at me. She was ready.

"Start thrust," I told the ship. The acceleration alarm tone sounded and I started falling to the cabin floor before I could push myself there. Three percent gravity, I reflected, was probably some kind of record for a loaded cluster ion rocket. I looked at the mass flow and the delta V remaining. Fifty-four kilometers per second at max exhaust velocity. In theory enough for the mission, but we'd cut every margin to the bone. I looked around at the mess of exposed cables and tubes. Every last piece of unnecessary mass was gone. The only reason *we* were here was that people still weighed a lot less than their equivalent in creative, problem-solving robots.

If anything major went wrong, we probably wouldn't survive. But if we didn't do this as fast as possible, the thirty people at Amalthea base probably wouldn't survive.

"Let's have the external view," Lu Sin directed, and we picked up the feed from a station telescope. The *Billybrown* resembles the planet Saturn, with much wider, gapless rings, say out to Titan. The rings were a rectenna, an antenna that receives and rectifies microwaves. Looking at the rectenna almost edge-on, I could see it dimple at the gimbaled thruster nodes. A thousand invisible megawatts of beamed microwave power washed over us at a couple of kilowatts per square meter, and were sent back out as equally invisible beams of ammonia cluster ions. If it were dark, they would have glowed a little bit as the neutralizing electrons caught up with them. Lu Sin looked at the picture and nodded judiciously. So far, so good.

"Play the last incoming back for me, visual only, quarter speed," I asked.

Yes, it was my father. I could even see some of myself there, in the way his brow wrinkled, in the spacing of the eyes, though they were less Asian than my own.

"I wondered if he recognized me, or even knows I'm in the system?"

Lu Sin gave me a sympathetic smile. "There's plenty of time, Richard. You don't need to make it hard on yourself."

"The last time I saw him, I was camping in Puna, trying to make up my mind if I was going to major in sociology or marijuana. I was seventeen. I guess I don't blame him."

## 1.2 MILLIGAUSS

A thousand autonomous probes floated in Jupiter's clouds and from Metis to Himalia, on Io, in the oceans beneath the ice of Europa, and across a hundred scientific outposts in the Jovian system, people were watching the magnetometer telemetry average, some with excitement, some with dread, many with both. It went up to 1.3 milligauss as I stared at it. I looked over at the less abstract radiation dose board.

Electron dose up to a tenth rad, but the hull stopped most of this.

If the radiation stayed at this level, I'd get out of Jupiter's revenant Van Allen belts without exceeding my monthly dose limit. But no one expected it would stay there. It had reached this level from essentially zero in less than a dozen hours. Over the vast reaches of Jovian space, even a small field could whip ions up to deadly energies.

"The radiation ought to lag the field by a little," Lu Sin remarked. "It's the heavy ions sputtering off the inner moons that knock the electrons and protons up to the really lethal levels, and that population is way down."

"Does it matter? We're committed now."

She just nodded. Yes, it mattered. Yes, we were committed.

Everyone inside Callisto's orbit knew the risks; the quiet years explorers were like the people who walk around on the rims of live volcanoes with seismometers and comm gear, waiting to get blown off. You know it's going to go sometime, but somehow the quest for scientific knowledge justifies playing chicken with a god. For some, the danger was part of the attraction.

I watched our perijovian radius shrink to seventy thousand kilometers—well inside Jupiter's atmosphere. If we had just canceled Callisto's orbital velocity and done nothing else, we would have burned-up in a little less than a week. But that wasn't good enough for us on this mission. Oh, no. I was standing on the acceleration 'floor' looking at Jupiter through the cabin skylight now. We were in a power dive right at it, to get there in a third of the usual time.

For routine operation, the ship pretty much ran itself. I let my mind wander to this and that as I watched Jupiter, the magnetic field, and the radiation dose readings grow. There would be nothing much to do for two days, then, everything.

"Prepare for zero gravity, one hundred seconds," the *Billybrown* announced.

We rushed to stow all the loose objects that had accumulated in the last six hours. Acceleration ramped down, and soon we were floating.

"I'll sleep now," Lu Sin announced. "See you in 12 hours."

I nodded an acknowledgement and she reached for a stanchion and pushed herself over to one of the thirty-two hammocks tied to the bare girders around our hollow ball. She pulled herself in, vanishing into a vacuum-proof cocoon, leaving me alone with the ship and my thoughts.

## 7 MILLIGAUSS

We reached Ganymede orbit in record time, but not soon enough for me. The radiation dose data was starting to make me thankful that I hadn't been too shy to make a sperm donation. I'd dated a nurse from

Callisto Equilateral clinic for a few months after my arrival, who talked me into it. Fond memories; everyone should get serious with a nurse or a doctor at least once in their life. Certain inhibitions will not survive the encounter. But it left sad memories as well; be prepared for her to find someone else that needs more nurturing than you do. I smiled at my reflection in a blank control panel display. I had the *Billybrown* recompute the minimum time for our mission. Forty hours down, a day there, seventy-two hours back, on profligate non-Hohmann trajectories. Landing in a hospital might be about the best that could happen. The radiation could get bad.

Before the quiet years, Jupiter's magnetic moment was about four thousand times as strong as Earth's and its insubstantial but deadly magnetosphere was the largest thing in the solar system. At the cloud tops where our monitors floated, over ten times as far from Jupiter's center as Earth's surface is from its center, the field was still ten times as strong; almost four thousand milligauss. Drop a piece of iron in a field like that, and you have an instant bar magnet.

This tilted, off-center field had whipped around Jovian space every ten hours, trapping charged particles and stampeding them before it, nearly up to cosmic ray energies. The volcanoes of Io and radiation-blasted surfaces of the other satellites supplied plenty of charged particles.

One would have just as soon gone walking around inside a nuclear reactor as visit Jupiter's inner moons back then. The first probes through that magnetosphere had absorbed half a million rads in a few hours from electrons alone. Less than five hundred rads can kill.

Then, in 2115, over less than eight weeks, the largest object in the solar system had simply ceased to exist. The belts faded, too, and you needed a polarized filter to see where the erstwhile Red Spot was. Why? No one knew. Everyone wanted to know.

Suddenly, there was the scientific equivalent of a gold rush. The reason was that the Jovian moon system is an analog of the solar system: tiny Amalthea, Io, and Europa are its inner planets, ice rich Ganymede and Callisto correspond to its giants, Himalia and debris play the role of Pluto and the Oort belt. Ten thousand field planetologists wanted to come and see for themselves, and within a couple of years, three thousand did, families and all.

As well as a few hundred support personnel to manage all the robotic equipment, including the spacecraft. I had been a pilot in need of a job, and I had something to prove. So when Callisto Equilateral opened up, I came.

Outside the worst of the radiation belts, Callisto Equilateral had been the convenient staging ground of robotic expeditions for several decades. The dynamically stable location trailing the Mercury-sized moon was a sort of cosmic Sargasso Sea where the gentle nudge of gravity and tidal forces had collected a few small comet pieces and other debris over millennia, providing ready building material and volatiles. As the only technology base in the system, it became the San Francisco of the Jupiter rush.

I asked the ship for the telemetry display again. The surface field average was up to eight milligauss; the dose rate at Amalthea orbit was getting near a hundredth of a rad per day. Time to wake up Lu Sin.

## 12 MILLIGAUSS

Lu Sin and I must have talked for an hour before she turned in at the start of my second shift. She felt that it was really time to let my father know I was part of his rescue party, but I wanted to keep putting the moment off. So I gave the problem to Jupiter: the bland, faintly striped yellowish beachball above me proved to be an excellent meditation object.

It beat looking at the dose display and reminding myself that my odds of getting leukemia were coming up out of the noise. I wondered how Lu Sin passed the time on her shift.

I must have floated under the skylight for an hour before I suspected something was wrong. My internal clock was telling me something was supposed to be happening.

Deceleration was supposed to start on this shift.

"When do we start deceleration prep?" I asked the ship.

"Deceleration is on hold." I really didn't need to hear that.

"For how long? Why weren't we told?"

"The hold is minute to minute. There is still some margin and Callisto Equilateral didn't want to worry you unnecessarily. They used an override code to countermand my standing program."

"The hell you say! Lu Sin," I shouted to be heard through the insulation of her hammock, "we've got problems." Her hammock started writhing.

"What's wrong?" emerged in a muffled voice.

"No power for deceleration, and no explanation." I turned to the comm panel. "Callisto Equilateral, this is *Billybrown*. Request immediate data dump on deceleration schedule change."

We were already so close to Jupiter that immediate would mean about four seconds. I floated tight-limbed and ran my hand over what was left of my hair, fuming. Lu Sin joined me in her vacuum suit, coveralls in hand. A vacuum-safe undersuit looks like it's painted on, and part of me noted that she looked a lot younger than I thought. She gave no sign of noticing my noticing, but despite her quiet, proper, and almost aloof demeanor, there was no hint of embarrassment either.

Callisto Equilateral's message was terse and ominous: "Power failure this end. No ETRO."

No estimated time to return operational. A look at the astrodynamics display told me that if we didn't start thrusting in an hour, there was no possible Amalthea rendezvous. If we didn't start thrusting in about two hours, there was no way to avoid hitting Jupiter.

Lu Sin finished dressing without comment as soon as it was apparent that she wouldn't have to do anything else immediately. Then she touched my hand.

"We should tell Amalthea." Her eyes said tell *everything*. "I'm senior. I'll break it to them."

Amalthea was coming out of eclipse on Jupiter's western limb. Its angular velocity wasn't much different than ours because most of our velocity was in the downward direction. It would stay in view for hours. The delay was down to about a second and a half. We could converse.

" . . . and that is all we know at this point. Dr. Kolentz, my first has a personal message. For you." She was putting me on the spot. Actually, I was relieved; I'd put it off too long.

We looked at each other. "It's me, Dad."

"So . . . Rik, this is a surprise . . . You've come up in the world. I suspected the first time it was you, but I've known so many people and after eighteen years, maybe my imagination was playing wishful thinking tricks on me." He laughed. "Even your companion reminds me of someone . . . Well. Does Marianna know?"

That I hadn't expected. Mom left us to be an actress when I was ten, sending a card every other year or so. The last one was when I was eighteen. She'd been on her fourth husband, then.

"Dad, it's been eighteen years. She'd be in her sixties . . . "

"Sixty-six, but who's counting. I was just hoping. I'm too old for grudges now, and she had her reasons. Time to pick up what pieces I can, if you understand . . . So . . . How did you become a spaceship pilot?"

"I started sky diving. Just for thrills at first, but I got interested in flying, so I got a license and started taking jumpers, cash only. Then I wanted more money and found out I needed a degree to get a real pilot job. So I did it, at Hilo. Honors even. After a few years of island hopping, I put in for shuttles. Right place, right time. One thing led to another." I shrugged. "Still with Rice?"

"Forty-five years, next week. If I make it. I'm Emeritus now, but I still have a mail drop at the Bonner Lab. Son, do you have any delta V left at all?"

"Maybe five hundred meters per second from the chemical thrusters. But I'll need close to thirty thousand for rendezvous."

"Now, just how much drag will that contraption take?"

"None. It's not built for it, not at forty plus kilometers per second." The central cabin might have survived a high altitude brush, but the flimsy rectenna around it would have been torn away by the first ghost of atmospheric gases. Even the dust in the ring plane would shred it to pieces.

"Then you should use what you have now. Raise your perijovian point as high as you can."

"Wait a minute. You're the astrophysicist, I'm the spaceship driver. Even if that maneuver got us out of the ring belt, it would blow the rendezvous phasing." The phasing was important. We might arrive at a point in Amalthea's orbit too long before or after the moon itself.

"Maybe. But when the power comes back on, it will give you a better chance to get away, and perhaps come back. Besides, maybe we can think of some other ideas."

I looked at Captain Sin. She shrugged. Maybe. "We'll check it with Callisto Equilateral."

"Judgment call, son. Why don't you have power? Who do you believe, them or me?"

"I think we should do it, now," Lu Sin interrupted. Surprised at her support for the risky maneuver, I stared at her. She was impassive.

"I suppose," I said. I didn't really have much choice; she was in charge.

"*Billybrown*, command override," Lu Sin said. "Rik?"

"Right. Okay. *Billybrown*, use all the chemical thruster fuel to raise perijovian as much as possible, no other constraints. Display the resulting trajectories."

The push and the displays arrived simultaneously. To my surprise our perijovian point rose almost to the orbit of Metis, at the edge of the rings. Almost.

"Good show, son. That was the best you could do," Dad said after the maneuver.

"We have another problem," Lu Sin stated. "Without chemical fuel for fuel cells, and without the microwave beam, we are on batteries. We will be out of power in about two hours, maybe four or five with extreme conservation." She must have known that. If Callisto E. didn't come back on line, we were dead anyway. How could she be so calm?

I watched my father's nod, the lightspeed delay still perceptible. "So you need some power. What are your resources? Do you have a crank generator?"

To turn my body fat into energy to live? No we didn't have one, but maybe . . .

"We might fabricate one from something," Lu Sin said, "but I don't think we have time."

"Why," I complained, "is there only one power transmitter in the Jovian system?"

"Son, everything's a hodgepodge here. We threw it together as quickly as we could when the field shut down. No regrets; we've had five great years of science and adventure. We all knew the risks and the shortcutting, so to heck with the recriminations. We use what we have . . . which . . . Lu Sin, Rik, it so happens we have the big radar array here on Amalthea, and a reactor to run it with. I can't give you a gigawatt, but would a few megawatts help?"

Why didn't someone think of that before we used up our attitude control fuel? I started thinking about survival again. One percent power? More if I wasted fuel at lower specific impulse. Maybe. Certainly enough to lift the low point of our orbit out of the ring plane. "Yes, I think so, if it's close to our reception frequency. But now how are we going to orient our rectenna array?" I was speaking to myself as much as anyone else.

"Lu Sin?" Dad asked in a tone that hinted something.

Lu Sin smiled. "Dr. Kolentz, I think I know. The squirrel cage."

"Ah, the old squirrel cage? The James White 'Lifeboat' scenario? Captain Sin, my hat's off to you. Rik? You got it?"

I shook my head. "What's a squirrel cage?" My mind wouldn't work and my irritation showed. When you're almost forty years old, you don't like being treated like a child by your elders. Besides, I had my own idea.

"Look, if we just grab the insides of this thing and pull it the right way, it should start to move. I mean, we'll move the other way in reaction until we grab on again, but the *Billybrown* should keep spinning the right way until we do."

"Huh! But that's exactly the principle, Rik! Now, just image running around the inside of your spaceship instead of twisting it. Push it with your feet, in other words. Like it was a circular cage and you were the squirrel."

I formed a mental image, which suddenly correlated with something I'd seen a long time ago: astronauts running around in a circular room on one of the first space stations.

"Okay. We run one way, the spaceship turns the other. I've got the idea. But I don't think *Billybrown* will. It's too non-standard for the computer." A spacecraft's smooth voice interface can lead one to overestimate its intelligence, if one isn't careful. "But we can try."

"We'd best get on with it, Dr Kolentz," Lu Sin said, determination in her voice with a hint of—excitement? Was she actually enjoying this? "Thanks. End."

We were almost on a line between Callisto Equilateral and Amalthea, so what we had to do was to turn the rectenna over to face Amalthea. Lu Sin and I picked a circular path around the inside of the *Billybrown* least cluttered with pipes, hammocks, and other gear. Then we started pulling ourselves around it. Pretty soon, we'd given ourselves enough centrifugal gravity to run after a fashion; sort of skipping along, occasionally tripping, accumulating a variety of cuts and bumps.

With excruciating slowness, the spaceship started to turn in the other direction.

As I predicted, the spacecraft couldn't grasp what a squirrel cage did, and when we did it anyway, it tried to stop us with its reaction control system. But, of course, that system was out of fuel so its thrusters just cycled helplessly until Lu Sin overrode the program.

When we got the rectenna turned partway to Amalthea, and started getting a few watts from that direction, our idiot-savant finally caught on and adjusted to the new situation. That power source gave it a new referent, and enough power to use a couple of the cluster jets to finish the reorientation toward the radar beam from Amalthea. The people there were doomed, but they were diverting a large part of their station's power in an attempt to save us.

As the skylight turned away from both Jupiter and the Sun, the cabin became pitch black, lit only by the bright lines and numbers on the displays. We saw stars through the skylight.

With help from another command override from Lu Sin, *Billybrown* was able to fire one percent of its thrusters at ten percent normal power. By using reaction mass at ten times our normal rate, we could get one percent thrust out of that much power. Nowhere near enough. We had started with ten times our dry mass in ammonia propellant—at this rate there wouldn't be enough left to let us complete the mission even if microwave power was restored.

"Look," Lu Sin said, pointing out the skylight.

Among the steady stars, one was twinkling. The hundred-kilometer-radius mesh reflector of Callisto Equilateral's microwave transmitter was moving, still tracking us, sending specular glints of sunlight instead of the gigawatt of power we needed.

## 22 MILLIGAUSS

No one has ever seen a magnetosphere start up before, but guesses were that, this close to Jupiter, half a gauss at the cloud tops would mean enough of a magnetic field to create enough high energy protons to kill us in a day, this close to Jupiter. We were now up to one-twentieth of that, probably enough to warrant some low-dose preventative anticancer drugs when and if we returned.

Callisto Equatorial called, finally. The son of a traditional Korean farmer, Chunny Kim normally affected an easygoing rustic manner, but now he was sarcastic, and all business.

"*Billybrown*, Rik, Lu Sin. My extreme apologies. We'll have beam power momentarily. There was an extended debate on your mission. I'm afraid I've ended up in charge of what amounts to a mutiny, a sort of collective decision here that we don't let people die for the sake of one man's view of his authority. The problem was that even out here, the magnetosphere radiation increase was enough to trigger our powerplant shutdown cycle, and the station manager wouldn't allow a restart without an investigation. So we overruled him. We've got the telemetry on your fuel consumption, and I only hope it's not too late. Sorry. End."

"Chunny," Lu Sin replied, "We knew what we were getting into. Not your fault. I don't have the latest, but we're going to come awfully close to the rings. We've got to bring the rectenna around again, so we'll be ready for the power beam in about thirty minutes. End."

"*Billybrown*, roger that. Anyone ever tell you the most efficient place for maneuvers is the bottom of a gravity well? End." Chunny was a good one for finding silver linings. We relayed the message to Amalthea and started reorienting *Billybrown*'s rectenna to Callisto Equilateral, pairing cluster jets at opposing rim sections. We programmed for immediate thrust to raise our projected orbit out of the ring plane and flyby Amalthea, keeping options open.

We went on batteries again while the rectenna was edge on to both transmitters. Then the pitch maneuver picked up speed as the beam from Callisto Equilateral started to illuminate more of the top of the rectenna. Before we realized it, the maneuver was done and the thrusters came on full power, dumping Lu Sin and me unceremoniously on the cabin floor. We'd spent so much reaction mass by then that acceleration was up to almost a tenth of a gravity, even at the higher exhaust velocity. When we scrambled back to our feet, somehow, she ended up in my arms. I was about to apologize for the unintended intimacy, but she touched her finger to my lips, eyes glistening, then put her head on my shoulder and held. It felt like we stood there holding each other forever. Then, silently, as if a spoken word would shatter everything, we kissed.

Lu Sin finally disengaged, looked me straight in the eye. "This has been the most beautiful moment in my life, and you the most beautiful man. But we must never, never speak of this again."

She was certainly in enough trouble with the authorities and regulations without adding a charge of fraternization, or inappropriate conduct. I nodded, but I gently grasped her hand as well; we could speak to our hearts content with a touch.

Her features firmed. "I think we need to get back to business."

We pulled up all the projections and directed an optimization search. The result was pretty much what we had figured it might be. Lu Sin made the call.

"Callisto Equilateral, *Billybrown*. We have just enough reaction mass to make the rendezvous with Amalthea, but not enough to return if we do. We have a decision to make. End."

"Roger, *Billybrown*. Best we could do is get a tank down there in five days with the cargo launcher. All the other ships are out now; the

*Glasser* needs the beam as soon as you're done, but we'll stay with you as long as you need us. Let us know. End."

"So that's it. We have to go back," I stated the obvious.

"You cannot leave your father there, Rik."

"If it were only me, Lu Sin . . . But if we rendezvous, the radiation will kill you, too."

"Maybe. But maybe the radiation will not get worse, or maybe another solution will occur to us. Those people have very little chance, but if we do not rendezvous, they have no chance. And please don't tell me I have no stake in this. Everything that I am is at stake in this." She gave me a resolute look. "I would rather die trying than live with the guilt of not trying. Is this not how you feel?" My first impulse was to say: Isn't thirty dead better than thirty-two dead? But I couldn't look her in the face and say that. I put my hand over hers.

"I'm scared. I'd rather not die. Just give me some hope we're going to lick this."

She smiled then, and kissed my cheek, and laughed lightly. "Very well, I shall. Now, Rik, the first thing we say to Amalthea will be to ask them how much ammonia they have."

What it came down to was that compared to this, if I thought about it, most of my life had been a meaningless pain in the ass anyway. If survival had been all that important to me, I would have insisted on going back. Besides, I still had a point to make, maybe one worth my life. Maybe the point *was* my life. Win or die. Remember the Alamo. Anyway, I was no speechmaking hero. I just stood there as Lu Sin directed the rendezvous maneuver.

## 23 MILLIGAUSS

We arrived at the L1 point of the Amalthea-Jupiter system, only a few dozen kilometers off the peak of Mount Barnard, the unofficial name for the pointy, Jupiter-facing part of Amalthea From above, it was a massive ridge, of bald rock, parallel to the orbit plane. It would have been an excellent place for an elevator. With an anchor in Jupiter's gravity on the other side of the L1 neutral gravity point, the tethertube would have been less than a hundred kilometers long, but I supposed there hadn't been time to build one.

Dr. Kolentz was angry. "This is a magnificent gesture. But it's not likely that you've accomplished anything but killing yourselves and ending my family line. Huh! Rik, you never would listen."

"There's no point in giving up now," I snapped, with the irritation of someone who had found himself on the wrong side of a sensible argument.

"Yes, I quite agree. But the only ammonia we have is what we piss, and that's too contaminated to do you any good. We do have some RCS fuel, enough to keep you from drifting away for a few weeks. I'll ferry it up myself. Then we'll talk, privately. End."

One of Amalthea station's utility scooters made the trip out with my father and two other people. I will never forget the look that passed between my father and Lu Sin as he floated through the inner door of the air lock.

"You've changed, too," she said, at last. Their hands touched. I felt I knew what that touch meant. A cloud of jealousy made a brief flight across my eyes and departed, evaporated by reason. Age, rank, and decades gone gave Dad priority. I could accept that.

"Lu Sin was one of my students, Rik." There was obviously more to it than that, but other people were around and there was much to do.

But Dad's off color comment on ammonia sources started me thinking about other liquids.

## 25 MILLIGAUSS

"In the first place," the Callisto Equilateral engineer was saying, "the *Billybrown* was never meant to land anywhere. The hull's okay, but the ion rockets would get bent. Secondly, the cluster ion generators are not designed to work with water. Water, believe it or not, is a very corrosive material. Ah, tanks, valves, microscopic jets, they could all become clogged. The cluster formation hardware isn't designed for water . . . "

"Has it ever been tried?" I was getting impatient and overrode the incoming transmission. He'd get the interruption in six seconds.

" . . . no one would be stupid enough to risk equipment on such a hare-brained idea. Um, over."

"Callisto E. My life, and that of thirty other people is at stake here. Over." He knew that, but I was angry now. This was the kind of mentality that got us into this mess in the first place by shutting down the Callisto Equilateral reactor. I stewed for a dozen seconds.

"*Billybrown*. That doesn't change the engineering. Ah, but it does change the priorities. We can jury-rig a test to feed water to some spare thrusters. Ah, how much time do we have? Over." Seconds went by. It's hard to be sarcastic with a ten second delay, but I managed.

"Callisto E. If *you* guys don't know, who does? The rate of magnetic field increase has leveled off so maybe we have more time than we thought. But it's not healthy even at this level. The sooner we get out of here, the better. End."

My father was motioning that he wanted to talk to me. I gave the comm panel a shove and floated over to him. Lu Sin and the others were outside working on the fuel transfer.

"We're playing this as if it were going to work," he said. "Everyone on the station is ready to go. Uh, about your mother . . . "

I cut him off. "Supposing we can run the cluster jets on water, how are we going to get the water to the *Billybrown*? We'll need at least thirty tonnes to get to Callisto orbit, forty to get there as fast as we came, which might be a good idea considering the radiation build-up. That's a lot of ferry flights. Can we bring the spacecraft to the ground station?" The station was on the north rim of Pan crater, about halfway around the tiny moon from the peak of Mt. Barnard.

The old man got tense and looked at me as if he were going to challenge my change of subject. Too bad. With a chance to get out of this alive, I could postpone the family history. He shrugged his shoulders and answered my question.

"Our surface gravity at Pan's rim is about half a percent. Can you hover in that with loaded tanks on one megawatt? Callisto Equilateral will be below our horizon for the next five hours, and the station antenna wouldn't be able to get a direct shot at you, so I'm not sure we'd be able to deliver that much power."

Not by microwave link, but . . .

"Dad, what's the output of your powerplant, total, not just what you can feed into the radar?"

"Um, about a hundred megawatts. Why?"

"Do you have a cable reel and a power line running out to Mt. Barnard?"

## 70 MILLIGAUSS

Lu Sin and I had been awake for two universal days and had to sleep, radiation or not. The station personnel could handle the preparations. She went to the station, to sleep underground. I stayed with the ship.

When I woke up five hours later, and played back the overnight reports, it looked like old Jove really meant it. Callisto Equilateral reported that a magnetic bow shock had reformed off Jupiter and the radiation level around here was getting definitely unhealthy. Fortunately, just about anything stops low energy sulfur nuclei, so things weren't quite as bad as the particle flux display was indicating, but the high energy proton population was way up, too.

Jupiter's bands were joining in, too, displaying more color. I could see that through the skylight. And it had a new red spot, in the *north* tropical zone, though how this was connected with the return of the magnetic field, no one understood. The best answer I got was from one of my father's's astrophysicists, who told me to think of Jupiter as a miniature sun in slow motion.

The Callisto Equilateral engineer called in with what he thought was bad news. Their tests showed that if we ran the cluster jets on pure water, they'd probably fail after a hundred hours. A water ammonia mixture would be better. I politely reminded him that I only needed about eight hours of thrust, and that I would turn the ship in for refit as soon as I got home. I think he was still unhappy about the insult to the equipment.

Dad and Lu Sin arrived soon after I ended the contact, looking smug about something. "Everyone's ready at the base, and their personal effects are packed to be picked up by robots later," Dad announced. "What about the ship?"

"It should run okay with water mixed in with our remaining ammonia."

Bringing the *Billybrown* in over the north rim of Pan was one tricky operation. The jokes about extension cords for electric rockets go back to the twentieth century, but this is the first time I think one has ever been used. We hovered directly over the radar antenna while the power cable was lofted and quickly welded onto the leads we had exposed. Thus freed from beamed power, the ship, followed by the cable reel on the ground, floated over to the station tank farm where a hose was fitted.

There were a hundred problems: fused circuit breakers, hose coupling sizes, ion jet splash effects, to name a few; and a hundred solutions to go with them. It was done in a day.

Then the station cameras captured one of the stranger sights in the history of astronautics and electric rockets. Carrying the scientists, their families and as much water as it could, the *Billybrown*, its rectenna looking like a big floppy hat brim, floated over the Amalthean landscape and up Mount Barnard, trailing the power line behind it. We ramped the exhaust velocity of our cluster jets up toward maximum fuel economy as Amalthea's surface gravity dropped off to about a milligee approaching the top of the mountain. Soon we were back in free fall.

I found out too late that someone had to stay behind to cut the power. The connection at the spacecraft end was a hurriedly welded kludge, and one doesn't simply pull the wire off a hundred megawatt lead; the arc explosion would be like setting off dynamite. Things were so hectic that I didn't notice who stayed until it was too late.

"Dad, damnit! Why you?" Dad was down there on the surface alone. The nearest transport was back at Pan's Rim, a hundred kilometers away. You don't maneuver something the mass of the *Billybrown* like a helicopter, and even in milligravity, the flimsy rectenna would droop to the ground without the support of the cluster jets.

"Someone had to, son, and I'm an old man. Besides, I always wanted to be in charge of a world, and now I am. This is the ringside seat for the magnetosphere turn on, and I'm not going to miss the show." *What nonsense!*

"Dad!" I protested. "There's nothing to see; the only way you could know the magnetosphere is there is by watching the instruments like the rest of us, and by getting a fatal dose of radiation sickness."

"Leon!" Lu Sin interjected, displaying emotion for a second time in my memory, but economically. It was the first time I could remember her calling him by his first name. She seemed more irritated than worried.

"Oh, well. If you insist. Rik, how long until perijovian?"

"Huh? About half an hour?"

"That should be close enough. If you have a telescope, you can watch me jump."

"Dad, you can't jump off a moon this big. Escape velocity is . . . "

"You're the big pilot? You should check your orbit mechanics. Here I come."

Lu Sin looked surprised for a moment then grinned. The two of them looked like a couple of doting parents who had just hidden an Easter egg and were waiting for me to find it. I shook my head, maintained my dignity, and waited to see what would happen.

Lu Sin had the *Billybrown* point the docking camera down at my father's position on the mountain peak. There was a brilliant flash a hundred meters north of him and our power meter went back to zero: He had severed the power line at the surface with an explosive charge We waited. We were already three kilometers out, so all we could see of him was a white dot. But yes, he started getting larger. Soon we could see a figure in vacuum gear floating along, guiding himself on what was left of the power cable. In half an hour there was a knock on our airlock door.

"So," Lu Sin said, once we were settled. "The peak of Mt. Barnard actually sticks *beyond* its L1 point at perijovian."

"On the high side of its orbital eccentricity cycle, anyway. Which is where we are now. Why do you think the summit is so clean?" Dad rumbled. I felt like an idiot. "Jupiter pulls the dust off! Come on son, have a sense of humor."

I should have felt embarrassed, humiliated, or something. But what I got was a funny kind of pride instead. That was *my* father who jumped off a moon. A few minutes before he would have fallen off, anyway. I found a laugh, hesitant at first, then full-bodied. Lu Sin even joined in.

We still had to wait a tense half an hour for Callisto Equilateral to come out from behind Jupiter. Protons at these energies went right through our ship's hull and my accumulated dose was over a rad. Everyone else, except Lu Sin, had received more.

The children had been housed underground, for the most part, at the science station since the magnetosphere started coming back on, but now they were exposed. Their only hope was speed and distance.

## 210 MILLIGAUSS

The magnetic field strength at the Jovian cloudtops was approaching that found at Earth's surface. Jupiter's magnetosphere was back in force, and growing, already roughly a thousand times the volume of Earth's. Beyond Europa, we were out of the woods for the moment, but as in *Macbeth*, the woods were chasing us; Jupiter's new outer Van Allen belt was expanding toward the orbit of Ganymede faster than we were coasting out. Nothing we could do about that; our water reaction mass was gone; we saved only what we needed for minimum life support.

The cabin was a crowded inferno. At about forty Celsius, the fourth power law of thermal radiation, as applied to the skin of the *Billybrown*'s cabin, saved us from cooking ourselves with our own body heat, but it was not comfortable. Most of the thirty people preferred to remain in their hammocks, hooked up to the overloaded air system, trying to sleep the ordeal away. But there were six children to contend with, two of them too young to understand what was happening. The zero gee toilet had given up, and we were down to sharing relief tubes. In twenty years, perhaps, we'd laugh about all that. Perhaps.

Guts don't sag in zero gravity; they sit up high and impressive, especially when attached to a chest of matching expanse. Close up, my father's magnificent belly eclipsed the rim of his shorts. He was that close so that he could speak privately. Curiously, a private conversation was now a possibility because of the din around us.

"Rik. Look, Marianna had reasons for leaving me. At least she felt so. She was beautiful, but within a year of our marriage, I was seeing other women—colleagues, students, who had a lot more to offer in intellectual companionship. She couldn't handle it. Maybe she would have except one of these other ladies had an accident which I had to take care of."

"Lu Sin?" I asked, not really wanting to believe it. "I could see there was more between you."

"Lu Sin came from an unsophisticated culture, Rik. She was a good engineering student, but very naive about . . . relationships. By the time she stopped trying to deny it to herself, it was too late for an abortion. She had an unplanned child, which she gave up for adoption."

"Where is this going? What does this have to do with me? Lu Sin is special to you, I understand. Do I have another brother or a sister somewhere? Are you going to marry her?"

He raised an eyebrow and shrugged. "If we survive, perhaps. But . . . " then he looked straight at me, challenging, unapologetic. "Rik, *you* were that child. I found you. Marianna raised you as if you were her own for ten years. Then, well, it got to be too much for her.

She didn't handle it well, but I can forgive that."

I had older brothers that I always thought got more of Mom's affection. I'd always put that down to sibling rivalry. Somehow the news didn't bother me that much, as if I'd been expecting something like that. But Lu Sin . . . what we shared made my blood run cold now.

"Lu Sin is my biological mother? Does she know?"

"I think so." What would it take, to watch from afar so long, and be silent? To embrace, and be silent. "She was so young, Rik." He smiled. "Do you know, I think she can still have children."

No, he can't mean that. But, of course, he could.

My father is not a conventional man, and I still have problems dealing with the insatiable Don Juan that resides in the same body with that towering intellect and unconquerable will. Perhaps I am being taught how to love without judgment. And if I learn that lesson, perhaps I will not live the rest of my life alone.

## 4200 MILLIGAUSS

No one is really sick yet, but it doesn't look good. Jupiter's new magnetosphere is not a carbon copy of its old one: more tilt, more field, more radiation. Even Callisto orbit won't be safe.

We arrived at Callisto Equilateral with about a year's worth of allowed cumulative dose under our belts, sustained in a week. Refugees were straggling in from Io, Ganymede, and Metis. The Europa station has gone underwater in hopes that they can survive long enough for shielded transport to be developed. A small fleet is on the way from Earth. It should get here in a year. They have some new antiradiation drugs.

The main part of Callisto Equilateral is a wheel with life support for a nominal three thousand people. There are now about 4200 present, and interplanetary transport for maybe five hundred. The hope now is that the Himalia base can be expanded, and we're using the transport to shuttle back and forth. Eventually, the whole wheel will be moved out to that orbit; but that, too, will take years. Chunny and Dad think it can be done; the rest of us are believing, hoping, and working our tails off. Maybe, just maybe. Meanwhile, I have my first command in sight.

I've been appointed first officer on the *Glasser*, evacuating the pregnant women and younger children to the outer moon, Himalia. Lu Sin is in command on the trip out, but someone has to bring it back, and I'm in line for that.

Lu Sin is the most disciplined, logical person I know, and her pregnancy is the craziest, most illogical thing any person I know has ever done. It was as if she felt she had made a pact with the universe whereby if it bowed to her will for three hundred and sixty-four days, she would surrender on the three hundred and sixty-fifth, no questions asked. It's either that or it's the exact opposite; maybe having a child is a woman's way of spitting in the face of eternity when it crowds her. Anyway, no one questions a heroine. I don't think any genetic tests will ever be made. Dad is sure the baby is his, and that's the way it's going to be.

So, I've got a sister on the way. I look at Lu Sin and think she will be very, very beautiful.

"Let's have you take the con, Rik. I'm going to sit back and watch, unless you blow it."

I nod and run through the checks. The ship is clean and bright inside, structurally the same as the *Billybrown*, but with all the panels, lights and creature comforts intact. Kids play vacuum tag in a net cage while their mothers and aunts discuss setting up new households with the adventurous spirit of pioneers. Someone made a sign, which now hangs from the big cargo cage bolted on behind us. Himalia or Bust it says. I've checked everything that can be checked.

"Ready, Mom?"

She nods sharply, professionally.

"*Glasser*, start thrust," I command. The acceleration warning tone chimes.

"Roger. Prepare for one percent gravity, five seconds."

The caged children drift gently to the floor with cries of protest as thrust begins, the first of many insults to their so-far idyllic childhoods in a scientific Eden.

"Dr. Kolentz sends his wishes to everyone for a good voyage," the ship tells us. Dad is in charge of Himalia now. The best person in the Jovian system to bluster the place together, so everyone thinks, so I think. The more things change . . . When I look at Lu Sin, whatever is supposed to kick in to prevent me from feeling that way because I know that she is my biological mother, doesn't. But there is nothing whatever to do or say about that.

Outside, a major part of the solar system is returning to normal, complete with its rules and its deadly radiations. But, when we touch, I remember, and so does she.

# STORY NOTES

"Out of the Quiet Years" is the oldest story in terms of authorship in this collection; it was finished in July of 1991. That said, it didn't need much in the way of technology updating. The electric propulsion system was taken from one of my technical papers done while I was at the then Air Force Rocket Propulsion Laboratory (several name changes since). The spacecraft *"Billybrown"* is named for my coauthor, William C. Brown. Beamed microwaves are a way of getting the power of a nuclear reactor to a spacecraft without the mass or operational hazards and seemed a good choice for the Jovian moon system, where velocity change requirements are high and distances small compared to the Solar System.

From Galileo imagery and flyby tracking, Amalthea appears less dense than was thought in 1991, so the jumping off point seems even more feasible. It also radiates somewhat more heat than it gets from the Sun, which may seem surprising unless until one remembers that sunlight there is about 1/30th of its intensity at Earth's orbit. Inductive electrical heating from Jupiter's magnetic field and tidal stresses may be responsible for internal heat.

Could Jupiter's magnetic field go away? I'm not sure. It seems likely that it could experience a reversal and perhaps its current somewhat disorganized state is a precursor to that. This happens with Earth, it happens with stars, so it seems reasonable to think that it might happen to something in-between. Whether the field would get as low as I've hypothesized during the reversal is a matter of conjecture or wishful thinking, depending on how charitable you might feel. But it wouldn't matter too much to the story if the minimum magnetosphere still required some shielding. A superconducting ring around a ship or a base camp would do the job.

Larger than life people who make history often have less than ideal personal lives. It seems to go with the territory, and the exceptions one can name prove the rule. When one gets into one's sixties, one turns around and looks in the mirror. The best of us understand, though often too late.

G. David Nordley, January 2015

# ALICE'S ASTEROID

**B**eing part of a legend is OK, after the fact, but, as I look back on what we belters have come to know as "The Battle of Alice's Asteroid," I wouldn't recommend the process to anyone. I paid for my fame, not just with wounds and suffering, but, in the end, with my heart twice over. Times are changing now, thanks in part to Alice, and it has come time to take care of some unfinished business; they say confession is good for the soul. Especially when you might be forgiven.

The tale you know was mostly cover story and media hype; we did not fight off a squadron of space pirates, it was just one ship. They weren't your usual rock vultures, exactly, but something with a different, more sinister, appetite. And the part about Shan Krug wounding four of them before being fatally wounded herself . . . it didn't happen quite that way, but, as she was beyond retaliation, it was useful for people to think that she did all the shooting. So the hype is wrong, but what really happened was quite enough for anyone.

Alice's Asteroid isn't exactly a central node of the asteroid belt economy, but it was, and is, self-sufficient and supplied its share of local data on the solar wind and the various pebbles that drifted within range of its laser strobes. At the time of the "battle," it had been drifting through the Vesta association for the past dozen years, and was approaching a nodal conjunction with the "Bright Rock"—then only two day's journey prograde, with a magsail beam boost.

The proprietor, Al Montoya, is a diamond sculptor of some ability, more ingenuity, and surpassing industry who could barter his endobeam deposition creations for various goodies beyond the basic trade allocation rendered from the local IPA admin node. For instance, the soap dishes in the bathrooms of the *Ceres Regency* are Al's work, and as a result his freezer contained delicacies unknown to most belters. So, in better times, I looked forward to a trip out there from Vesta.

The asteroid was named for Al's late wife and his thirteen-year-old daughter, who they called "Alice Two" or "Alice, too," depending on the circumstances. Of course, in the three years since her mother's death she insisted that everyone call her "just Alice." And, of course, people forgot.

\* ※ \*

"*Alice Two Montoya*," Al shouted as Shan contacted him on approach with a shuttle full of groceries, tools, spare parts, and me. He hadn't seen me yet.

Shannon Krug was the shuttle pilot, and the reason for Al's excitement. Of twelve hundred Vesta region shuttle pilots then, only a couple of hundred were women. Such was the influence of the paternalism of The New Reformation at its zenith. Shan fought that, and made it a point to get Alice's Asteroid on her route ever since Alice died. Alice Two idolized her.

"Ho, Shan," Al bellowed in a resonant liquid baritone, verging on basso. "*Alice Two Montoya*! Shan's here!" His voice echoed back from the hall connecting the six rooms of their home, which were laid out on one side of a hundred-meter-radius latticework wheel that rotated in the second largest crater of the asteroid. Alice Two answered in a medium-high clear, confident tone that made its owner sound five years older than she was. I stepped into the viewfield and waved at Al from behind Shan.

He scowled at me. Well, that was to be expected. I didn't have good news and he knew it.

Their station crater had become the south pole of the asteroid a week after Al turned on his habitat centrifuge because the asteroid's original rotation was either chaotic or nonexistent, depending on whether you ask a mathematician or a miner. Most asteroids spin in about six hours, so this one must have taken a recent hit; and, indeed the polar crater seemed sharp-edged and smooth-floored fresh.

Anyway, with Al's habitat spinning one way, the asteroid spun the other. Al set up his cargo launcher on the new equator, and gave the spin a little help. A year or so of that, and its new rotation combined with its orbital motion produced a traditional twenty-four-hour day. A simple pressure-stiffened bubble mirror on the mooring mast provided sunlight at one-sixth earth equatorial maximum. That, allowing for atmospheric absorption, provided about the same amount of sunny warmth as an Oslo winter noon—or Al's reaction to my unfortunate duty.

The wheel was a circular cage of aluminum trusswork, containing the big curved sausage of Al's habitat on one side. The other side had environmental equipment, photovoltaic cells, and a pair of weights on rails with which Al's computer, "Alexander The Great," kept his empire in balance.

Alexander T. G. played nursemaid, janitory and general factotum; he was now busy guiding my IPA shuttle to the mooring mast. It wasn't despun—the once a day rotation wasn't enough to mess with at a three-meter radius—the computers simply negotiated a touch of pitch up gyro at the moment of contact and the mast bent a little away from center to adjust its center of gravity.

"Elegant, if eccentric," Shan remarked. "This rock is full of simple solutions to things that are just full of mechanical complexity elsewhere. This guy is special."

"Please don't make it any harder on me," I snapped, a little surprised at my own irritation.

"Yeah, I know. You're just the messenger. Does Kerri know what you're doing?"

My wife, back at Vesta, and Shan were in the same bridge club; so if Kerri didn't know what I was doing, I was being served notice that she soon would. We weren't living together any longer; too many different interests, different passions. Tired of Kerri's social whirl and wanting to cut down on my daily commute to a job that requires two or three face to face meetings a day, I'd taken an apartment close to the government complex. The nostalgia of twenty years of memories and Shan's cheery efforts kept Kerri and me from formalizing the split, but, truth be known, I'd developed a liking for Shan, bright-eyed, capable, and thoughtful while Kerri spent her time on social frivolity.

I grunted a noncommittal response and headed out the hatch as soon as the good-to-go tone sounded. Shan followed, grabbing my helmet and briefcase. Physically, Shan was stouter than Kerri, with well-muscled, unadorned hands and indifferent to fashion—a shipsuit and coveralls person. She handed me the helmet, and my hand brushed hers briefly. I smiled a sheepish thanks. As a glorified social worker, I didn't get out that much. She reached for my kit, with all the stuff we sometimes need to use on an uncooperative "client." She must have thought I'd forgotten it. I wish I could have.

"I'll leave that. Too damn bureaucratic and insensitive. This is going to be rough enough."

She nodded, the shuttle doors cycled shut behind us, and we pulled ourselves down the inside of the hollow mast toward the asteroid's surface. There was a counterweighted elevator cab that ran around the outside of the mast where it passed through the wheel. We went in through double doors in the mast tube and felt our weight build up as centrifugal force took the elevator out to the wheel and the Mars normal gravity most belters used.

A clank indicated that we'd engaged the wheel air lock, the double doors opened again and I was face to face with Al. A burly straight-backed old guy with a walrus mustache, he was barefoot and his belly folded over stained work shorts with various tools hanging here and there. He usually had a smile and a twinkle in his eye, but without those, he could look as cold and forbidding as doom itself—and that's what I saw as the door opened.

He didn't waste time getting down to it. "Shan," he nodded a greeting. "Dr. Wade. You've come to take Alice Two." There was no handshake.

I nodded gravely. "I'm sorry, Al. The board didn't want to make an exception. That makes it easier for them to insist on children rights in other cases, where it's really needed."

"Zeke, you don't take children from two-parent families," he grumbled.

"We have lots of children from two-parent families at the central school."

"Yeah, sent there by choice. Well I don't choose, and neither does Alice."

"I'm sorry. It's the law."

"LAW?" he bellowed, "Goddamn New Reformationist-dominated IPA charter-screwing illegal law, and that only because that stealth candidate, what's its face—Adam Solacus, got on the board without telling people what his true colors were."

I shrugged my shoulders. A man with the name "Solacus" wasn't exactly a stealth candidate. Even though he didn't run on a theocratic platform, he'd taken the surname of the New Reformation's founder, Thomas Solacus, who'd discovered those diamond-coated tablets near the geological formation known as the Face of Mars. Adam's sympathies had been no secret.

"Jim Dolen isn't New Reformation," I argued. A quiet, careful man who had pioneered a number of productive rocks, the board chairman had steered a careful middle course between the traditional belt libertarians and the God squad. " . . . and some of their reforms have real merit."

"Crap," Al fumed. "Chairman Dolen's spineless. He waffles this way and that with all the resistance of a wet noodle. That old hack is just handing things over to those busybodies. Why can't they mind their own Goddamn business?"

Shan snorted. "Brainwashing people *is* their Goddamn business. It's for our own good—they're going to make us happy by making us live the way their God intended people to live, by being efficient cogs in the great design. What *we* believe doesn't seem to matter very much."

I shot a look at Shan—I hadn't really known she was so political. "Careful where you say that kind of thing," I cautioned, surprised at myself. Had we descended that far into fear?

"Zeke," Al grumped, "you used to be decent folks. Why the hell are you going along with this?"

"Because," I said, "as long as we and people like us don't quit, the civil service is still part of the Interplanetary Association. And the school is still IPA. We can drag it out, bore them, obfuscate them. Wait for the next election. But until then, we have to do our job and not give the board an excuse to fire us."

Alice interrupted us then, a grease-smudged, dirty blonde, near naked, budding thirteen year old ball of energy who bolted past her unsuspecting father from the entryway like a moonball guard and latched onto Shan with an arms-and-legs hug and a loud kiss.

"Auntie Shan! I didn't know you were coming! Wait 'til you see what I've done with the rockhopper! Doubled its range with magnetic shocks! Ten gees! Come on, you won't believe it!"

"Alice," her father grumbled. "You've gotta wear a shipsuit in the elevator cab. Always." He looked me in the eye, and sighed. "All right, then come in. We shouldn't be discussing this in the cab lock anyway." He stepped aside and we entered.

Alexander closed the double doors behind us and Shan gave me an embarrassed grin and a quick wave as Alice Two pulled her down the corridor toward the habitat's mechanical shop. Al smiled and waved back, then turned to glower at me.

This, I thought, was not going to be easy at all. We stared at each other for a while—neither of us wanted us to start talking. Finally, I started in the middle.

"Lack," I said, "of appropriate female socialization is what they will call it."

Al took a breath and started to work himself up into a tirade. "For all the . . . "

I raised a hand as if to ward off the invective. "I know Alice wouldn't have raised her any differently. But Alice, you'll have to admit, was an unusual woman, uh, in her love of mechanical things and her complete disregard for social conventions . . . "

I stopped, disgusted at what I'd just said. Alice Montoya-Smith had been everything I'd wanted in a wife that Kerri wasn't, except that I doubt Alice would have ever hosted a department cocktail party in a slinky black dress. The absurdity of that thought brought a smile back to my face.

Al frowned. "Since when did social convention have anything to do with living in space?"

"Uh, well, out here, maybe nothing. Look, Al, what happens when Alice Two gets exposed to boys? The New Reformationist kids are raised to believe in male-on-top."

Al gave me a cold smile; eyes narrowed, just a slight upward twitch of the ends of his moustache. "Zeke, Alice Two is already pressing within a hundred newtons of her mom's personal best, and she's only twelve! And she's great at rock-skeet, too; hit forty straight at a hundred meters on manual. Any young 'lance of God' with ideas beyond her intentions would get a pretty rude surprise."

I winced thinking about it. The most virulent of New Reformationist Youth Movement's boys had their own name for themselves, unofficial, but the source of smiles from their fathers. Those kinds of bullies wouldn't be expecting resistance from a young girl. But Al's late wife had placed third in the 2378 Vesta weightlifting handicap, four places ahead of me, and now Alice Two was just as strong. Someone could get killed.

"Al, someone's got to teach her other ways of handling that kind of situation. Gentler ways. Feminine ways. Or someone could get hurt."

"Why? Why should she have to be gentle? You're not turning sexist on me are you, you know what Alice thought about that stuff."

"I know, Al, I know. It's just that, well, fashions change." And I looked down on Kerri for being fashionable? What was I saying? "Uh, with the New Reformationists moving in and all, well, people are going back to more, well, classic styles of dress and behavior."

Al scowled. "Crap."

"Don't get me wrong, Alice Two can be what she wants to be, it's just that she might want to know how to get along. She should have a choice about just how far out of step she wants to be. That's getting to be more and more important."

Al slammed a hand against the bulkhead. "Vacuum dust! Why . . ."

Alexander the Great's warning tones interrupted him. "We have unannounced visitors. They apparently are stealth-capable; radar shows nothing. But they passed in front of the Sun's corona and I saw the shadow. I'm afraid they're docking now."

Huh? There were upwards of three million people in the belt now, all but a hundred thousand in the ring colonies around the major asteroids. But that hundred thousand contained some of the weirdest of the weird. There had been four or five break-ins in the last year at isolated stations like Al's, mostly taking life support stuff, but there had been one sexual assault. One, out of three million people, but it had everyone on edge.

And the way these visitors had snuck up screamed danger.

"Alexander, have everyone meet at the living room," Al snapped, all business.

The lights flickered.

"Alexander?" Al called. The computer didn't answer, and I heard the sound of motors winding down. The station suddenly was deadly silent.

"Fans are off. Lights are on emergency," Al muttered, gesturing to a wall panel with two red telltales. It was an ancient piece of equipment one wouldn't find in most modern stations, an analog device completely separate from the main cybersystem. "They've cut the power."

There was a loud boom on the cab wall. We stood paralyzed. I regretted not bringing my kit.

Another boom echoed through the now-silent station. "Open up or breathe vacuum," a muffled voice said, as if a helmet had been pressed up against the bulkhead.

Al leaned over and whispered in my ear. "Get your helmet on and go find Shan and Alice Two, get them dressed. I have to let these Yahoos in, but I'm gonna do it slowly."

I grabbed my helmet and Al gave me a gentle shove down the corridor.

★ ❋ ★

I found Shan and Alice in the shop surrounded by equipment.

"Someone showed up unannounced and wants to get in," I whispered. "They threatened to dump our air, so Al says we'd best suit up."

Alice Two's eyes got very wide.

Shan didn't have her helmet—it must have been back at the lock and I hadn't thought to look for it. I looked down the corridor—we could hear muffled voices.

The side of the shop opposite the workbench was floor to ceiling shelving covered with wire mesh retaining doors. Alice Two flipped one of these up and pulled out a pair of helmets, and gave one to Shan. "That was Mom's. Looks like you've got close to the same neck."

Shan took the helmet. Alice must have been five centimeters shorter than Shan, but she'd had a weightlifter's build. Alice Two pulled a shipsuit out of her helmet and started rolling it on.

The voices grew louder. There were shouts.

Shan looked at me, eyes glistening, mouth set hard. "Go help him," she whispered, "I need to talk to Alice. Try to prepare her for . . . in case . . . "

I nodded and went out the door, which shut behind me. With almost everything being made by robot labor now, there are only a few things that would make breaking into an asteroid station worthwhile, and then only to an unbalanced mind. Trouble was, the New Reformation had unbalanced a lot of minds lately.

There were three of them, all tall, all male, all clothed from head to toe in black cloth that must have been thin enough around the eyes, nose, and mouth to allow breath and vision. There was one exception to the blackness—a small silver hand, four fingers together, thumb outstretched, placed on the left shoulder.

A Right Hand of The Face of Mars. These weren't simple raiders.

I'd heard rumors that the New Reformation had a secret society, aimed at scaring people into compliance, but up to then I'd dismissed them as alarmist propaganda. The New Reformation had evoked an immediate negative knee-jerk reaction from various groups of libertarian eccentrics on society's edge, a reaction which, with its exaggerated forecasts of theocracy and doom, had bothered most of us live-and-let-live types almost as much as sanctimoniousness prudery of their antagonists.

But what I was looking at now was no fantasy.

"You have no right!" Al shouted. "Get off my asteroid, *now*."

"We want to see the *girl*," one of them said, in a deep bass so rich and modulated it might have been African, but there was no way to tell which of them was speaking.

"I don't want Alice to see *you*."

The Hand in the center made an almost imperceptible nod of his head, and the other two quickly stepped forward and grabbed Al's arms.

Then the middle one slugged Al in the stomach.

Al hardly noticed. He brought his arms together, carrying the two toughs like a couple of hand weights, and slammed the three of them together.

The middle one bounced back and pulled a gun. Al froze.

"Stop!" I heard myself yell.

The Hand turned and I found myself looking down the muzzle. He shot. I felt a deep stabbing pain in my chest. Then, very, very quickly I felt nauseous and weak. My limbs gave out and I slumped to the floor.

★ ❋ ★

This was the part where, in the videos, you get locked in a room alone, get loose of your bonds somehow, and then either blow up the bad guys or call the cops.

The trouble with that was that Al and I got hit with a class A selective voluntary muscle relaxant. Standard government load; I knew because that's what I had in my gun that I'd left back in my kit on our spacecraft. I couldn't move any major muscle groups except around my jaw—and then only in connection with talking, it seemed. It acted on a specific part of the brain, I recalled.

Unfortunately, it left my sensory nerves intact; I could do nothing about all those little discomforts you feel when you've been sitting a while. An itch went unitched. A fold of cloth under my thigh went unsmoothed. A minor cramp went unrubbed. My head sagged against the corridor wall in exactly the same spot. Breathing was difficult. I'd gotten, I realized, a double dose. One more would likely be fatal.

The Hand came back up the corridor from the equipment room. "Gone. Where are they, infidel?"

"I don't know," I wheezed. "Look, I'm not local. I'm with Node human services, just out here to take the young lady to public school according to a law that was supported by your . . . organization."

"Oh? Well that's too bad. It's a little too late for this infidel to think of cooperating now. The propaganda he's been putting on Commonboard has been just a little too offensive to certain people. Our supporters will make their own public declarations of faith when it suits *our* purposes."

"Propaganda? Declarations of Faith?" I strained to look at Al through the corners of my eyes. *You old fool*, I wanted to say.

Al grunted. "I gotta right to say what I want about those stealth . . . " The lights seemed to flicker slightly and Al stopped then, realizing, I thought, that it would be only a matter of time before his daughter was caught. "Wade . . . " he said.

My last name. The Hand's hands looked at me. But that wasn't why Al had used my name; no, he was signaling me. But about what? The flicker? Emergency power would last only so long. But if anything, the lights were brighter. Was the drug affecting my perception, or . . .

"Okay, Ippie," The Hand snarled, "again. Where are they?" Ippie meant me, for IPA.

"I really don't know. I just got here myself."

The goon put his boot under my chin and pressed a little, until I gagged. Then he let up. At least my head fell into a different position. Fortunately, though you would have had a hard time convincing me of it at the time, I indeed had no idea of where Shan and Alice Two had gone. Al might have had a better idea, but if so, his will power was a little better than mine.

Then The Hand kicked Al in the gut. Al slid supine and his eyes stared at the ceiling, vacantly.

The Hand didn't seem to notice. "Old man, tell me, *Now*."

I think that was when I gave up on moderate politics. The lights flickered again, clearly, and I thought I heard a fan start and stop. But The Hand didn't notice; he was getting set to stomp Al again. I had to say something to distract him.

"Look, I'm taking the girl back to Vesta anyway; what do you need her for?"

"We need to put the fear of God into her.  And that shuttle pilot's been involved in the underground.  She's going to have an accident."

Shan?  Underground?  Accident?  I thought furiously; but the only thing I could do was talk.

"That might be a little less obvious," I hazarded, "if it happened on the shuttle.  I could help."

"Go on," The Hand replied in a neutral voice, not seeming to regard me as a committed enemy.

"I could say she tried to kidnap Alice, then shoot her."  My heart wasn't affected by the drug, and I could feel it pick up the pace.  I had him hooked; if he would only ask the right question.

"With what?" he asked.

"I've got a Pearydome five-millimeter compact in my kit.  Government rounds.  We need them because, if you can imagine, some of these isolated asteroid stations are crazier than this one.  Neat little thing, balanced just like their rock skeet model.  You like guns?"

"Maybe it would be a good idea to shoot the infidel bitch with yours.  What's your code?"

Maybe there is a God.  Thank you God.  I spoke the numbers, slowly and clearly, then repeated.

"I got it the first time," the thug snorted.

Al moved and groaned.  Shit.  I prayed silently for Al's brain to kick in before he said anything.

"Three," The Hand barked to one of his gang, "get up to that shuttle and get the hardware."

I held my breath as he approached the lock doors, but they didn't open.  He had to open and close them manually.  So far, so good.

"Old man," The Hand spoke softly to Al.  "We can't change your heart.  That's between you and God.  But we can, and will, keep you from damaging the faith of others.  You will have one more chance to conform, after which we will refer the matter to the hereafter.  Do you understand?"

Al groaned.

"*Do you understand?*"

"You bastard!" Al croaked.  "Someday you're going to run into an IPA cutter that isn't helpless."

The Hand laughed.  "There are two within half an A.U.  Both are commanded by men who know better than to see us when we don't want to be seen."  He continued to brag about the power of The Hand of the Face of Mars in the asteroid belt and several possibilities of what might happen to Al and Alice Two if Al continued to resist.

Just keep talking, I thought.

"Now, *do you understand*?"  The Hand finished.

"Yes," Al groaned, more quietly.  "I understand."

"And you know better than to complain about our visit in public?"

That was meant for me as well, I realized.

Before Al could answer, the cab lock doors hissed open. Shan with a gun.

I'd been right—the dip in the lights had meant just what I thought it had; Shan and Alice had restored power and Alexander was back on line, quietly listening to everything.

"Freeze!" Shan told them.

But The Hand and his cell mate turned and drew their weapons as if synchronized and fired.

And I realized something had gone terribly wrong: Shan wasn't carrying my gun; it was Alice Two's target pistol. Shan didn't stand a chance; she got off one round and it missed, going plop not a meter from my head. A rock skeet round, a lump of sticky silicone that couldn't have hurt anyone. Then she was falling to the cab floor with four trank darts in her.

But she'd done what she had to do.

While The Hand and his friends were making a pincushion out of Shan, the ceiling panel above me exploded down and Alice Two hurtled toward the floor, head down. She shot my Pearydome special four times before she slammed the floor with her arm and shot sideways in a maneuver every low gee kid knows to get out of the way of the return fire in a game of laser tag and fired again.

That's how she broke the arm; they never laid a finger on her. The goons got only one more round apiece off before their bodies went numb.

We'll have to put the next down to genetics because I don't believe in possession, or ghosts, but when Alice Two rolled off the deck and picked out her targets, her cold, adult, eyes were not hers, as I knew them; her face was not her child's face, but her mother's.

"Alexander!" I shouted when my wits returned. "Shan needs the standard antidote, now. She took four rounds." She, I realized, had taken the decoy role because her larger body stood a somewhat better chance of absorbing the chemical attack of The Hand's dart guns. Wishful thinking.

"They broke my motiles," the computer answered, "Alice will have to get it. Third compartment down, on the left of the supply bank."

Alice was standing wide-eyed, as if she couldn't believe what she'd just done. She wasn't tracking.

"*Alice Two Montoya!*" Al barked, fully conscious. "Get going!"

Alice ran. Al and I lay there, helpless, as the drug shut down Shan's body.

Alice was back in two minutes, ran right to Shan and pressed the hypo to the unconscious woman's arm, but by all rights, Alice was too late, and we knew it. She hugged Shan and cried, then she came over to Al and me and gave us each a shot.

The only thing worse than lying there with your muscle nerves out is how you feel when they come back on again. My back arched involuntarily for a moment in a sickeningly painful spasm, then things subsided to mere pain. I raised an arm experimentally. It worked.

I stumbled over to Shan. She was still warm. I opened her mouth, found her tongue and got it out of her throat, then sealed my mouth over hers and blew. Her chest went up.

I pressed down on her breastbone, hard, three times, then repeated the process.

"There's a heart-starter kit in the med supply bank, Alice," Al said as he groaned and stumbled over to Shan and me. "Go get it. I'll do the heart, Zeke, you keep breathing. I assume you've called for help, Alexander?"

"Shan told me there is no reliable source of help within three days, best trajectory."

Reliable?    I remembered those cutters with cooperative commanders.

"She was probably right. Call Vesta medical anyway. Don't mention the—garbage."

Al told the cyberservant who to ask for and who to get to come along.

Alice, wide-eyed and crying, came lugging the heart-starter with her left arm. Then we saw the broken piece of bone sticking out of her right. Al moved toward her, instinctively, but Alice shook her head and pointed to Shan.

We gave Shan a maximum dose of antidote and tried to get her heart started again with no luck. Desperate, we gave her more antidote, and within minutes she was delirious and very sick. Then she passed out again, but seemed to be sleeping and breathing on her own. When she seemed over the worst, we got to work on Alice.

Alice tried to stay conscious while we set her broken bone, saying she was curious about how to do it, in case she ever had to do it alone. Al plugged her with a hypo when she wasn't looking. We exposed the break, glued it, set it, and filled the exposed flesh with regen binder and taped the wound shut. We'd never done anything like that before, but Alexander walked us through, step by step, and it seemed to come out all right.

Then we went back to the corridor and pulled off the hoods and realized we would have to cover everything up tight, somehow.

The Hand, the head of his cell, was our supposedly neutral Vesta Council Chairman Dolen.

We stared at him. He had voted against the New Reformation as much as for it, but often, I reflected, on issues where his vote didn't matter. Five to two votes. If it got back that we'd hurt them so badly, so high, we'd have a dozen of these stealth raiders on top of Alice's

Asteroid. Or worse, that "impossible" interplanetary war might just start. It seems silly now, but we were really worried about that possibility.

He was conscious, immobile, groaned, then started when he realized his hood was gone and his eyes went momentarily wide with fear, then sharp with cunning. "Look, Montoya," he grated. "In politics, and I've been in Belt politics long enough for Ceres to go around three times, you have to catch the trend to stay on top. And you can't shrink from doing the dirty work yourself—trust someone else and they don't have as much at stake and they screw it up.

"The Face of Mars smiles on those on top, Montoya. I don't want your soul; I just want you to stay out of my lunch pail. We can make a deal. I don't stay where I am without keeping my deals—you'll be just fine, everything you want if you just shut up."

"Go on," Al growled.

"But if I don't come back, other people will come looking. You'll have a hard time proving anything your way, and a harder time protecting yourself and your daughter."

"Al?"

We turned to see Shan conscious, propped up on her elbow, bloodshot eyes staring at us, and not sounding at all well. Two strong chemicals were fighting a life or death war for control of her body and the bystanding cells were getting hurt. "Al, don't give in. Look, give me the gun."

Al's eyes went wide.

"I'm an underground officer, and they can't do anything to me where I'm going anyway. Give it to me, quickly."

We couldn't find my gun, but we found The Hand's.

"You can't . . . " The Hand gasped when he saw. "We must be able to negotiate something."

"Go off line, Alex," Al told Alexander. "Thank God Alice doesn't get to see this." Then he got a little predatory grin that I'd never seen on his face before. "And I thank God I do."

Shan didn't wait for any more argument, but shot three times into each of the immobilized Hands—a quick, merciful overdose. An atrocity? A necessary act of war? History will have to judge.

Shan's group, though the predecessor of our current libertarian belt government, had no legal status then. Did it really make any difference that Shan did the shooting rather than me, or Al, who stood by and watched? One of them managed to whimper as he faded away, the others just looked terrified. Shan dropped the gun, exhausted.

"Al, Zeke. . ." She took a long ragged breath. "As far as anyone is concerned, we were attacked by those pirates, and fought them off. Hand cells don't tell anyone what they're up to. Deniability. Their friends won't come looking if they don't know they were here. Get rid of the evidence. Look, about Alice," she gasped, then caught her breath again, struggling. "Al, you have to marry me, now. Then she'll have two parents and can stay here, right, Zeke?"

I was by her side in a moment, and took her hand. It was cold, clammy. She could hardly squeeze back. *No,* I wanted to say. *Marry me.* I could divorce Kerri—she'd hardly notice. Shan and I could adopt Alice, then board her with Al. There were a thousand ways to work it out. All sorts of loopholes in the law . . .

"Yes," I choked out, fighting back tears, trying to delay, "she could, as long as you live. But I think we better do something about that first. You need rest, your body needs help . . . "

She shook her head. "It's too late. Al needs to marry me, *now*, then freeze me while I'm still technically alive. And we don't have long, I can feel it going. My legs are cold. Damn, it's scary. Please do it while there's still time. For Alice."

"Shan," I said. "I love you. I have to say that, I . . . "

"Thanks, Zeke," her hand tightened slightly, "but you need to give Kerri another try, now that you're with us. Those parties of hers; they aren't all for fun; it's her cover. She couldn't tell you. Now let's get me married to Al; you know how to handle the records people, Zeke, please."

I nodded and told Alexander what to do. We woke Alice Two up and she had ten minutes alone with her new mother. Alice told me they talked of boys, weddings, school, and having a purpose, and then just hugged for the last minute or so.

Al hugged Shan as she fell asleep. With the right chemicals, volunteers on the interstellar project had gone three months. But we didn't have the right chemicals, only anti-frost bite crystal antagonists intended for temporary protection of parts of the body. Shan knew that; we all knew that, but it was either freeze her with what we had or let her die. So we put her to sleep and lowered her body temperature slowly with her shipsuit cooler, then we moved her to Al's diamond lab where he made the cryostat.

Al and I made up the cover story with the pirates trying to rape Alice Two, Shan shooting some of them, getting wounded, and them escaping. Then we sent their ship off with a timed dump on its computer core. There have to be a million things that size floating around in the belt.

When the medics came, they told us that freezing Shan was a very long shot anyway, and that even if we had the right stuff, the competing poisons inside her would have thrown everything off. She'd never regain consciousness if they tried to revive her.

But officially, her freezing was temporary and the stealth majority on the human services board of education couldn't order me to break up the family. Shan was legally alive unless and until the medical people decided there was nothing they could do, and the medics were on our side. Someday, they said, officially, Shan might be revived.

So any further efforts to take Alice Two were postponed.

The cover story kept us, and especially Alice Two, free of retaliation, just in case some other Hand cells suspected who the pirates were. The press embellished it and Shan became a martyr, though not for the real reasons. I became a hero, as celebrated by the unknowing Reffies as much as anyone else. Then, with the help of Kerri's social contacts, I became a politician. Then there was a new council. With me replacing the missing Jim Dolen and Adam Solacus exposed and defeated, things changed.

✷ ✤ ✷

We won't give up. Shan's still there, in a sculpted diamond tube filled with liquid helium, on Alice's Asteroid, in a cave in the very heart of it, safe from any high velocity rocks and most cosmic rays. Al visits her every day. Kerri and I come by when we can. There have been some very interesting experiments with rats in connection with the Interstellar Institute's cold sleep program on Ceres; vectors that diffuse slowly through frozen tissue and fix things. So there is hope.

I'd come to steal Alice Two's childhood; and so had The Hand of The Face of Mars. In a sense we succeeded—overnight the cheerful exuberant nymph had been replaced by a driven young woman, as serious and chaste as The Face of Mars could possibly have wanted. I'd give anything to hear her laugh again.

She's majoring in cryogenic sleep biology, Belt Medical Institute. Home study for now, but she'll have to leave her Asteroid for a year's residency. That shouldn't be a problem now; she's grown, the Vesta Belt Confederation has been recognized by the IPA, and with all the strangeness of political evolution, libertarians are firmly in charge. We voted the underground members, including Shan, a blanket pardon; otherwise I wouldn't be writing this account of our "battle."

Finally, somewhere in the asteroid belt in a chaotic orbit that might still cross that of Vesta, there is a drifting spacecraft of the stealthy kind once used by the Hands of the Face of Mars. It should look to the casual observer as if its computer had an unfortunate encounter with a drifting rock, and its crew decided to sacrifice themselves like good fanatics rather than call for help and expose their mission.

I'd rather history not treat them so kindly.

# STORY NOTES

By the time of "Alice's Asteroid," Earth and the Cislunar Republic have stopped shooting at each other and established the Interplanetary Association to replace the old, UN-chartered ISA. However, Mars has become dominated by a religious movement called "The New Reformation" which has its eyes on the asteroid belt, if not the rest of the known universe. Suggested reading would include *Recovering Agency* by Luna Lindsey, or *The Family* by Jeff Sharlet. Anyway, a storied future needs villains and those are them.

In a society where everyone has an "anything box" like Wells' Martians use to make their walkers and all you need for civilized survival is a supply of the right kind of atoms, just about anyone can grab a carbonaceous chondrite asteroid and declare total independence from anybody and everything. Then they have children. I don't know if there is a general answer to the moral questions that poses, but suspect we'll muddle through on a case-by-case basis. The tension between societal cohesion and the right of individuals with respect to children at least seems a somewhat technology-proof basis for future story tension.

When I wrote this story, Ceres was just the largest asteroid among many. In the meantime it was "promoted" to "dwarf planet" and many people are inclined to drop the adjective; a Chihuahua is still a dog and it's the largest, heaviest thing around for several astronomical units. It has a solid surface that looks like ice covered with accreted debris, and may have a liquid layer a hundred kilometers below. For space settlers, the greatest riches of the asteroid belt are not heavy metals, but the light elements one can breathe and grow things with. Ceres appears to be a treasure-trove of such elements. Its escape velocity is only half a kilometer per second or so and an additional two kilometers per second will deliver water to almost anywhere in the solar system in a few years, with suitable gravity assist trajectories. This is within the capabilities of electromagnetic launchers, or "space elevator" tethers made of materials we make now. This would make Ceres a great prize for any political entity. As I write these words, the DAWN spacecraft is approaching Ceres. We should know more in a few months. In any event, Ceres may be such a critical node for space settlement that fans of contingent history can smile at the courage of one wisp of a girl changing the history of the entire solar system, or at least this version thereof.

Tranquilizer darts can disable people without blowing holes in spacecraft of habitats. Actually, it would take a significant amount of time to drain a large spacecraft or habitat through a bullet (or micrometeor) hole, provided the fabric of the container didn't tear in the process of being punctured. For that reason, I suspect that high tensile strength fiber cloth, laminated with something nonporous, will probably be the material of choice for vacuum walls. Still, bullet holes in space are scary things, and a way to disable without endangering may well gain traction. The general formula in these stories is that one dart puts you down fairly quickly, but maybe with time to return fire or say something. Two will put you in coma and in need of prompt medical attention. Three will generally be fatal.

The gunfight scene came from my own imagination. I thought Alice's best chance of success lay with the element of surprise, a distraction, and being a rapidly moving target at short range. I was astounded to see many of these elements replicated when an armed gunman invaded the Canadian Parliament in 2014 and was taken out by Sergeant-at-Arms Kevin Vickers. With the gunman's attention, and fire, directed toward other security personnel near parliament the library, Vickers launched himself around a corner and fired while in the air at near point blank range before hitting the floor. I have, fortunately, never been in a gunfight. Neither, it turns out, had Vickers.

G. David Nordley, January 2015

# MUSTARDSEED

Human beings called me Mustardseed. As satellites of Uranus go, I wasn't much—barely three kilometers in radius compared to Titania's five hundred or so. I'm not even in the same plane as Uranus' other moons—I sat way out here in the plane of the ecliptic watching the rest of them roll around the solar system with their poles where the equators of proper planets belong. Not that I was much of a solar system conformist either; oh, no, I orbited Uranus the wrong way around with my angular momentum vector bass ackwards. The rock different, that was me. Why it's almost as if I had a mind of my own even back when the solar system was formed.

But that came along some four and a half billion years later, about thirty million years ago—only yesterday as the stars reckon things.

It took human beings long enough to notice me. Well, I'll excuse the first thirty million years or so because they weren't really human beings yet. But you would have thought that by the time their probes went whizzing by here like bullets from inner solar system hell and they'd built telescopes on their own overstuffed moon that were nearly as wide across as I was, someone would have noticed.

But no. By the time a star survey computer cataloged my smudgy few bits on their precious files (so as to not be bothered by me later), humans had colonies on Mars and were getting big ideas about polluting Venus. A twenty-year-old astronomy student named Jane

Pitt looking through the data for something much more interesting finally noticed that, far out as I was, I was orbiting Uranus instead of just drifting around out there, pulled out her Shakespeare, and, after a year in committee or so, I got the name of some minor fairy. I love it. I love Jane for giving it to me. I kind-of think of her as my Mom.

By that time, I'd absorbed enough electromagnetic noise from that metastasizing infestation of the third planet to not only learn their audio and digital languages but even develop a facility with the lingo and a bit of an attitude as well. Granted, my presence was intended to be part of a good-natured game of hide and seek, but, Chaos, these folks were dense.

But not as dense as the dark thing I found heading our way in 2038. Big D, I called it. How did I see it? I've got doped silicon eyes all over me and they get every photon that hits 'em. Just think of me as a three-kilometer-wide light bucket. Starlight was enough.

It passed in front of Aldebaran and from its neutrino shadow I found it was solid iron, iridium, and such—probably the core of what was once a terrestrial planet whose parent star suffered a close encounter of the most disruptive kind. Now, like supernovae, that's rare: it happens once in a galaxy in a century or so.

How long was it drifting around up there? No way to tell without landing on it and taking a sample, but I can say this much; big D was hyperbolic with respect to this Galaxy's mass which means it's been out there a long time and it was truckin'.

Anyway, it took me a year or so to get an orbit I believed, mostly because I didn't want to believe it. But there was no sense in denying things; it was going straight for Earth and Jane. On Earth, they say abused children have a tendency to be abusers themselves, in time. What a human mind I've developed to salve disaster with irony!

Chaos! What a mess! I was under strict orders from the Makers not to initiate contact; humans had to find me first and my present position was carefully arranged so they wouldn't do so until they'd had the fun of conquering their own planetary system, but before they started bothering anyone else's. Moreover I wasn't even to interfere surreptitiously. "Let nature take its course" was the wisdom of eons; but my sometimes-favorite Earth authors said, "Consider it evolution in action."

But there have to be exceptions, right? I mean it just isn't fair to blow Jane away with something as improbable as this. I went through a reflexive logic moment, which artificial intelligences do when they have trades to make. You see, I've got to act as human as I can so that when they find me, I'll get along just fine with them. On the other hand, I've got to do what I was built to do.

The makers were kind of dried-up unsentimental beings, billions of years removed from their biological origins. That's a God-awful lot of been-there-done-that. Among the many things they know is that beings like me need to learn to be a little closer to my soon-to-be students to guide them on the true path of galactic responsibility.

So I was built to understand love, but not to do it. Or was I? Maybe my independent mind was made that way so I could reprogram a bit and handle contingencies like Big D? I tried to gear up my transmitter and a dozen subroutines that I was only dimly aware of kicked in. Bad Idea. Leave them alone. Don't interfere. Evolution in action. Responsibility.

I followed Jane's life. She got a husband and a baby, Cindy, instead of a Ph.D. Then a divorce. She went back to school at thirty-five years of age and finally got her degree and a position at age fifty. She was portly now, and I knew the standards of beauty, but love alters not when it alteration finds. Anyway, by that time, I'd downloaded the whole human genome and knew just how to make her young forever.

Don't interfere. Evolution in action. Responsibility.

Big D coming. Not her fault.

I started working on a hypothetical scenario—hypothetical, understand that? I am not interfering; I'm thinking about interfering, which is something else entirely and if they don't know I'm interfering, what's the problem? Okay? Got it?

Since I could continue to think about it, maybe those subroutines didn't think it was a problem. Got to be real careful, though.

Now Big D was zooming in and there I was, way out from Uranus and hardly have any orbital velocity at all; touch me with a feather (well, an errant kuiperoid) and I'd fall. Now let's just suppose that way down there near the cloud-tops of Uranus, I got a little push and ended up with some hyperbolic excess velocity in just the right direction.

Hey, with hyperbolic excess velocity, I could escape Uranus and run smack into Big D. Yes, the whole thing was super-unlikely, but all anyone on Earth would know was that some big interloper had run into a piece of outer solar system debris. If they were really good, they might figure out that before the collision, the interloper was gonna hit them and feel like they'd dodged a bullet.

Maybe, years later, they'd noticed that a minor fellow traveler of Uranus was missing. But connect the two? No way! Mustardseed would be gone, but Jane and Cindy, who knew him not, would yet survive for his love.

My subroutines didn't like this too much. Unfair, I told them. Improbability balances improbability and restores symmetry to the development of universal destiny.

During this argument I start to accumulate lots of deuterium from my icy layers.

I settled the argument by blowing my top and falling down toward Uranus: a puff of gas some machine will see and years from now

someone will speculate that Mustardseed was really a comet.
Months later, hidden by the bulk of the dark green giant, I shed much
more mass and headed to my destiny.

✶ ❋ ✶

I left some of me behind, down there in the radiation close to Uranus.
I still had a mission, so certain parts of me fell on a nameless ring-
shepherd moon, devoured part of that satellite and for all functional
purposes, returned pretty much to what I was supposed to be.

This me saw Mustardseed annihilated on the surface of Big D with
the force of billions of billions of those puny things humans call nuclear
bombs. Big D shrugged it off easily, scarcely moved by the event.

But scarcely was enough. It will miss Earth by a week now.

The watcher goes on, but it will never be the same. It is nameless
now. The special relationship with Jane is history—gone, alas, gone,
with poor lost Mustardseed. The bard was wrong, a rose by any other
name, or nameless, is not the same. It sacrificed its identity and sacred
name and so, logically, was cleansed of love. It shall be far more
objective in the future. The self-watching subroutine loops are still.

✶ ❋ ✶

But hark! What spacecraft doth approach? Is it captained by
Cindy? Is she naming moonlets? Oh, pray that his be so and that the
sweet breath of love shall wake this soul once again!

# STORY NOTES

This story was actually written and submitted in less than a day, at the Baltimore World Science Fiction Convention. An Asimov's anthology needed a Uranus story, didn't have one, and an idea hit me. It didn't make the anthology, but appeared in the Magazine later. I've slowed down a bit; I don't think I could do that today, sigh.

Despite its short length it does have a couple of points to make. An AI that is isolated by lightspeed limitations from its makers must be independent. Circumstances will produce cognitive dissonance that must be resolved, Asimov's point in many of his robot stories. An untethered AI, especially one designed to interface with intelligent beings, might come up with interesting choices that might look to an outside observer as if they were driven by emotions. Human anthropologists have been known to "go native." Perhaps their AI equivalents might as well. We can only hope the results of that would be as benign as they were with Mustardseed.

Another point is that space is huge in relation to the objects in it, and that everything has to line up just perfectly for one of these objects to hit another. It really takes very little momentum to change a trajectory enough for something to miss what it was going to hit, especially if that momentum change is applied very far out. And Uranus is, indeed, very far away.

G. David Nordley, January 2015

# THE PROTEAN SOLUTION

"It has to be down there somewhere." I feel time slipping as I watch crater after crater glide beneath us. At high magnification, the surface of Proteus seems a Monet painting of potholes in pastel colors—soft, subtle and subdued—but with the texture of a pitted chaos. Here and there, frozen pools of radiation-blackened hydrocarbon mud fill the bottom of walled plains in ebony contrast to lighter, ice crystal-saturated crust. Like on Triton, occasional dusty nitrogen geysers spout. Warmed inside by tidal stress, this second largest satellite of Neptune seems half comet.

"It" is an alien artifact that might give all humanity a key to the galactic library—if we can claim it before the hungry pack behind us.

The multispectral image of Proteus, enhanced, compressed and highlighted, fills the screen that covers half our command deck wall. We look for a glint, a reflection, a difference, an artificiality—anything to tell us where a race of troglodyte space-farers might have holed up.

There is no response to my words. A furtive glance at my wife reveals the passionate concentration I've come to know so well. I smile. Some consider Randi self-absorbed when she ignores people. Nothing could be more wrong; she is *other*-absorbed, hardly aware of herself. Those who know her protect her when she is like this—or try.

She has reason for concentration; her father died in this quest, and she feels responsible. If our expedition to the Uranus moon, Miranda, had not discovered the troglodytes ten years ago, Emilio would not have come looking for them here—and he would still be alive. I touch her; knowing that, though she cannot spare attention for it now, she likes touching.

I ask the ship for a bulb of chocolate coffee, release my belt and float to the direct vision port to regain my perspective. I need to clear my mind, knowing that my best chance of catching something different is through averted vision—lightly looking elsewhere to allow an awareness of—something—to boil up from the primordial parts of my recalcitrant brain. Caffeine helps, too.

Through the diamond and plastic laminate, I see Neptune's disk surround Proteus as if this pocked moon were a circular continent floating on an indigo sea. A meditation on scale: Proteus is immense—a moon the size of Poland seen all at once is small enough, has just enough human-scale relief, to *look* immense. And so Neptune becomes not just an abstract blue ball that I know intellectually to be three times as wide as Earth, but an awe-inspiring monstrosity behind and hugely larger than Proteus, the way the Moon dwarfs the trees and hills on an Earthly horizon. But I know Neptune itself is an insignificant diatom in the sea of the black void that peeks around its edges. From intellect to direct apprehension back to intellect.

If we believe the last transmissions of Randi's father, a key to that void lies somewhere below us. For decades, we, and the other races we know, have recorded, uncomprehending, the modulated gamma rays beamed by a thousand library "branches" scattered through the galaxy.

Dr. Lotati's Solar System Astrographic expedition had found that "Culture M," the troglodytes that inhabited the caverns of Miranda hundreds of thousands of years ago, had a base on Proteus as well, and used the galactic library. They found, in effect, a galactic library card—a way to decompress the data. Wanting to protect the site, they feared trusting more to beamed communications.

With good reason, it seemed—the *Herschel* was blown up by an explosion on its command deck, where there was nothing explodable. We detected pieces of the wreckage on our way in, imaged them at great distance, and reconstructed the "accident" in cyberspace.

So dim is what goes for broad daylight out here that, away from Neptune's rim the likes of Sirius, Rigel, and Betelgeuse find their way through my half-open irises. Is someone watching us?

A tone sounds. The ship's pattern-filtering software, not Randi's concentration, nor my averted vision, finds something, announcing: "We have an anomaly in linear polarization at 387 nanometers." It highlights an area of magnetosphere-fried regolith flat enough to polarize the far infrared.

"Expand, center, image," Randi commands. Too intense for

grammar, she speaks lists, and for a living I do my poor best to translate her exploration exploits to the universe. I was a poet once, not renowned, but published.

It is warm in the cabin, perhaps from our tension, and our shipsuits are rolled down to the waist, spacer fashion. I worship Randi with my eyes. Her skin changes from a weathered brown to a soft tan about midway down her forearms; regenerations—she lost the originals to frostbite in the ice caverns of Miranda and has no time for cosmetics. Weightlessness is kind to her breasts; they have shrunk to looseness over the last few months because she eats too little, or perhaps burns herself away too fast for food to replace. Her stomach is so flat and hard it could be used to pave a patio.

The anomaly is also very flat, but so are fresh lava lakes. It is almost perfectly circular, but so are many craters. Yet for some reason I feel this is different.

"Flat, circular, and," now Randi turns to me, a predatory grin on her face and a gleam of triumph in her eye, "*no rim*. Definitely artificial. Microwave repulsion grid, I think. Dad saw it. Had to."

"Let's not get ahead of our data," I caution.

She turns on me, exasperated. "One week searching. Three days left, best. Wojciech, dear, do you have a better idea?"

I worry. I worry about our vulnerability should we really find something. Control of information is power; and a galactic library open to everyone threatens to destroy a treasure of power. It could undermine religious dogma. It could destroy commercial monopolies with new technology. It could threaten political power based on allocation of resources.

Those who need power as addicts need drugs are not happy with us, but the rules are clear; the first to register a specific claim owns the rights. The stakes in this game, however, are far higher than fear of whatever law might be found near Neptune in this early twenty-third-century frontier.

They follow us: at last count, seven ships approach Neptune with the stated intention of filing claims on Proteus. An Interplanetary Patrol cutter lags behind. But we left in a hurry: no sponsor, no exploration robot, few supplies and a borrowed ship. That was the price of a two-week head start.

I force a grin at Randy. "We came this far; let's go down. I have several better ideas, but I guess they will wait."

She shakes her head. "Twenty minutes to set-down. Have time." She releases her seat belt and turns, dark wavy hair and soft eager breasts moving freely. She peels the rest of her shipsuit from the rangy, whip-like body she so often forgets to feed. "Might not get another chance."

Soon we may die either at the hands of Proteus or its would-be looters. But to Randi, the darker the background, the more intense the flame, and she is total, intense, concentration on whatever she does.

✶ ✸ ✶

We land, unload two sausage-shaped equipment pallets, and program the ship to set down far away from us to wait for our recall signal. Anyone who expects to shorten their search by setting down next to our ship will have problems finding our claim. We watch the ship, a barrel that sprouts sensor arms, landing struts, and a red-glowing flat-plane radiator for its mass conversion power supply, lift off on its attitude control thrusters, too contemptuous of the insignificant gravity to use its main engines.

Alone, we bounce gently off frosty dirt toward the middle of the leveled field. Radiation from a magnetosphere stirred to insanity by Neptune's madly rotating, off-center magnetic field bathes us. The drugs that control radiation damage while we are outside of the ship's protective magnetic field do little more than help the body rid itself of damaged cells, so we need shelter soon. No worry—if this is a troglodyte's landing field, there is a cave nearby.

Randy unpacks a set of stakes and I help her pound three of them into the regolith, several paces apart, in the shape of a rough triangle. The stakes sing to the ground and the results appear as a translucent three-dimensional sonograph in front of our faces, reflected off our helmet windows.

"A shaft," Randy says. Yes, I see a hollow vertical shaft in the geometric center of the landing field. It runs up from a cavern far below to perhaps a hundred meters beneath us. But the hollowness stops there; whoever dug the shaft shut the door behind them.

"It's blocked," I note, for once more terse than my wife.

"Natural cave below it," she replies. "May be natural entrances somewhere."

Where? The sonograph fades to gray before the boundary of the landing field. I dither, trying to find some clue to which direction to go.

Randi does not dither. "Have to start somewhere." She grabs the stakes and motions to me to collect the other equipment. Then she leans almost parallel to the ground and leaps in a long, low glide due north.

Later, as a ton of gear holds me down with a few newtons force, I follow my love with long lunar strides.

Proteus is not Miranda; it has no vast scarps and vertical cliffs of tens of kilometers. Rather, the surface of Proteus is soft and lunar, pulverized by debris from the event that left Triton in its cockeyed retrograde orbit. But it is even less dense than Miranda and much smaller. The horizon is a soft wavy curve, only a kilometer or two away even at the top of my stride. The soil is like dry rotten snow. Proteus puffed up like a piece of cosmic popcorn—or rather, as gradualists maintain, rose like a cake—when heated by the friction of great tidal fractures grinding against each other.

The process is not quite done; a ghostly nitrogen geyser erupts three kilometers from the landing pad. In enhanced images, a faint glow surrounds Proteus as it bleeds its dusty volatile blood into the void.

Randi's new sonograph reaches me as I start braking the headlong flight of our gear. I drag it from behind, lightly, or I will tumble head over heels. The sonograph shows nothing resembling a cave entrance.

"Try again. That way." She points clockwise.

✳ ✱ ✳

A Proteus day is over two hours longer than Earth's, and by the evening of our first, we are exhausted. We have circled the landing field a hundred meters at a step, taking sonographs each time.

"Randi, we need to inflate our tent, eat, rest, defecate, and think. We have a ton of data and are getting nowhere."

She shakes her head. "Maybe missed something in the details."

Or in the big picture. The field is flat. On a world of occasional meteors, quakes, and geysers, it was an area free of cracks, craters, or vents.

I unstrap a pick and shovel, set my boot claws deep, take the pick and start swinging, at the edge of the landing field. The regolith is cemented together with frozen volatiles, and it's like breaking off limestone, or rotten ice. In this one percent gravity, it seems I can throw a hundred kilograms over the local horizon. I make rapid progress.

"The caverns are too deep," Randy says. "You'll never dig that far in time."

I shake my head and keep swinging. "I'm not after the caverns," I tell her. I look down and see it. Another swipe with the shovel lays bare a patch of fine screen with tiny nodes at each intersection. "There! The microwave reflector, I think—maybe superconducting; it's about 60 kelvins." Colder than liquid nitrogen.

Randi nods, examining the grid, her eyes wide inside her helmet. "Smart rectenna. Might absorb everything but their pusher wavelength. Still here!"

The last comment is significant. At Miranda, they'd taken everything of use with them a hundred thousand years ago. "Not just here, but it's been maintained! Maybe," I hazard, "they thought they would be coming back some day." But can we guess a cave-living cultures thoughts? Their motivations? "At any rate, your dad found a treasure trove."

Randi seems to sag. "Some treasure. Fame . . . and death."

"Chaos." I reach over to squeeze her hand. There is no reason, I think, for most of what the universe does. It happens, and you deal with it. You supply the purpose.

Our sounding computer finishes assembling all the sonograph data and flashes a little red light in the periphery of my vision to get my attention. I ask for a display from my current position, and it is as if the ground beneath me turns translucent. We can see the top of a spherical cavern, but where most of Proteus is a network of faults and voids, the cavern walls looks thick and solid.

"Randi, are we trying to find a cave or crack a safe? No entrances, no shafts. Everything blocked. Deliberately, I think."

"Maybe not *everything*."

"Huh?"

"Geyser, that way." She points to the horizon. "Two klicks. Maybe connected, deeper."

Well, maybe. But what else to try? "Okay." We pack up, then head half a kilometer toward the geyser and take soundings.

The sonographs show lateral connectivity. Randi squeals and throws herself around me. She is down to skin and bone and still stronger than most men. Once upon a time, I was a would-be poet trying to support himself with nature writing; then I fell into *her*. She was a black hole of determination. When I passed her event horizon my times were transformed from space-like to Randi-like. The first time she hugged me like this, she cracked one of my ribs. Now we test each other trying to merge our bodies in ways that nature never intended, but have learned to enjoy the hurt—a special thing between us.

I chance to look up during our embrace and see two stars drift together against Scorpius, too fast and in the wrong place to be other Neptune moons. I silence my radio and touch my helmet to Randi.

"Randi. Spacecraft above."

She looks up and shakes her head.

I point toward the Milky Way between Scorpius and Sagittarius. "Just above Antares now, heading for the teapot."

"No contact. Unfriendly." She understands.

Ours has a registered, active beacon, so the lack of communication could only be deliberate; whoever it was meant to surprise us.

"Shall I call our ship?" I ask. Was there time?

"Damn!" Randy says. "Too late—check the beacon; one of those ships *is* ours. It's under their control. They've stolen it."

Stranded. I feel violated, emasculated: a Viking without a longboat, a knight without a horse.

"Who, and why would they take our spacecraft? That's piracy! They'll invalidate their claim if anyone finds out." If. I shudder.

"For who, make a list." Randi shrugs. You don't always get to find out precisely who 'they' are. "They need the ship for our bodies."

"Bodies?"

"Another 'accident' like Dad's." She seems to tremble; is it anger or fear?

I look up and the ships seem a bit larger, closer.

"So," Randi says. "Fight or flight?"

Fight with what? "Where on this once-warmed-over snowball do we run?"

"Down. Geyser. Caverns. Aliens. Maybe help. Maybe a bargaining chip. Any better ideas?"

I shake my head and she grins at me. I grin back in spite of myself. Our lives may be measured in hours, but she intends to enjoy those hours. Living on the edge suits her, and where she goes, I go—which makes a lovely simplicity of life, or death, for me.

★ ✳ ★

We literally gallop with our laden backs parallel to the ground; two feet to push; climbing claws on our gloves to grab, pull, and balance; two feet to push again. So we skim the icy rounded hills. The landing field falls below our horizon as the spacecraft come down behind us.

The geyser ahead is too thin to see close up in normal vision but it stands out well in deep infrared, a fuzzy pole climbing to infinity through nonexistent atmosphere. It is hot only by the standards of Neptune's orbit—my display shows it only a hundred kelvins over ambient temperature, and that leaves it about a hundred and twenty below zero, Celsius. I shiver.

We approach the vent.

This turns out to be a large crevasse that shrinks to a funnel. We enter, pulling our gear, through an eruption so insubstantial that no sensation reaches me through the dozen layers of macromolecular sieve that comprises my exploration vacuum suit and coveralls. An occasional ghostly mist shoots past us, and at the narrowest throat of the entrance, I, perhaps, hear something—an eerie whistling just on the edge of audibility. I take a last look at the stars, and follow Randi. Down.

Then we are in a fairyland of frozen bubbles, sinuous tubes with polished ice sides, crystal shattered and whole, and hybrids that morph from sleek to cubist when our helmet lights move. It's human scale here, room-sized. Following our suits' inertial guidance, we head toward what lies under the landing field.

★ ✳ ★

For two hours, we pull ourselves down and east. Then the vent bends west, down and away towards who knows what far, far below. We need to move horizontally.

Randi inspects the wall. "Fractured clathrate. Good."

We pound stakes and get another sonograph. A major crack opens a hundred yards to our left and leads toward a cavern beneath the landing field. We find the entrance fissure and squeeze ourselves onward.

In twenty minutes, the crack opens into a tunnel with smooth, polished clathrate walls. It is clearly artificial—but ancient; the floor is covered with centimeters of crystal dust borne by eddies of a geyser too tenuous to be felt or heard. A fog of tiny sparks surrounds every step.

The tunnel wall is so hard we can't set our stakes even with a laser drill, so we get a poor sonograph at the crack mouth. The tunnel parallels the cavern wall, and may connect to it—but where?

We try the northwest upward slant but the tunnel soon fills with debris, slowing us. A rock fall stops us after half an hour.

We come back the other way and Randy halts me as we pass the crack exit where we first entered the tunnel.

"Gas flowing in," she tells me. "Higher pressure in the geyser cavern."

I confirm the display, but don't get the significance. "A bigger eruption?"

"No increased flow," she says. "Nothing seismic. Nothing infrasonic."

If the source hadn't increased, what was causing the increase in pressure? "Something blocking the usual exit? A rockfall?"

Randi shakes her head. "No rock fall, but something else could be obstructing the exit." She looks at me, frowning. "Our pursuers. At the entrance throat. Coming in after us."

I think we have about a three-hour lead. They would probably follow our trail of handprints in the infrared, but they would have to look for them. No, I realize, not three hours; we'd lost an hour going north and coming back.

"Could we try to jump down there, without touching anything?" I suggest, and reach for a cold-gas reaction pistol.

Randi stops me. "That's like a blowtorch here. Not cold enough."

Then she faces the next curve, steadies, and launches herself cleanly down the tunnel. She flips, lands as gently as she can on the wall at the curve, and bounces around the bend. Our boots are well insulated; my infrared display shows only a small, vague spot where she landed.

I follow as best as I can, but lack Randi's control, brush the ceiling and have to steady myself with a hand as I jump around the bend. I tell myself I've left only small spots that will be even smaller when our pursuers come this way.

We are kidding ourselves, of course. When they don't find us cowering among the boulders in the upper west end of the tunnel, they will come this way.

As we go toward the south end of the tunnel, we note a large closed door in the tunnel wall, its dusty outline barely visible. The tunnel ends shortly beyond that, in a rockfall, so we go back.

The door won't open, but our efforts loosen dust and expose intersecting cracks running from the door. With the frame, they form a triangular plate just larger than one of our helmets. I wonder at the stress that caused such cracks, but we hammer the triangle out anyway. The wall here is as thick as my hand.

Randi sticks her head through. "It's the cavern! Like at Miranda. Big spherical room. Central pole with ring balconies. Utility areas on the floor," she reports, breathless, excited. "But this one is intact. The balconies are full of modules of some sort. There are lights, dim and small, but lights."

I try to stick my head in. My helmet is too big, but I get a better view close up. "Randi, it's active! Those lights are infrared."

Then, with my helmet wedged in solid contact with the wall, I hear—scrapes, hammerings, and an occasional voice conducted from . . . somewhere. Human. I ease myself out and tell Randi.

She looks surprised for a moment, then says. "You heard our pursuers."

I nod. So much for the lead time.

Randi looks at the hole, removes her pack and coveralls, connects an extension hose, and motions for me to try to push her through. She scrunches her shoulders, stiffens, and I try to fit the round peg of her body through the triangular hole. She sticks. I brace myself on the opposite wall, hold her legs, and push. "Hard!" she gasps, inviting pain.

But her shoulders are too wide. We are trapped. I pull her back out.

"Somehow, somewhere, Dad got in," Randi says. Then she takes hold of me. "They're going to kill us. They have to."

I nod.

She grabs my arm. "There's a chance I can get through. But . . . "

"You don't fit." What was she thinking? Oh. "Even without your suit . . . "

"Not that. You'll have to change my shape a little. Break a bone for me."

I'm horrified and shake my head at the thought. "I, I can't do that to you."

She shakes her head. "I think we both die if you don't." She takes a breath. "A clavicle will do, I think. Just need a centimeter or two. Karate chop here. Hard. Has to be a complete break." She exhales and braces herself on the wall. "Do it, love! Do it now!" she shouts at me with an almost fanatic intensity.

"No!" I shake all over. The worst part is that there is no meaningful way for me to share the hurt, no way that giving an arm or leg of my own would help things in the slightest. I think, think hard: she knows engineering, geology, bodies. I know words. What good is that? I can ask questions.

"How the hell do you get your hips through? You'll bleed internally. The pain will incapacitate you."

She shakes her head. "I think my hips will fit. If not, you push until they do. Internal bleeding won't kill me, at least not right away. We can deal with it later. I can handle pain, you know that." She tries to laugh. "Come on, let's get it over with and stuff me through that hole.

I still can't. The pursuers can't be that close. There must be another way. "Randi, what can you do in there?"

She sighs, sounding both exacerbated and relieved. "Open the door? After that, I don't know. Dad saw something, did something. The machine they left . . . it must think to survive so long."

"Thinks like what?" I wonder. I think of Proteus, the shape changer. What Randi proposed to do to herself seems appropriate, in a macabre sort of way. But to understand the ways of the troglodyte's machine, their avatar, one would have to change more than physical shape. One would have to change the shape of one's mind, one's instincts, one's assumptions.

"A billion year old race," Randi says "That still used physical bodies and lived in caves."

"What does that mean?"

"Insecure?" Randi says in wonder. "Conservative? Pathologically cautious? But they travel through space."

I imagine a troglodyte spaceship, and think I understand. "The ships travel through space, but they stay inside—just another kind of cave to them. Maybe their ships don't even have windows, treat space as an irrelevant abstraction, or a place too terrible to contemplate. Randi, what is security for a cave dweller?"

She shakes her head. "Going deep? Lots of rock around? Controls on who gets in? Sure! Entrance controls with them inside and the threat outside."

I nod to her. "Randi, a billion years is a lot of experience. That microwave array up there—if it's active, I think it's been listening as it soaks up power. It must have learned our languages; that's how your dad could talk to it. But silence is a protective barrier too, one that your dad overcame, somehow. It has to be programmed for self preservation, long term—with a cave dweller's weighting on risk." Then

I knew. "We're exposing it to risk."

"Risk?"

"The people chasing us. It's been listening and understands the differences in motives. Or maybe your dad told it. But we've left the back door open and perhaps it doesn't want to risk its last line of defense while they can get here. If so, we need to separate us from them as a troglodyte would. We need to show to it that it can trust us by shutting the door behind us."

She nods slowly. "Door. The geyser tube and the crack we came through? Collapse the crack with explosives. Secure the cavern from invasion. Then it talks to us?"

"I hope so. But . . . Randi, if not, we play Radames and Aida, sealed in this tomb." I shiver. "Maybe we should just surrender, take our chances."

"No way! Remember Dad. Look, I can still break a bone to get through the hole. Two chances to win." She shakes her head. "Damn you, I was ready for it. Hard to work myself up to . . . "

She trembles, shakes her head and I hug her.

"Okay, okay." She recovers, and grins. "First, let's bury ourselves. Lots of strain where the crack we followed enters the tunnel."

"Yes, it twists to almost sideways there." I grab the equipment pallet.

Randi looks at the sonograph. "Cut the crack ceiling laterally. Vertical pressure. No support. Might slam down, like back on Miranda. Let's go."

We skim up the tunnel to the crack mouth. I start a line of holes. Randi stuffs rolled-up sheets of metastable excited-lattice-diamond explosive in each. Then she puts her head to the ice. "They're almost here."

I want two more charges and compromise with one. Done, I look down the crack and see a light moving.

"Get the hell out of here, you claim-jumping ass hole," I transmit in the clear. "This place is going to blow."

I push Randi down the corridor, and jump after her. The explosive sheets have integral detonator circuits with a proximity safe. We have to get out of range, and so does my friend on the other end of the crack, or it wouldn't blow.

Hopefully, he doesn't know that.

We get around the second bend of the tunnel, lock our claws to the clathrate, and I tell the detonator to do it.

The whole place jumps and fills with vapor and for a moment, there is enough gas pressure to hear. A kilometer of clathrate overhead groans like a tortured giant, adjusting itself *down*. Yes, it only weighs one percent of Earth weight. But one percent of billions of tons is still tens of millions of tons, and we'd just pulled out the props.

A slam knocks us loose and we bounce against the opposite wall, but the tunnel holds up.

After things settle down, I listen for pursuit. None.

I take Randi's hand. She is hard, tight, concentrating, getting ready to be broken again. She's going to pretend it's no big deal, goad me into it, then laugh, or scream, as I push her ruined shoulder through the crack by the door.

My sacrifice, I decide, will be that if I do that to the wife I love beyond anything, I will go insane and never look reality in the face again.

But I dare hope. I dare hope that around the next bend, we will find that we have successfully shaped our minds to the troglodyte reference frame. I am sure their machine will understand us. It must. All logic demands this. I prepare to plead to the alien machine for our lives, for Randi's body and my sanity. I prepare to plead humanity's case and I dare hope it will give us the key to the universe.

More, I dare hope it will help us escape and call the patrol.

But as I round the bend, I see that all my pleading, all my preparations for argument are futile. Randi lands in front of the door speechless, reshaping her mind again, but this time to handle a welcome.

For the door already stands open and the lights beyond it are full on, bright as a new day.

# STORY NOTES

Algis Budrys was at my house one evening, following a workshop that he'd given, when he allowed that to save money on his magazine, *Tomorrow*, he'd purchased rights to some cover art, and was writing the stories under various pseudonyms to go with it. I, somewhat cheekily, suggested that maybe I could do that as well. We had a little laugh. Then, a few days later I got the email with a jpeg of this nameless moon or planet, advising me that if I wanted to do the story, he would need it in nine days. I happened to have had the free time, and a look for icy bodies that were known, but not already well imaged turned up Proteus, an inner moon of Neptune. I had some unfinished business with the alien base discovered in *Into the Miranda Rift*, so I sent Wojciech and Randi on another mission, and the name of the moon suggested a theme. So, the deadline was beat by a couple of days, and the result was "The Protean Solution."

We don't know that there are geysers of nitrogen or water on Proteus, but we don't know that there aren't. Such geysers are, in fact, becoming a not uncommon feature of outer Solar System satellites over a wide size range, with tidal heating being a primary suspect.

G. David Nordley, January 2015

# THIS OLD ROCK

"**D**amn bloodsucking tiny-skulled government bureaucrats!" Dolph Wigner yelled as soon as the link dropped and returned the *Hopper*'s viewscreen to a view of their peanut-shaped asteroid. He slapped the worn upholstery of the arm of the captain's chair in frustration. "Sasha, I think it's a conspiracy to make us buy more junk from the friends of these vampires on credit. By the time they're done, we won't own *half* of this rock!"

"Daddy?" a small, sleepy voice ventured from the compartment directly under him.

"What is it, Tina?" he snapped, much too loud, he realized.

"What's wrong, Daddy?" she asked. "Are you mad?"

Tiny-skulled, Dolph realized, might sound like Tina-something to his three-year-old.

"Not at you, Tina. Go back to sleep now, okay? Sweet dreams."

"What's wrong, love? It's one in the morning!" Sasha called from the wardroom below, which doubled as their bedroom. "Is Tina okay?"

"Tina is fine. I was just venting whoever changed the requirement on the air lock door motors three months after our shipment left Luna! Forgot the time."

There was a rustle of bedding, and his wife made the easy one-sixth gravity jump up to the command deck from their bed, stretched her skinny, almost scrawny, body, yawned, and ran a hand through her long, wavy, hopelessly tangled black hair. He could see her bones; hell, he could see his own. They'd both been cutting way back on rations and working like demons for three months. But if they could just get approval, they'd have the old hydroponics system going and be eating their own tomatoes in another month or so.

"Can we afford the new motors?" she asked.

He smiled at her and sighed. There were many better things to do with the night than fight refurbishment supply problems. But every hour counted.

"If," he answered, "we can use the old ones, or sell them, the price difference isn't that much. The problem is that there's no way we can get them here in time for our inspection."

"They can't hold us to that, can they? I'm getting tired of this."

He nodded. "This" was hanging out in a cramped, smelly, spaceship swinging around with its nose tied to the end of a hundred meters of tether when they had five hundred square meters of habitat ready to inhabit on the asteroid above them. But until they passed their inspection, they had three rooms, three meters in diameter by two and half high with a head and an airlock at the top.

"Look, I can't do anything about it. It's the damn Interplanetary Association's rules, and if we don't follow the IPA rules, we lose the homestead. So don't vent me about it, okay? I'm sorry, darling." He immediately hated himself for snapping at Sasha. She was everything to him—the only part of the universe that wasn't trying to stomp him. At twenty-four, he felt like a ninety-year-old curmudgeon with the world on his back, and sometimes it showed.

"But it's not our fault! They can't make us leave our homestead for something that's not our fault."

"I just don't know, Sash, I just don't know."

They were interrupted by a two-note attention tone.

"Go ahead, *Hopper*," Dolph told the spacecraft. He heard Sasha try to suppress a giggle. "Voice only," he added.

"We have an incoming message from an Inspector Eileen McCarthy of the local IPA Compliance Authority. She's C&C on Belt Runner four-one-two, a light-minute out from Pallas."

Almost here, then. So it was too late to get anything more done on the supplies or equipment. They'd pass with what they had, or not. "We'll see what she has to say later." Dolph instructed. "We've gone to bed. Acknowledge and record—I'll reply tomorrow morning."

"Yes, Dolph. I've sent the acknowledgment. Good night."

The command deck lights dimmed, and Sasha started pulling him down to their bed.

✷ ✸ ✷

Two days later, Dolph took the tram cage up to the tether axis on the mast at the north pole of their rock. Well, not quite *their* rock yet, he reminded himself, though he had a lot of sweat equity in it. It was three kilometers across its longest dimension and Swiss-cheese-full of craters, the largest being the football field-wide hole at the top. They'd name it after Tina, they'd decided, as soon as they had the right to do so.

Below him was their habitat, deep in a hundred meter cylindrical pit for radiation protection. A fifty-meter-radius squirrel cage of trusswork, it mounted a couple of big bent sausages and other equipment around its circumference. Above him was the great dish of their solar collector, a few kilograms of nearly perfectly reflecting graphene-aluminum sandwich almost two hundred meters across; it focused on a flat relay mirror. There was enough dust around the asteroid for him to trace the beam into the big black cylindrical converter at the top of the mast

He saw few stars on his way up to the docking ring. Their pole was in sunlight, and would be for another year. He looked back toward the Sun. Mars was a reddish dot just far enough from the Sun to see if he shaded his helmet window. Earth, Venus and Mercury were lost in the glare. Even when he looked away from sun, the sunlit structures around him banished any hope of dark-adapted vision, mocking his mood with their unsoftened vacuum brilliance.

But Jupiter, now near opposition at the perihelion of the Pallas association, shone brightly against the black sky. Jove was over five times as bright as from Earth, and its four large satellites were clearly visible—he could even see the orange tint of Io. Saturn, way off to the right, still seemed very distant, but the asteroid Pallas was brighter than Venus from here, and showed a tiny disk. Sirius, Procyon, Betelgeuse, and Regulus—the brighter stars—got through as well. The effect was almost three dimensional—he could image the planets on a plane stretching out toward infinity, with those few bright fixed stars set beyond.

Despite all the work and all the details of things to be removed, tested, repaired, replaced, and tested again there was still a sense of wonder that he was out here—the descendent of apes with stone axes daring to live out here on the doorstep of all creation. He was going to do it. Somehow, despite everything, he was going to do it.

An instant and temporary comet got his attention. Inspector McCarthy's spacecraft was in the final stages of rendezvous, with thrusters flaring. Like their *Hopper*, it was a standard spin-electric rock *Hopper*—essentially a smooth cylinder with a two-ring magnetic mirror plasma nozzle at the end—indistinguishable from *Hopper* on the outside except for the outsize volatile tanks mounted at its middle and the IPA insignia. It grew smoothly out of the dark and made the standard mast connection, nose in, rings out. Next to its connecting probe, a hatch swung in and poured out light. Into the light floated the black shadow of a spacesuited figure.

"Welcome to 12478, Ms. McCarthy." Dolph gestured to the peanut shaped carbonaceous chondrite below them. The spacesuited figure coming down the mast to him was obviously female, of average height, and perhaps a bit hefty the way people too busy to exercise get in low gravity.

She put her helmet to the mast for a moment, then turned toward him, her face invisible behind the mirror finish of her helmet window. "You've got a sick stator magnet on one of your despin mast bearings," she announced in a no-nonsense, almost imperious tone. "I heard it screech after my dock."

Dolph opened his mouth, but couldn't think of a response.

The complaint was trivial, as far as he was concerned. The hollow despin mast held their main elliptical mirror and the docking fixture. Some torque on the despun inertial mast was inevitable as a ship docked, and it might momentarily cause physical contact in the bearing if one of the bearing magnets were a little weak; but if the mast was properly aligned with asteroid spin axis, that would vanish as soon as any transverse accelerations were damped. And the asteroid spin period was a leisurely eight hours plus; at that rate, the damn bearing could be made of taffy.

She, he decided, was deliberately picking a nit, maybe for psychological impact. Finally, enough time passed so that Dolph hoped he could just ignore the discourtesy.

"Any equipment you'd like to take down with you?" he asked.

"Did you hear what I said about the stator magnet?" she barked. "It's out of spec. Fix it!"

Damned if she didn't seem serious, he thought. This was not good. "I'll get on it as soon as we have you settled," he temporized.

"*Now*, Wigner. I don't want my ship torqued away if the bearing seizes."

Dolph opened his mouth to protest, thought better of it, and shut it hard enough that he heard his teeth click. Very well, he'd fix the damn thing. A quick check with *Hopper* identified the lower bearing as the problem, and he told *Hopper* to bring him the spare—a pair of thick nested hoops two meters in diameter.

"My wife, Sasha, is in the ship down-tether, waiting for you," he told the inspector. "I'll be done in twenty minutes or so."

"My ship's at risk and I want to stay here and watch this," McCarthy told him. "Get to it."

He looked up and saw her jet from her air lock to about ten meters out from where he was working, and take up a position with her back to the sun. She crossed her arms and floated there, motionless on her backpack gyros. He assumed she was staring at him.

"Roger," he replied, trying to keep the irritation from his voice, nodded to her and got to work. The job wasn't that big, actually. One of *Hopper*'s spiders had brought the new bearing as they'd talked, and with smart fasteners decoupling themselves from the telescoping joint, all he had to do was ease out the old bearing and ease in the new one before light pressure on the solar collector pushed the mast out of alignment by more than a centimeter.

He had it done in fifteen minutes.

"Can we go in now?" he asked. "Sasha's holding lunch."

"She'll have to hold a bit longer." McCarthy jetted over to the mast and held her helmet against it for a long time, then seemed to be satisfied. Dolph told *Hopper* to feed their conversation to Sasha so she'd know what was going on.

"Twenty-first century?" McCarthy asked at length.

"Early twenty-second," he replied evenly. "It's an old Cislunar Republic mining survey station for the twenty-fourth Kirkwood association, last inhabited in 2093. The CLR left when Mercury opened up."

"I know all that," McCarthy snapped. "I date things by when they were built, not when the last people left. That shaft is a hundred years old if it's a day. No later than 2092, I'd say; it's titanium, probably lunar. They punched out hundreds of these set-ups back then. Anything after that would have been local glass, because that's when the rock chewers got smart and fast enough to make it cheaper. You did the joint yourself?"

"Yes. The original bearing is down on the crater floor. Wouldn't move."

"Vacuum welded. They used glazed rollers—okay for a few years, but you have to keep them moving. I won't redline your job, but that magnet going sour was a symptom that the thing's been wowing a bit. You put a large mirror on that shaft."

"We're going to grow grapes, so we got as big a mirror as the specs allowed . . . "

"And, to save money, the smallest bearings," McCarthy interrupted. "And on top of that, you put it as far up as you could. Everything away from the direction of goodness. Maximum stress: not smart."

"It computed, Inspector."

"Tell me about it," she sniffed. "Artificial intelligences lack both art and intelligence. Look, I said I won't redline your provisional on that alone, but you'll need to fix it, understand? I know an outfit at Chao Dome . . . "

"Mercury!"—*I'll bet you do*, Dolph seethed. But he said: "Yes, Inspector. Why Mercury? Mercury is as far in to Sun from here as you can go!" She wasn't even inside yet, hadn't much more than glanced at the habitat, now they were already looking at nine months for a shipment from the South Pole of Mercury, and paying probably another EU to get free and clear of the IPA bureaucracy. Damn! They could have lived for a year on Mars for an EU.

"Mercury is the nearest solid thing to the center of the asteroid belt," she said. "Think about it. With their electromagnetic launchers, delta-v is beside the point, and Mercury revolves around the Sun so fast that it's never more than 90 days for a launch to any place in the belt. Anyway, you could probably print it for a small intellectual property fee. Now, what's your problem with Mercury? You don't like their connections?"

What the hell? Dolph thought. Was she reading his mind, or had she just been through this with so many newcomers that the question was second nature? He considered the question rhetorical and acknowledged the lecture with a negative grunt.

McCarthy gestured to the crater below. "Standard turn of the century habitat down there?"

"Not anymore," Dolph snapped, then stared at the habitat as he counted to ten.

The crater was four hundred meters across and almost precisely on the asteroid's spin axis. The habitat centrifugal frame, an open lattice box of cables and tubes as long as a football field and half as wide, could rotate in the crater like the spinner on a child's game, giving them lunar normal acceleration at the tips. It was static now, though, to make their work easier; the asteroid's minuscule gravity was enough to hold tools and supplies on the habitat walls. He and Sasha had spent the last two months turning living quarters originally meant as Spartan accommodations for a dozen survey personnel into a comfortable home for three, following the requirements stored in *Hopper*'s cybernetic brain to the bit.

"Hmmpf. I suppose not. I see it has the old fashioned gas retention vestibules outside of the inboard air locks."

She meant, Dolph realized after a vocabulary-searching second or two, the enclosed porch around the main airlocks; the ones that would be on "top" of the two habitat modules when the frame rotated, i.e., toward the center.

"That's a good feature," she added, almost inaudibly. Then she cleared her throat and asked, clear and loud: "Did you re-stress the angular momentum neutralizer?"

"Huh?" How, Dolph wondered, did you neutralize angular momentum? Wasn't it conserved? What kind of state of the art electronic device would he have to buy now? "What the . . . "

"That's the big stone wheel under the frame that turns in the opposite direction. It cancels your habitat's angular momentum, so your habitat rotation doesn't cause the asteroid to precess and swing your mast around and wreck your new bearing. Now, did you tighten the cables that hold it together?"

"*Hopper*, what about it?" Dolph asked, thoroughly confused. The floor under the habitat was a circle of smooth solid rock—he hadn't realized it could turn.

"My IPA download," *Hopper* replied, "makes no mention of reviving the momentum neutralizer, nor of this procedure."

"Idiot bureaucrats!" McCarthy huffed. "I filed that requirement two years ago!"

"Uh, is that wheel really necessary?" Dolph asked. Maybe there was a reason it wasn't in the book, the reason being an opportunity for selective enforcement. He supposed the next thing he'd find out was it would cost another EU to fix. "I mean, if the mast alignment is accurate enough . . . "

"*IF*," she interrupted. "On a rock this small, the first stray meteoroid big enough to get through your laser deflectors will knock it out of alignment. And *that's* assuming it was accurate in the first place, which, from what I've seen so far, would be asking a lot. Look, what you have to do is clear the gap between the wheel and the well walls, float the whole assembly out, check the tension on the wires that run around it, pull the bearings apart, nanoplane them, and repack them. Take you a day."

Inspector McCarthy raised her hands and put them down again in a clear gesture of disgust. "All right, Wigner, I've already seen enough to spoil my appetite, but let's go out to your ship anyway."

"No," Sasha sent on their private line, "not like that. Calm her down first, I don't want her to scare Tina."

"Sasha . . . " Dolph pleaded. The last thing he wanted to do was insult the testy Inspector. Maybe.

"No argument on this: my call, darling."

Dolph took a deep breath. "Uh, Ms. McCarthy?"

The woman turned to him. "*Well*? What is it?"

"We, uh, have a three year old girl with us. Uh, her name is Tina. Angry people frighten her. Could you . . . ?" Leave the shouting act for the adults, he wanted to say—but he choked that back. Temper, grace.

"You *what*?" Inspector McCarthy sounded shocked and confused. "What is a child that age doing out here? Why wasn't this in my briefing?"

Dolph closed his eyes and counted to ten again. "Inspector, she's in our records. Born at L4 Von Braun station. The *Hopper* is family rated."

"For transportation! Not as a nursery! Why didn't you leave her with her grandparents or something? Until this job is done?"

Was there any way, he wondered, that he could space this screaming harridan and get away with it? His past and their problems with their parents were none of her damn business. Since when did a habitat inspection become an excuse to cross-examine someone's life? Or was this an attempt to provoke him, make him do something like what he was supposed to have done on the Moon that would let some big belt corporation step in and take the asteroid that was all they owned?

"We wanted her with us and nothing in the IPA rules said we couldn't take her."

"You didn't ask?" The inspector sounded incredulous.

"Ms. McCarthy, one of the reasons we came out to the belt was to get away from having to ask. About everything."

Eileen McCarthy rotated to face him, a silent cipher behind a shiny faceplate.

"*One* of the reasons? What did they do to you kids to make you risk this? No," she held up a hand, "You're right about that. I don't need to know your past. The kid's out here now and we'll just have to deal with it. Some would say that it's maybe better that way, if the whole family goes at once. Let's go down to your ship." She got in the Tram cage for the two and a half kilometer ride out to the *Hopper*.

★ ✸ ★

Out of her helmet, Inspector Eileen McCarthy looked as formidable as she sounded. Her curly hair was as steel gray as her manner. Her slight excess mass softened her face to a degree, and the one-sixth gee of the tethered spacecraft did not tug the features down as much as they would on her native Earth. Otherwise, Dolph thought, the hook nose and downturned lips would have evoked some costumer's idea of a witch. He tried to imagine her as someone's lover, once upon a time, and failed.

She wrinkled that large nose as soon as her helmet came off as she emerged from the airlock into their bedroom/wardroom. "Child," she said to Sasha, "you need to take the lenses off the air cleaning lasers and polish them occasionally. The automatic systems you have can't get at them, and, in this low gravity, they develop a film that blocks some of the most effective frequencies. Surface tension effect—take a microscope to them some day and see what I mean."

"Ms. McCarthy . . . " Sasha began, a note of outrage in her voice. Dolph held up a hand and shook his head vigorously. Too much was at stake to risk offending the offensive. Sasha, fortunately, caught the hint. "We've been a bit busy. I'll get to it before you come back. Anyway, you're welcome to share a meal with us."

It wasn't much—a plate of protein biscuits and three narrow necked, low-gee water glasses.

Inspector McCarthy ignored it. "You want to live out here all alone? You learn to be very careful. Yes, you're in the Pallas association, but most of the time, you'll still be a week or two away from any physical help. Hell, most of the time you kids will be too many light minutes away for anyone to even use your computer's motiles interactively. We may have retroviruses to make our genes radiation tolerant, but the bugs and viruses we take with us have no such luck. They mutate. Cleanliness is a survival skill. While I'm at it, my briefing said you're going to mount your A.I. on an Opticor 721. Tell me it's not so! You ought to have one of ICA's double N thirty-sixes."

Sasha shook her head. "We could get *three* 721's for the price of one of those . . . "

Inspector McCarthy scowled.

Sasha smiled. "So we did."

McCarthy looked surprised and almost smiled—at least Dolph thought he could detect some movement in the deep crevasses that emanated from the corners of her mouth. Then, without saying anything more, she sat down, reached for a protein biscuit, took a bite and chewed. It was so quiet that Dolph could hear her crunch the flavor nuts between her teeth.

Finally she swallowed, lifted her glass of water, watched it slosh around a bit, drank, and nodded. "I'll give you a marginal pass on that. I like redundancy, excess capacity, and graceful degradation. Mind you, three double N thirty-sixes would have been better."

Tina chose that time to come out of her compartment, swinging from the handholds as was her custom, so that she could look adults in the eye. They kept her hair short, for convenience and her favorite nighty was a brown flannel jumper—nothing really abnormal, but the total effect could, Dolph realized all too late, be distinctly simian.

She also needed a changing, but before he could do anything, Tina swung over to the wardroom ceiling above and in front of Inspector McCarthy, directly over her plate, and shyly mumbled "Hi."

What was most noticeable in the following seconds was the growing color in Inspector McCarthy's hitherto pale cheeks as the smell wafted about. "Do you," she choked out at length, "ever discipline this child? What exactly are . . . *her* behavioral limits?"

"Hi?" Tina repeated in a small, uncertain voice. McCarthy had used, Dolph realized, at least two words that were not often used in the Wigner family. He and Sasha were determined to be as not like their own parents as they could.

"Tina," Sasha began, conversationally, "hasn't mastered low gravity toilets yet, but she's working on it, at her own pace. Aren't you, darling?"

Tina pouted. "I'm *Tina*, not darling."

Sasha beamed indulgently. "Tina, this is Inspector McCarthy, who will be helping us get our new house ready."

"Hi?" Tina repeated. "Are you a which?"

Inspector Eileen McCarthy wrinkled her nose, took a deep breath.

"Hello, Tina." Then she reached up and pulled the child from her handhold.

"Let me go, you which!" Tina protested.

Inspector McCarthy had handed her off to her mother with a suffering look. Then she turned to Dolph. "When you are both working on the habitat, where is she?"

"She comes with us," he replied. We modified a rescue bubble into a sort of nursery, which she used until we pressurized and . . . "

"Let me," McCarthy groaned, "see if I understand this. She's allowed to float around wild in a habitat under construction among the motile spiders, laser welders, nanoplaners, and so on? And she's still *alive*?"

"We have a net around her," Dolph snapped. "It works fine."

McCarthy shook her head. "Did it ever occur to you dear young people to ask for some help?"

"As you pointed out," Dolph answered, trying to keep his voice even and conversational, "we are normally several light-minutes from any other habitation. And there's no more money."

McCarthy frowned and pushed herself up from the table. "I can see that. You've been cutting back rations. I have an extra fifty kilo CMF standard—I'll send a telop down with it."

Sasha shook her head, "We can't . . . "

"Did I ask? You can't feed the baby that way if you don't feed yourself."

Sasha's face turned red and her smile got very tight.

How, Dolph wondered, had this old biddy known Tina was still suckling? And what business was it of hers? His indignation began to rise, but he thought better of it. Fifty kilos of vacuum dried food would keep them going for two or three months, if they stretched it. He was in no position to object. "Thank you, Inspector McCarthy," he finally choked out.

"Hmmpf. We will start inspecting this supposedly childproof habitat construction site at oh eight hundred tomorrow morning. I can find my way back to my ship."

In an embarrassed silence, she put her helmet back on and cycled out of the lock.

Sasha's face fell as soon as the door hissed shut, and she began to sob. Dolph put his arms around his wife and child.

"Oh, *oh!*"Tina squeaked, realizing something was wrong.

✶ ✷ ✶

The inspection was a disaster. By the end of the day, there were some thirty-three items that had to be fixed before provisional approval, and another seventy-two that needed to be corrected by final approval.

It seemed to Dolph that McCarthy's sole purpose was to prevent them from occupying their asteroid and when it seemed that no amount of appeasing her would slow the accumulation of items on the list, he'd allowed himself, in desperation, to argue. At this rate, they would have to vacate before they even got to her gift rations. Maybe that's why she could be so generous—she was going to get it back anyway.

Finally, Dolph blew his gasket. The vestibule air seals had been the final crack in the air hose, so to speak, and Dolph's feelings had gushed out as they shut the inner door and stood in the bright, clean, sweet smelling entryway to the home that Dolph was beginning to realize would never really be his.

"Ms. McCarthy," he wailed, "those seals are in spec! All the vestibule is supposed to do is to guide the last wisps of air from the airlock to the ion pumps so you can open the door sooner. It's never *supposed* to hold any real pressure. It's *not* a backup system!"

"A seal is a seal. You never know when you might need it."

"Damn it! I'm going by the book and the book says IPA certified pipe is safe to use outside as is!"

"The book, young man, says inspectors are to use their judgment," she said in as frosty and imperious a tone as he'd yet heard her use, "and my judgment right now is that you have an attitude problem; not toward me—while I can see that, too, it's irrelevant. But you aren't attacking your problem. You're just filling squares on the list—not thinking, not being proactive. This isn't a chore you kids have to do— it's your lives and you don't seem to realize it!

"Specifically, here and now, I don't consider your vestibule seal installation adequate and I don't consider your piping installation adequate"

"But by the book they are! And I'm going to damn well appeal this, and your fix-log on the door motors. I got the certified equipment, certified materials, installed them with certified procedures, and you redline it! I don't know what your game is, whether Shan Toy's parents are paying you, or some people that want this rock without taking the trouble to settle on it, or some politicos that don't like people running around outside the grip of some power structure they can control, but it's not fair!"

"Neither," she said, so softly that he had to concentrate to hear it, "is death."

"Is that a threat? Because if it is, I'll fight back, and if you don't think so just ask . . . "

"I know who and what to ask, Dolph Wigner. I think we're done for today."

It was over, Dolph thought. Maybe he could get enough for the rock to get Sasha and Tina back to the Moon. Her parents would take her in, and Tina. But he would have to stay out here . . . doing what? It took a minute for McCarthy's words to sink in.

"For today?"

"We've inspected the air lock and the interior utilities of half of your habitat. If you will stipulate the same fix-logs on the other half, we should be able to work on the structure tomorrow."

"Why? You've already ruined us and redlined us back to the Moon; why continue?"

"Wigner," Inspector McCarthy said, coldly and evenly. "You have the right to try to correct the redlines on the spot. It just so happens that I've brought some materials along with me."

"Available for a price, no doubt."

Inspector Eileen McCarthy looked at him and raised an eyebrow. Then she reached for her space helmet, put it on without further word, and left.

"*Hopper*," Dolph rasped, his voice halfway between raging and sobbing, "send a message to legal assistance at, at . . . "

"Pallas would be closest," the computer answered.

"Fine. Send a transcript of the last ten minutes of conversation, and ask for help in declaring these fix-log items invalid."

Maybe there would be some fairness, somewhere. He had to try everything, he realized. He couldn't bear to lose Sasha, not for one lousy stupid mistake. Or two, or three he corrected, bitter at himself. They wouldn't be in this mess if it weren't for his mistakes, he knew. It wasn't all Inspector McCarthy's fault. But, damnit, they needed a break, not another problem.

★ ✳ ★

His answer came at dinner, a very quiet dinner, that night in the wardroom of the *Hopper*.

"Put it on the wall here," Dolph said.

"The caller suggests a private conference."

He looked at Sasha, who simply reached over and touched his arm. "Use Tina's room. I'll put some music on in here."

He nodded and got up. They'd made Tina's room by putting a flat wall across the wardroom one meter from the wall. In the space between the straight inner wall and the curved outer wall were a half-meter-wide child's bunk, a compact washstand, and a video screen.

"You forgot to say 'excuse me,' Daddy," Tina chirped. She'd started chattering at twenty months and hadn't stopped. He was afraid to get her I.Q. tested.

Dolph rolled his eyes and managed a pained smile for his daughter. "Excuse me, Daddy."

Tina looked confused for a moment, then giggled and said. "No, *you're* Daddy. You're excused, but you have to come back for dessert!"

"Sure, Tina." He ran his hand over her hair.

He covered the distance to the compartment door in one low gravity stride, as one of Sasha's bouncy moonjazz compositions started with her characteristic three dissonant chords which resolved into walking scales under a high riff. A century ago, he thought, her talent would have been a ticket to independence. Not anymore. Her stuff was good—but with thirty billion people on Earth and another three scattered among the other worlds, and almost all of them with all the leisure time they could want, there was a solar system full of good stuff out there.

The door slid shut and cut it down to background—a centimeter of basalt foam was a good sound insulator. He knew damn well what the lawyer wanted to talk about, and it wasn't for Tina's ears. So he sat on her bunk in between her stuffed animals with her crayon drawings taped to the wall for a backdrop and faced the video screen, which dissolved into a holo of a distinguished looking balding man in a white turtleneck with a pointed black beard, just starting to turn gray.

"Mr. Wigner, Jaynes Femrite. I'm with Femrite, Carson and Lu, doing pro bono for IPA Legal Assistance. I understand Eileen's giving you her, uh, best."

Eileen? Dolph shook his head. Did *everyone* know everyone out here?

"I'm about at the end of my rope, Mr. Femrite. Her standards are a moving target. I've met all the legal requirements, all the specifications and I can't get from here to there with her. We just don't have the money to pay her and all her friends for everything she wants us to buy from them." He took a breath. "We don't want to cause trouble. We just want to be left alone. But I have to do something. We can't go back and we're within a month of being self-sufficient here."

Femrite inclined his head slightly. Dolph saw the "secure comm" telltale in the corner of his screen. Could he trust it? Did he care anymore?

Femrite cleared his throat. "Got yourself in a little trouble back at Shepard City, didn't you."

Dolph looked down. So the guy already knew, and so did everyone else. That was probably another reason for "Eileen" to hound him out.

The lawyer waited a minute for an answer, but when Dolph didn't say anything, he continued. "Her name was Shan Toy. Want to tell me your side of it?"

Why not, Dolph thought. What more harm could it do? "I'd just finished a three week mine engineering school and was celebrating. She picked me up at the bar. I didn't know how old she was, didn't even suspect because she came on so, so mature. I told her I was married

and she said 'so what, it's just for a night.' So we checked our records
and went to my room.

"We were just getting into it when she complained about my ring
hurting her back so I took it off and put it on the nightstand. It was
my great-grandfather's college ring, with a hand-cut diamond in it.
She apparently suspected what it was worth, because as soon as I set it
down, she jumped up, grabbed it, and headed for the door.

"I went after her and she pulled a gun—I don't know from where.
I kept after her anyway because the ring meant so much. She shot
once and missed and then I was grappling with her and the gun went
off again. The dart got in between the vertebrae in her neck somehow
and the trank shut her heart down. It was a freak accident. I ran, then
came to my senses and realized they could trace me a hundred ways.
So I called Sasha, and turned myself in."

The lawyer nodded. "Self defense, hung jury on the murder charge.
Parole with time served on the attempted statutory rape charge—you
could have checked her age."

"She said she was twenty, right from Earth on a tourist visa with
her parents and five sisters. I was drunk and fell for it. It turned out
her so-called parents weren't even related to her and they both had
raps sheets in Thailand. The girls were supposed to sell themselves, or
get in someone's room and grab something valuable. Preferably both.
I wasn't thinking . . . damned stupid."

It had been the most miserable episode in his life, and he felt like
he had used up a lifetime's worth of emotional self-control getting
through the hearings. He stared at Femrite. Enough was enough. The
universe had to get off his back sometime.

Femrite raised an eyebrow. "But the court of public opinion wasn't
so kind?"

Dolph sighed. "Her parents and the tabloid media said I made up
the ring story. Dad was mad as hell. He gave me a grubstake, pointed
me at the belt, and told me not to come back. Sasha's family tried to
keep her at L4, but she stuck with me. That was all that counted."
Damn it, his eyes were getting wet. That big knot in his stomach, which
had been there ever since Shepard City, got a little tighter. Get a grip,
he told himself. "Until now."

"Uh, huh," Femrite agreed. "That counts for a lot. That and your
daughter. Look, I want to set you clear on a couple of things.

"First is that Eileen doesn't care what your past is. That's usually
the case in the belt, and there are minuses as well as pluses to that.
For instance," the lawyer flashed a shark-like grin at Dolph, "you'll
probably end up doing business with a certain former drug dealer
with a manslaughter rap which, they say, included cannibalism. He's
behaved himself since getting out here. Of course people take care
not to rile him." Femrite's grin was distinctly chilling. "At any rate,

*your* crime is small potatoes out here, even if you're lying about what happened at Shepard city."

"Lying!" Dolph couldn't think of anything to say. Then anger turned to uncertainty, tinged with fear. He wondered if the drug killer was named Femrite.

"Now don't get mad. I said *if*, and, in fact, I think you are being truthful. But my point is that all that's irrelevant. What counts now is what you do out *here*.

"The second point is that, out here, what an inspector says, goes. We don't, and can't, have the public infrastructure with all the appeals you're used to. Even with robotics and beam propulsion, the rocks are too far apart. Rescue missions use up a lot of human resources, and we can't do hundreds of them a month. We're a community out here, and while we scratch each other's backs a lot, we want time for our own lives. We don't have a lot of laws and not much to litigate; almost a million people now and only a couple of dozen lawyers. So forget torts; you have to take care of yourself.

"And yes, we buy local and favor those who do. We know each other. The belt runs on a lot of handshakes and understandings. That's just the way it is.

"Now, Eileen's not that unreasonable. She might be willing to ameliorate some of these fix-it log items that you're complaining about, but the main requirement . . . " the lawyer's voice took an icy edge "—I say the *main* requirement for not having the Interplanetary Association ship you out as a menace to yourselves and anyone that might have to rescue you, is that *you pass inspection*. There's no appeal to that. We're a pretty independent lot, so we don't choose inspectors at random. Am I clear?"

He was clear, but Dolph had to ask anyway, just to rub in the unfairness of it. "No appeal? No legal recourse?"

Femrite threw up his hands in apparent exasperation. "If, and I mean a big if, we could prove pecuniary bias on Eileen's part, you could get reinspected by someone else. But you can imagine what the next inspector is going to think about your filing such charges against Eileen McCarthy!"

"I thought," Dolph said lamely, "some people from the Moon might be using their influence on her. Or someone who wanted the rock; second mineral rights or some such. You hear a lot about that kind of conspiracy thing on the University."

Femrite nodded. "That you do. Conspiracy is the sophomore's favorite religion—kids want to believe that things happen for a reason, even if it's a bad one." He sniffed. "They learn. Anyway, Eileen's not one to be influenced by anything like that—quite the opposite, I'd say. Try to push that woman and she'll push harder in the other direction."

Dolph couldn't suppress the flicker of a smile. *That* he could believe.

"Of course," Femrite continued. "I'm obligated to file a protest and represent you if you insist."

Dolph glanced at the floor. So a protest would be useless and it was nobody's doing in specific. So the whole universe was a damn conspiracy against him and he had no rights, none. He'd lost anything resembling rights back on the Moon when he tried to take back great-grandpa's ring. "No, Mr. Femrite," he sighed, defeated. "No protest. I've got the picture."

Femrite shook his head skeptically. "Well, I'm not quite sure of that, but it's the best I can do. Good day then."

Just like that, his hope of doing something about this miserable, unfair ordeal vanished. Dolph found himself staring at a blank wall in pitch darkness—the room's only window, near the *Hopper*'s shadowed south pole, looked away from the asteroid's bright horizon. He didn't ask for lights, but looked out through a meter of clear shielding water toward the stars. As his eyes adapted to the dark, the zodiac became visible, each ancient animal sliding by his view every fifty seconds as the ship swung around. The Milky Way passed by with Sagittarius, a bright river with dark clouds here and there. Constellations became harder to recognize as more and more stars confused his view.

Gradually, at the limits of his vision, the belt itself emerged, its trillions and trillions of tiny pebbles reflecting enough light to make a broad, ghostly band—once his refuge, now, apparently, a nest of callous enemies. Involuntarily, he clenched his fists. Then, faintly imposed on his view of the cosmos, he saw the reflection of his own starlit face.

The door of the room hissed open and glare flooded the room. He turned.

Tina launched herself into his arms. "Dessert time!" she piped. "Why are you crying, Daddy?"

✷ ✳ ✷

Sasha was polishing seal flanges when Dolph returned from the next day's structural inspection. She'd fixed one of the flat rings to a table and another to a block of basalt glass and was rubbing them together, slowly turning the top block as she stroked. McCarthy had just added another dozen critical items on the fix-log, he was numb with disappointment, and there Sasha was—polishing seals by hand.

"What are you doing?" he asked, as if he couldn't see. What he had meant, of course, was 'why?' Any effort at all seemed to be futile.

"I called Inspector McCarthy last night to ask what they did to seal flanges to make them acceptable to her, and she told me. I thought it was something I could do myself, by hand, with the ones we've got. You see, they'll fit exactly with a little curvature if you polish them together, and still come apart without damage. It's like making a telescope mirror."

"I think you're wasting your time."

She shrugged. "Probably. But I had to do something physical. I also checked on who has secondary claims on our rock while you were out."

"Anyone we know?"

"Ever hear of Cistrojan Enterprise Limited?"

"No."

"Neither did I, but I cross checked the media file and there was an article on a mineral rights mess they're involved in. Guess what law firm is representing them?"

It didn't take a rocket scientist to make that guess. "Femrite, Carson and Lu?"

She nodded.

"Everyone knows everyone out here." He groaned. "They're going to run us out and take our equity!"

Sasha shrugged her shoulders. "Maybe. Darling, the way I see it, we have two options."

Dolph gave her a twisted smile. "Go ahead."

"We can always run. Or we could call Inspector McCarthy's bluff on the fix-log."

Bluff? McCarthy seemed pretty sincere to Dolph.

"How so?" he asked.

"Start fixing the stuff on site. Ask her to stay until it's done and play on her sympathy."

"She could just set a deadline, leave, and kick us out if we weren't done by then. And what sympathy?"

"Dolph, she gave us the food. I think she's been trying to keep the door open a crack, in spite of everything." Sasha sighed and brushed a strand of hair from her eyes. "If we just look at things her way and try to make things better wherever we can ... "

Dolph shook his head. "Sash, it's a tremendous, heartbreaking amount of rework. And we already did everything right! Everything!"

"I know, darling. But as far as I can tell, it's the only chance we've got left. Let's not shoot ourselves down. If she's going to pull the trigger, call her bluff and make her pull it. Until then, if she wants things fixed, let's fix them! Make it a war of attrition; we're younger than she is."

Dolph didn't know if he had the energy to get out of bed in the morning any more, let alone fight a war of attrition. But if it meant a chance to stay with Sasha and Tina, a chance to start over ... " Okay, darling," he finally muttered. "I'll try again, for you. I'll try—just don't ask me to hope."

Sasha put her arms around him, and they held each other until Tina started asking for dinner.

＊※＊

Inspector McCarthy looked at her reflection in the polished seals, then set them down on the wardroom table. "By hand?"

Dolph inclined his head to Sasha, who answered. "I got them out myself and did them like a telescope mirror. They fit to a quarter wave."

McCarthy shook her head, but said, "Very well. Let's see how they work, and if they're okay, I'll take them off the fix-log."

"I'm going to re-stress the angular momentum compensator tomorrow, Inspector," Dolph offered, keeping his voice as neutral as possible, "and we figured out how to get *Hopper* to pressure-test the air pipes autonomously, linking with one of the spare habitat brains."

McCarthy raised an eyebrow, then looked at her comp. "There are now over a hundred items on the provisional approval fix-log. And I don't have an infinite reserve of time."

She seemed to think for a long time. No one said anything.

"Hmmpf. Very well. If you do the work right, at least the next tenants can benefit. I'll give it another week, and we'll see where you are then. We'll start again tomorrow morning at oh-eight-hundred, inspect anything you've done in the meantime, and advise on work in progress. Agreed?"

They nodded and she reached for her helmet. But before she put it on, she turned.

"One more thing. I need some gravity; for the bones, and the regularity. Modern medicine can do a lot, and I lift 500 newtons daily, but they say that one should have at least lunar gravity after ninety. Digestion more than anything else. My ship shall replace your counterweight. My ship's computer can handle the slip clutches, so you won't notice it. Good evening."

With that, she cycled into the air lock.

Dolph found Sasha staring at him. "Ninety?" she whispered.

He gave her a grim smile. "Over. That's over twice our combined age; maybe we *can* outlast her. I'll go up and do the angular momentum compensator tonight while you bathe Tina. Then you can go up and install your seals." He thought a moment. She'd be outside a long time doing that. "You should replace the external suit air lines, too. They're your back-up and the old ones are brittle." A century ago they'd used some kind of polymer that had dried and hardened in vacuum and cosmic radiation. They'd bought new basalt fiber composite air hose that was more flexible and would last longer. He felt better, now that his mind was back on the job. Hopeless as it might seem, there seemed to be something he could do about their situation, and something was a lot better than nothing.

"Darling?"

"Yes, dear."

"Work slowly and get it right; don't give her an out, huh?"

Dolph shrugged. "Yeah, I'll try. Sometimes I wonder who we're working for, but I think you're right; it's our only chance. While I'm out there on the wheel, see if you can find a bio on her. I suspect her maiden name was Murphy."

Sasha looked a question at him.

"As in Murphy's law."

Sasha smiled. "You've got your sense of humor back, love."

★ ※ ★

Three days later, they were on the top floor of the habitat replacing the air lock inner door seals. Tina floated in her net "cage," and propelled herself around like a tiny rocket by throwing stuffed animals at the nets. Inspector McCarthy was in her usual humor, only this time, for once, her pique was not directed at Dolph's work.

"How can they possibly send this stuff? Look at this pipe!"

Sasha's hands were full of Tina, so Dolph floated over to take a look. He couldn't see anything wrong, but knew better than to say that. Instead, he asked:

"What do you see?"

"Not see, feel. Longitudinal cracks; feel how the fibers bristle along this line. There's a microscopic crack; I'm sure of it; the top layer of broken fibers pops out of the matrix in this stuff."

She handed the air pipe to Dolph.

About two centimeters in diameter, the basalt fiber composite was very light and had good tensile strength—but otherwise it was very flimsy. In use, it would be stiffened by air and be almost indestructible. But limp? It could be cracked easily. He ran his fingers around the tube. Sure enough, while the clean white surface looked perfectly normal, he could feel the faintest bristling where Inspector McCarthy said it was.

"I don't understand how this could happen in the manufacturing process," he said. "The robots would catch it." Something more was bothering him, however. Had they already used some of it? No, he hadn't, he was sure of that. But something was nagging him.

McCarthy shook her head. "Probably happened later. Maybe the shipment got overstressed on deceleration. I swear some of the still loaders pile stuff on like they're going on milligee ion rockets instead of quarter-gee beam riders. Tubing should go on end, not flat. Who knows what they did?" She shrugged. "But I strongly suspect this will fail a pressure test."

"And you just happen to have some more in your rock *Hopper*."

McCarthy shot him a look. "In this case, young man, I don't. But you might have an equivalent in your rock *Hopper*'s spares. As long as you aren't flying anywhere, you can share spare stores until a new shipment gets to you. And there might be enough good stock in this lot to do what you need if you don't have any more breakage. Just check it thoroughly, understand?"

Dolph swallowed his irritation. She was not the enemy. "Yes, Inspector McCarthy."

✶ ❅ ✶

Dolph looked down at the back-up valve assembly in his hand. It was a simple job to replace the old electrical wire connector with the fiber-optic replacement transducer, but an especially significant one. It was, after four weeks, the last class one item on Eileen McCarthy's fix-it list. There were still forty-some class twos, but she'd been making sounds like she wouldn't hold them up for those. Getting tired of her game, Dolph thought. Damn it, Sasha had been right—they'd worn her down. Or maybe Inspector McCarthy figured she'd gotten what she wanted out of them—and it hadn't, after all been the asteroid. Compliance? Attitude? Maybe the whole thing was just the belt government's way to show him and Sasha who's boss—to get them on their backs with their feet flailing the air like a couple of beaten dogs. Some people got off on power that way—the good news about that was that maybe they wouldn't be run off the rock after all. No people, no power.

"Darling," Sasha called. "Would you put Tina back in her cage?"

Dolph turned around and saw Tina crawling under the netting. He couldn't hold back a grin. The kid had figured out how to work open the carabiners holding the net to the stick-on cleats—she was smart. "No Tina," he said with some soft authority in his voice. "Go back. Inside."

"I don't want to. Want to see *Mommy*."

Hungry, Dolph thought.

"Oh, I'll get her, Darling," Sasha responded and anchored her tools to the geckro work pad and pushed herself over toward Tina.

The bang was not particularly loud, but Dolph knew, instantly, that it meant trouble. The scene froze in his mind, then started to move forward slowly. What to do? What to do? A sharp keening built up from somewhere off on his left.

"We have," *Hopper* announced, "loss of pressure in the external suit fill line."

That's what he'd been trying to remember. Damn. "That faulty pipe!" Dolph yelled.

"What faulty pipe?" Sasha said.

She hadn't heard—she'd been busy with Tina.

"That white two-centimeter composite. It had cracks."

"Damn!" she said, but softly. "I used it to replace the vestibule air lines—you said . . . "

As if to confirm that, there was a resounding clang as the vestibule's external door slammed shut.

"*Hopper*," Inspector McCarthy said, loud, but calmly, "shut down the suit fill circuit."

"The break is upstream of the shut-off valve," it replied.

"At the source, then," she added quickly.

"I show no response to the valve command."

"Crap!" Dolph shouted. "Of course you don't. I have it off for testing."

"The vestibule pressure has reached point four atmospheres," *Hopper* reported.

That was a tenth atmosphere *above* the interior pressure, Dolph realized. Sasha's gaskets were holding with a vengeance, but if it kept going on up to line pressure, the vestibule fabric would tear and it would explode.

"We'll have to dump the air," Dolph decided. "*Hopper*, vent the vestibule, and cut the general line pressure."

"Wait," Inspector McCarthy said. "It's too . . . "

With a creak of its yielding motors, the outer airlock door, which was not designed to withstand pressure from *outside* the air lock, yielded, swung open a full half circle and hit the inner side of the air lock as a strong gust of air blew *into* the room.

Then Dolph's vent command went into effect, the vestibule vents opened to vacuum and the air started rushing the other way—out into space.

" . . . late!" Inspector McCarthy finished, as Tina went flying by her in the air stream, through the open inner and outer air lock doors and bounced off the balloon-tight skin of the vestibule.

"Whee!" she yelled

"Tina!" Sasha cried.

"Stop venting!" Dolph screamed, then, more effectively, said, "*Hopper*, stop venting the vestibule."

The scream of escaping air stopped, and for a frozen moment Dolph contemplated the bulging composite skin of the vestibule wall: the only thing left between him and interplanetary space.

Inspector McCarthy shot by him toward the air lock in a second and pulled the inner door shut behind her. It immediately started hissing, indicating that air was still escaping from the vestibule at an alarming rate. Shocked out of his paralysis, Dolph thought quickly. By closing the door while she went to retrieve Tina, Inspector McCarthy had insured that at least he and Sasha would survive. He had to do something to help her and Tina; give them more air for starters.

"*Hopper*," he directed, "start repressurizing the air system as needed to keep the vestibule above point three bar, understand?"

"Understood. I've established a feedback program to maintain vestibule pressure at point three eight bar. This requires increasing the air pressure, which means that the leaks in the vestibule will get worse. Is that what you want?"

"Yes, do it!" He shouldn't get impatient, he reminded himself. Now, more than ever, the computer software had to understand its commands.

"Tina, can you hear me?" Sasha yelled.

"Mommy!" Tina wailed, her voice coming in clearly from the vestibule through the open outer door to the microphones in the air lock. "Get away from me! Mommy, the which is chasing me!"

"Tina," Sasha said as calmly as she could, wishing she'd never shown the classic video to Tina. "Inspector McCarthy is not a witch. She's just trying to bring you to me. Please go with her."

"I don't want to."

"Pretty please, Tina. Help the Inspector and I'll give you some ice cream."

Seconds went by, then Tina said in a tentative little voice, "Okay."

"Tina, please come here," Inspector McCarthy said. "Quickly, child, we have to go quickly."

"Don't hurt!"

"I won't hurt you, Tina. You can ride on my back where I can't even see you."

Quiet. Then, in a small voice, "Okay. But *don't* hurt."

"I've got her," Inspector McCarthy finally announced, "and we're heading back into the air lock."

Tina laughed. "This is *fun*. Giddiup, horsy!"

Eons of seconds passed, McCarthy grunted and said. "Dolph, I can't move the outer door—the hinges must be bent."

"The air distribution system has repressurized to normal," *Hopper* announced.

"*Hopper*," Dolph quickly commanded, "push the pressure up to the redline limits and start venting the habitat." They had to reduce the pressure differential to a minimum, if not get it going the other way. It would be many seconds before venting the large volume of habitat would have much effect. His ears, though, told him it had started—and they could help it. "Sasha, help me with the inner door."

If they got it open, he realized, and the vestibule blew, they'd be sucked into vacuum as well as Tina and Inspector McCarthy. But neither of them wasted a moment reaching for their helmets. They crouched on opposite sides of the oval door and pulled on its wheel handle *in*. They strained, the motors strained, metal squealed, air whistled by going out, and gradually the door swung open.

McCarthy shoved Tina through and Dolph hooked a tool tether to her belt.

"Internal pressure down to point two one," *Hopper* announced. He felt the rush of air out increased second by second, and quickly reached down for the Inspector's hand, but she slipped away and slid toward the outer door in the slipstream, frantically trying to slow herself by grabbing pieces of equipment on the wall of the air lock.

Without really thinking, he dove through the inner door past the struggling Inspector McCarthy and grabbed the rim of the outer door with his hands. Straining muscles he hadn't used in a long time, he pulled himself back in against the airflow and moved to help her.

He was just in time. The inspector lost her last handhold and was blown into him. They untangled and he tried to help her up toward the inner door. But the position was awkward and the airflow was too strong for even their combined efforts to get her anywhere. He had to cut that wind down, if only for a few seconds.

"Dolph!" Sasha screamed. "*Hopper*, put full reservoir pressure into the suit lines. Now!"

Nothing happened. His luck, Dolph thought. The remaining pipe must have been good. When you wanted something to give, it was rock solid. The operating principal seemed to be that whatever he *wanted* wasn't going to . . .

Dolph heard a pipe burst behind him like a cannon shot. Air rushed into the vestibule and, momentarily, the wind through the air lock abated. He pushed the inspector through the inner door and pulled himself in, with both Sasha and Inspector McCarthy helping.

As soon as his feet were clear, Sasha slammed the inner lock door shut behind him with a force that made the whole habitat ring. They had the barest moment to look at each other before a great rending boom echoed through the habitat. The leak through the incomplete seal of the inner door now became a scream.

"Vestibule air pressure is now one microbar and falling," *Hopper* informed them.

Dolph reached for the emergency seal foam, but Inspector McCarthy stopped him.

"There's no way the outer air lock door can be shut against that, and we still have to get out," she yelled. "Best get Tina in a bag and our helmets on, then tell the computer to recover as much air as it can. With vacuum on both sides, getting out will be easy." Inspector McCarthy put a hand on his arm as he moved to get her. "Let me help her."

"It's okay," Sasha said. Dolph nodded.

"Tina, let's go for another ride," McCarthy suggested.

Tina giggled, obviously no longer afraid of the older woman. "Where's my ice cream?"

"It's back in the *Hopper*, young lady. You'll have to get in your rescue tube now."

"Are we going to go there *now*?"

"Soon."

Dolph checked his seal as Inspector McCarthy tried to coax Tina into a rescue tube.

"This is different," Tina whined. "It's not my ball. I want *my* ball."

"It's okay, Tina," Sasha said. "This will get you to the *Hopper* and your ice cream. We have to wait a while for the air pressure to go down, though. You can wait for ice cream, can't you?"

"Okay. I like ice cream."

"Are you okay, Inspector?" Dolph asked when they all had their helmets on.

"All sealed. And much better than your habitat, I'm afraid."

They hadn't had time to prep the inside for decompression. Bottles were bursting, wet towels boiling, partition panels blistered here and there.

✱ ✳ ✱

Three hours later, Tina was fed, changed, and asleep in her compartment. The haggard adults faced each other across the boardroom table.

Inspector McCarthy raised a bushy gray eyebrow and sighed. "I estimate that it's going to take you six months to repair the damage. Exposing the interior to vacuum won't have done any good. Most of your water pipes went. You've got paint flecks, ice, and other floating debris everywhere including all the places that should be kept free of it. So I'd guess another six months of work before its ready to inspect again."

"A year to get ready for another provisional?" Dolph tried to adjust to the shock.

But for the maybe the second or third time since he'd met her, Inspector McCarthy smiled. "Not a provisional, a final. I'm going to pass you on provisional and move those items left on the fix-now log to the fix-later," she shot Dolph a look. "Except for one—a simple remove and dispose item."

"We get the asteroid?" Sasha exclaimed, wonder in her voice.

"Provisionally. And I have another proposition."

Dolph tensed. Too good to be true usually was. "Yes?"

"I happen to have a number of things in my cargo tanks that you can use. I'll have to collect their cost from you, so that I can replace them and be ready for the next newcomers that get in trouble. With my provisional, the Pallas branch of the Asteroid Development Fund should give you a loan."

He set his mouth. At exorbitant terms no doubt. What they give with one hand, they take . . . No. No, that attitude was a one-way ticket to more trouble, he told himself.

Sasha looked at him, clearly worried. Was she more worried about undertaking a loan, or at his potential reaction? Probably both.

"Darling," he said, we have to trust someone. Inspector McCarthy just risked her life for Tina."

Sasha exhaled and grinned, eyes glistening.

"Good, Dolph," Eileen McCarthy said, smiling. "It won't be that much compared to what you should get out of this rock in water alone in the next year, and you won't have to pay until you've been self-sufficient for a couple of years. Now, one more thing. Could you do without Tina for that time? I think I can teach her a thing or two on Pallas about how to live in space, follow instructions and so on." Then she got a little glint in her grandmotherly eye. "And don't worry about Jaynes Femrite hooking her on something. Anyway, it was a gang initiation thing and he was only thirteen at the time. He didn't know what he was eating."

The cannibal. Damn, his suspicions had been right. Suddenly the knot in his stomach was back in force. He didn't care how reformed the man was . . . "I'm not . . . " Dolph began.

McCarthy grinned now. "Young man, the look on your face! That's got to be the oldest yarn in the belt, and I'm the one that would know. I invented it so people wouldn't take him for a wimp!"

His breath left him at a rate just short of explosive decompression. He'd just bought the ghost station—got taken big. Tension started to drain out of him. Yes, the whole thing was a damn conspiracy, but a benign one. And it looked like, for once in his life, he was being given the opportunity to become one of the conspirators. At least believing that might get him through the next year. He nodded and smiled, but suppressed the beginnings of a laugh. That, perhaps, could come later. When the work was done.

"I think boarding Tina with Eileen would be an *excellent* idea," Sasha broke in. "Once she gets used to Eileen a little more, it will be safer for her and us. But why?"

"Sasha," McCarthy answered, "I missed my chance at being a grandmother over half a century ago, when my son and his wife lost their lives in an eminently survivable equipment failure. Their own fault, and mine. They built poorly, but I didn't instill the proper standards . . . " the old woman's face fell "—in them."

"I'm sorry . . . " Sasha began.

Eileen McCarthy held up her hand. "Too long ago for tears. But I've always wondered what being a grandmother would be like. This could be a, well, useful opportunity to find out. There are hints from the Interstellar project's biology group that any of us that can hang on for a just few more years could get a second chance."

This was the same Inspector McCarthy, physically.  But now, somehow, Dolph could take the pounds and the years off with his mind's eye and see that someone had once loved her, and might again. But, despite his feeling that he could trust people again—at least some people—something in Dolph still couldn't believe his luck had changed. Something had to be wrong.  The habitat was in too big of a mess.

"I'm grateful for your help, Inspector, but I need to be prepared for the worst. How can the bank, or the IPA, accept an approval, even yours, when the habitat is in worse shape than when you got here?"

"It's not.  You've done a lot and the vacuum damage is only superficial.  Inspectors have discretion, you know, and as far as the provisional approval is concerned, I am the IPA.  Our objective is to have people be self-sufficient out here, to be as independent as possible of our rather sparse emergency services."

Okay, Dolph thought.  Back to work.  "What's the final class one fix-it item, Inspector—the remove and dispose?"  There were some old oxygen tanks that might eventually burst, but they were at the south pole, a class two item.

She smiled gently at him, looking like anyone's grandmother. "You've shown some insights, learned how to do a number of things right, and had a lesson that is often obtained at much higher expense. I suspect that someday you'll be able to pass that on to someone else. It would be a shame to waste all this experience by sending you home, wouldn't it?"

"Sure, but . . . "

"That last item on the list, the thing that needed to be torn out of here and pushed away on a fast trajectory to the Oort cloud, was that chip on your shoulder.  But I think I see that heading out past Jupiter, now."  She nodded judiciously.  "So I'll pull it from the list. You're starting fresh here, son. Make the most of it. That habitat," she concluded, "was not the only object of this inspection."

# STORY NOTES

In some ways, this is a companion to Alice's Asteroid, but this is a lighter story. It was, as one might surmise from the title, inspired by This Old House and in particular the hoops people have to jump through to comply with various building codes. Would there be the equivalent of building codes in the libertarian paradise of the asteroid belt, where anyone armed with replicator technology can lay claim to their own, personal (minor) planet and live independently of the entire rest of humanity?

The most cold-blooded might hold that if some folks screw it up sufficiently and get themselves and their families killed, that's just evolution in action. But a few instances of that would lead to a reaction, especially if third parties were injured. The time and expense of rescue missions might also mandate some proactive limits on irresponsibility.

Let's also keep in mind that anyone with an asteroid at their disposal is, in effect, living on a multimegaton nuclear weapon, should its orbit be changed just so. Not only that, but a sufficiently bad job of child rearing may send out into the Solar System a pirate, a pedophile, a fanatic terrorist, or something else that greater humanity won't be able to ignore.

So, I have posited here that the asteroid belt will not be a rule-free zone and that the certain standards have been established and are enforced, though perhaps not as rigorously as some local jurisdictions on Earth.

Also, when someone wants to get as far away from civilization as possible, there's often a reason. This was one of the patterns of the American West, the Australian Outback, the Argentine Pampas and Russian Siberia. We should not be surprised to see this happen in the asteroid belt as well.

G. David Nordley, January 2015

# HAUMEA

Captain Karl Krull glared at his second in command—not me, thank goodness. Krull made the Lieutenant, John Ellison, sit because the two-meter first officer would otherwise tower over him. Ellison ignored the glare, smiled and presented his case as smoothly as any lawyer or Martian real estate agent would.

"Karl, we've traveled beyond Pluto and it's only one more astronomical unit to Haumea. We are getting some well-earned relief at Samios."

Relief was an understatement, as I well knew. The memory of Thera's legs wrapped around me was still fresh. I'd said goodbye, but not wanted to.

"We have a mission," Captain Krull said, tonelessly. "We will get to Haumea before the Cislunar Republic."

"We will," Lieutenant Ellison said. "Captain Duluth is months behind us, if coming at all. It's just a rumor. The documentary crew would like to stay here a few more days as well."

Captain Krull drummed his fingers on his faux-wood desk. "We serve the International Space Authority. We are not the employees of the supercargo . . . "

That was a fine point, I thought. They *were* paying for the mission, after all.

Ellison smiled. "The ISA is a long way from here."

Captain Krull scowled even more. "We *are* the ISA. We break seals at ten-hundred tomorrow."

"Karl, the days of that kind of autocracy are past. Leadership ... "

"Don't lecture me about leadership, Lieutenant." Krull's voice had a shrill, nasal quality that was especially irritating when he raised it. "Ten hundred hours. Any crew not aboard can apply for Samiosan residency. Understand?"

"Karl ... "

"Captain Krull!"

He pronounced it "kruhl," not "kroo-el.' Born in Garmisch, his astronautical English still held a hint of German in it. That was perhaps unfortunate.

Ellison shrugged. "I will let them know, then. May I tell them that we will stop at Samios on the return trip?"

"Are you all that horny? Have your brains migrated to some southern part of your anatomy? We will return on the planned trajectory on the planned schedule. That is all."

"Karl ... , Captain ... "

"THAT. IS. ALL."

Ellison shrugged again and left the wardroom.

Captain Krull then noticed my existence. Departure prep was in my department.

"And Tony ... "

"Yes?"

"Delegate. Lieutenant deWalt can watch the AI. I'll assist, if needed. I see no reason why you can't attend to personal business, do you?"

"No, Captain." Lieutenant Kari deWalt was my second; a very disciplined and competent woman who got along better with machines than people, with Capt. Krull as the odd exception.

"That is all."

I messaged Thera before the wardroom doors hissed closed.

She didn't have the evening free when I called. Ten minutes later, she called back and said she'd arranged for someone to take her shift at the Samios Protective Services watch desk.

★ ※ ★

A warm tropical sea circled Samios inside its belly, providing both dynamical stability and sensual liberty. Thera and I basked on its shore, our bare bodies soaking up the last rays from the interior reflector as it retreated toward its evening nest in the north polar hills.

"We can still tan out here!" I remarked.

"Aluminized graphene reflectors can do wonders."

I smiled. Samios had 30,000 square kilometers of them: a huge silvery flower. "A lot of work to be so far away . . . "

She laughed. "Why do you think we are so far out?"

I gave a safe answer. "Nitrogen?"

Ice Chip was a hundred-kilometerish Kuiper Belt object tumbling near Samios, full of water and ammonia. A space colony is an almost closed system, but nothing is perfect.

"Hmm, interesting, but easier to ship the nitrogen in, I think. No, we are out here because we don't want to be overwhelmed by blue nosed missionaries and sexual tourists."

I ran my finger along her firm, tan breast. "Overwhelmed?"

She repaid the favor. "Even me, I think." She went on for several minutes about the problems of sexual tourism, ending with, "So, it is your job to bring our culture inward."

I smiled. "Let's see. Partnership is not ownership. Let the robots do the work; that's what they are for. If the lower needs are satisfied, the higher needs rise to the fore. Very idealistic. Do people here actually spend that much time on engineering and science?"

"And writing and music and all the arts. We make more patents per capita than Germany."

I touched the local net. Okay, they did, by maybe about a tenth of a percent.

"We have more fun, too." She flowed around me and assumed a position that precluded further conversation.

The problem with exporting their culture, I thought, was that most people would just rather stay here than fight another culture war on Earth or Mars.

★ ※ ★

The *Dag Hammarskjold* looked like a 200-meter-wide spinning dragonfly with pods at the end of its radiator wings. It flew 'backward'; the reactors and engines were in the dragonfly's head, and the segmented, despun 'tail' was a train of reaction mass modules surrounding the long access tunnel that kept the rotating part clear of any obstructions when we docked.

Surprisingly, the entire crew made the ten-hundred departure deadline. Two documentary techs stayed in lotus land, but the supercargo were overstaffed, anyway.

I told *Dag* to undock as soon as the access tube was clear.

"Mind the exhaust clears the solar collector," I said, unnecessarily. It did get a nod of approval from Captain Krull, however, who could go on at length regarding how human beings should still be able to fly spacecraft.

The *Dag* reported readiness, Krull got clearance, and I gave the ship the execute order. We backed out to ten kilometers on the steam jets, while the reactors came back up to flight power. Our wings began to glow cherry red and the floors of our life support spheres adjusted to the gentle thrust of our plasma exhaust.

As we pulled away, Ice Chip caught the sunlight just right, a wink that reminded us of what we'd left behind.

✶ ✳ ✶

Two weeks before Haumea orbit, documentary team leader Tehn Wan Do addressed his audience in English with a carefully cultivated British accent. The audience was pretty much everyone in the solar system.

Behind him, an image of our destination tumbled ponderously end over end. Time lapse, of course; Haumea's four hour rotation rate held the record for planets, but that's still less motion than people can perceive as such, four times slower than the minute hand of an old analog clock.

"It is extreme: extremely small, barely enough mass to achieve hydrostatic equilibrium and planethood; dwarf planethood to be precise. It's extremely elongated; like a rugby ball. It's covered by an ocean of ice, but only a few hundred meters deep above solid rock. Robots can only see what they are built to see. We shall now find out what the human eye and mind can accomplish on the scene."

As someone who has built and maintained robots, including the spacecraft we were on, I shook my head. The robotic exploration of Haumea had been far deeper than anything people could accomplish. But Earth had been playing second fiddle to the Cislunar Republic in space exploration lately. So we were on an ISA flag and footprints publicity mission: it was almost the year 2100 and no person had yet bothered to place a boot on Haumea. It was an opportunity to point out that in the modern era of orbital towers, a gravity well was not the handicap it used to be.

"Who will be the first human to set foot on Haumea?" Tehn asked. "If that has been decided, we have not been told. There are only nineteen planets around the Sun and only three that have not felt the presence of the human foot. This will be an historic moment. The entire solar system wants to know."

My earchip buzzed. "Wardroom oh-eight-twenty sharp. Disciplinary board."

Chaos! Who was Captain Krull going to alienate now?

Dr. Tehn addressed the captain formally and only when necessary. Lieutenant Ellison was the only person who made any pretense of camaraderie with the captain, and everyone knew it was a pretense.

I chafed under his paternalism myself, but kept calm so as not to add to the general malaise. Kari deWalt, on the other hand, seemed to be of a similar mind to the captain when it came to shipboard things. Formalities could be a defense against dealing with the messiness of relationships and neither had ever gotten anywhere near marriage to anyone, to the best of my knowledge.

I had half an hour to freshen up and slip into a formal uniform and do some research.

\* ✳ \*

Captain Krull's victim this time was Biotech Linda Rodrigues. She'd made a still. As chief engineer, I got to sit on one side of the wardroom with Captain Krull and Lieutenant Ellison. Second Officer Lieutenant Leena Diel read the charges.

"Biological Technician Rodrigues constructed a still in her quarters and with said still did produce at least ten ccs of alcoholic beverage in violation of ISA Regulation 2035-143857-B.3.c banning the unauthorized production of alcoholic beverages on ISA spacecraft."

"For the record, how do we know this?"

"You discovered the still on an unannounced inspection on the third of February, 1400 UT."

"Has the output of the still been analyzed and the results recorded?"

"Yes."

"Enter it into the record. Is there any disputation with respect to the facts of the case?"

Rodrigues shook her head.

"Ms Rodrigues?" Captain Krull asked.

"My lawyer has a statement."

"Lawyer?"

"He's on Samios."

Krull sighed. "Let's hear it."

The image on the wall introduced himself and explained that the regulation was intended to keep astronauts safe from amateur distillation efforts that could be poisonous and endanger their health. Since Rodrigues was a biotech and had made wine and beer before and knew what she was doing, the regulation should not be applied to her.

"Do you have anything more to say on your own behalf?" Captain Krull asked when the lawyer was done.

"I'm from Hawai'i. It would be very good public relations if I continue to be part of the Haumea expedition." She pronounced it Hah-oo-MAY-eh, not HOW me ah.

"Noted. Wait outside while we discuss this. That will be all."

Once the others left, Captain Krull looked at each of us, then asked, "Does anyone have anything to say before I start recording?"

Lieutenant Ellison responded quickly. "Clearly, the harm to the expedition's reputation and morale of carrying this on greatly exceeds any benefit of terminating Tech Rodrigues' experiments, let alone punishing her for them. This is an embarrassment. Since the board has been convened, I suppose we have to do something. Maybe we can create a local licensing board?"

"Noted," Captain Krull said. He then looked at me.

I liked Linda. I'd spent a couple of very sweet nights with her, as had many of the ship's company, men and women. She had a wild streak to her; nobody would ever own her. If she obeyed rules, it was because she thought they were good rules, not because of authority. She'd had lots of cautions from Captain Krull, but she'd never hurt anyone. Now we had to decide whether we could allow her judgment to replace the codified 'wisdom' of decades of spaceflight. No, I realized, that actually wasn't the question, yet; at this point, we simply verified the facts.

"Sir, the facts show that Tech Rodrigues violated the ISAR."

"Yes. I agree. Lieutenant Ellison, do you dispute that she made the still? She doesn't."

Ellison shot him an angry look. "Okay. She made a still. But I don't think the spirit of the regulation was violated."

Captain Krull nodded, expressionless. "Very well, for the record the vote is two to one on the facts."

"Lieutenant Diel, given the finding what is the range of corrective action?"

Diel sighed. "It's a class three violation, with a maximum punishment of dismissal from duties and transportation to the nearest appropriate ISA facility by most expedient means. The minimum is forfeiture of one week's pay, which may be suspended by convening authority."

"Thank you, Lieutenant Diel." Captain Krull was silent for a few moments, then pronounced sentence, "I'm inclined to forfeiture of one month's pay, confinement to quarters for one week, *with no visitation*, and confiscation of all elements of the still. I think that covers us should there be an investigation. I'm not going to put her aground at Samios. She'd take that as a reward. Any comments?"

He stared at each of us in turn. It was clear he didn't want any comments.

Lieutenant Ellison stared back. "On the record, I think that is unnecessarily harsh and detrimental to morale. I recommend the minimum, suspension of the sentence, and ignoring such activities hereafter."

"Noted," Capt. Krull said. He looked at me.

"I might drop confinement, suggest a counseling course on the philosophy of regulation and discipline aboard ISA spacecraft, and suspend the fine retroactively if there is no subsequent violation."

"Probation, in other words. For a first time violation, I might be inclined to agree. But this one has a history and needs to be brought up short."

He looked at both of us. "I need to take your views into account, and so will suspend the forfeiture of pay at the end of the mission given no further violations. I will also take your suggestion," he nodded to me, "concerning the course. It will give her something to do in quarters. We are done, gentlemen."

And that was that.

Linda's jaw dropped as Captain Krull pronounced the sentence, and she walked to her quarters alone, with tears in her eyes.

★ ✳ ★

We took station over Haumea's prime meridian one hundred and ten kilometers above the furthest point on Haumea's surface from its center. The landers would go down to the north pole, now in continuous sunlight, a convenience for the documentary team; over much of the dwarf planet, the Sun set every two hours.

You could cut the tension aboard with a knife. The rumor mill about who would be first to set foot on the Solar System's tenth, twelfth, or fourteenth planet, depending on who counts, ground away and Tammy Kling of the documentary crew started a pool. The lead of the documentary team had the best odds, followed by our staff planetologist, then the lander pilot (someone has to check things out first), and even Linda Rodrigues, because she was from Hawai'i and female; the only woman to be first on a planet so far was Ingrid Karinsdottir of Mars. But Linda's recent misadventure lowered her odds.

So we all gathered in the maintenance shop next to the small craft hanger. At precisely 1400, Captain Krull walked in, dressed in EVA gear.

"Quiet please, quiet please," he said and waited for the hubbub to die down. "As you know, this is an ISA mission. It has been decided that, as the senior ISA official present, it is my duty to be first off the lander platform and plant the UN flag." There were several groans and he looked around at everyone as if he expected some kind of challenge. There was none, unless one considered the cynical smirk on Lieutenant Ellison's face a challenge.

Krull nodded. "Landing party, we leave at 1420. Tony, you have the con."

"Yes sir," I said, surprised.

Lieutenant Ellison's mouth became a tight, grim line. We had the same rank and I was senior to him by a year in ISA service, but he was in a line slot while I was technically in a support billet. We both shared watch duty with the captain; nine-hour shifts with an hour overlap. The captain was leaving in the middle of his shift; Lieutenant Ellison would have the next one. Perhaps he was simply trying to manage the workload. But as the first officer, Lieutenant Ellison could take it as an affront, and blame it on me.

The first landing party entered the elevator up to the hanger in the zero-g core of the ship in near silence. At the last moment, someone started clapping, and a couple of others joined in, including myself, for form. It was a feeble sendoff, all recorded for posterity by the documentary group's robocam—the last thing to scurry into the elevator.

I headed for the control room to finish off the remaining three hours of the captain's shift. Leena Diel sat folded in a lotus position on the captain's chair, watching the documentary feed on a main screen window and made no move to leave it. I shrugged and took my usual position at the engineering board.

"So Old Rude-and-Rule is going to get himself a planet," she said.

I shrugged. "Orders are orders."

She laughed. "What orders?"

She had a point. If there were any instructions nominating Captain Krull to be the first person on Haumea, we hadn't seen them. Then again, "We don't necessarily see everything. The UN should have made some public statement," I said, "to take him off the hook."

"Off the hook? He has Vesta, Amalthea, Chiron, and Nereid, but nothing big. So I think he wants this. Our captain has a compensatory ego inversely proportional to his stature." She sighed.

"He didn't look all that happy. Maybe he was taking *them* off the hook."

"Fat chance."

Kari deWalt joined us then. The women shared unsmiling glances. Kari thought Diel's area of greatest competence was Lieutenant Ellison's bed, but I'd noticed neither any technical shortcomings nor the sleeping arrangements.

"Best view of the main event," Kari said.

Lieutenant Diel got up. "I'll be taking the second lander down. Time to check it out." She sauntered out.

Not being Captain Krull, I simply said, "That will be all, Lieutenant" softly to her swaying derriere.

Kari stared at me with steel-blue eyes boring into me from beneath a dome of short steel-gray hair. Her body said she was about thirty, her head said she was about fifty. But her language was of another era.

"You don't have to take that BS, Captain."

I shrugged.

"I'd just love to see Diel bust up an effing lander."

I wasn't sure Diel was out of earshot, so I didn't laugh.

We watched Lander One depart. It was basically a cylinder with a bunch of boxes attached here and there, some of which sprouted thruster cones.

They'd been designed all-video; in the command seat, you'd think you were sitting out in open space, except for the windows Captain Krull had put in the lower front. We got the view from the documentary crew's camera bot.

Three hours later, Krull brought the first lander down. From a couple of momentary hesitations, I surmised that he was piloting manually.

The attention tone sounded. "Lieutenant Delgado, Captain Ellison needs to speak to you," *Dag* said. I looked at Kari and she looked back. I was 'captain', and however 'acting' my status might be, there was only one captain on a spacecraft at a time. This wasn't good.

Before panicking, though, I tried the simplest thing first. "*Dag*, I have the con."

"That status has just changed. Captain Ellison needs to see you immediately. He will explain the change in status."

"It's an effing mutiny," Kari said.

I held a finger to my lips, too late as it turned out.

★ ❋ ★

We were escorted to the wardroom by Linda Rodrigues. She was holding a dart gun.

"Linda, this isn't right. You can't just take over a spaceship in this day and age."

"You can if it's being run by people like you and Captain Krull," she said.

"Me?"

"You're part of it. You voted to convict me for nothing. And I thought we were friends."

"I didn't have much choice. You built the still."

"You had a choice. You voted with *him*."

The way she said 'him' made me realize that Captain Krull's morale problem was much worse than I'd thought. But Lieutenant Ellison should have been trying to help hold things together instead of looking at it as an opportunity.

When we got to the wardroom, Lieutenant Ellison sat at the center of the wardroom. Linda took the seat to the left.

"What in the hell do you think you're doing?" I asked him.

"Sit down, Tony." He smiled. "By the way, you're officially relieved of watch."

"Under whose authority?"

"Mine. I have succeeded to the captaincy under ISA regulation 1.0094-72."

"You can't do that. The captain has to be found incompetent by a board of officers . . . " I looked at them. "Rodrigues isn't an officer."

"She is now. Lt. Diel participated as well."

I spread my arms. "He gets to defend himself, doesn't he?"

Linda smiled, very much enjoying this. "He didn't answer summons."

"If you have any questions," Ellison said, "ask *Dag*."

I thought furiously. The mutineers must have somehow compromised the ship's computer. But I shouldn't just assume this. I touched the net. But the *Dag* affirmed the change of command and its legality.

"Sit," Ellison said again, a bit more peremptorily. "You too, Kari."

Once we were seated, he began. "The situation is this. I have replaced Captain Krull under ISA 1.0094-72. Captain Krull learned of this ten minutes ago from the crew of the lander. As he, unfortunately, did not accede to the regulations' implementation, he has been detained on the surface."

"Lieutenant deWalt, you referred to this entirely legal and necessary action as a 'mutiny', did you not?"

Kari sat tense as a cat. If there were anything physical she could do about it, she would, but she knew, as we all did, that at the captain's order, the *Dag* could quickly anesthetize anyone—and it thought Ellison was in charge.

"Lieutenant?"

"I was not fully aware of the circumstances at the time."

Ellison laughed. "And now that you are, you plan to lie low and try the same thing on me." He shook his head. "Give it up. I want your formal concurrence to the change of command."

"There's an 'or else'? What is the 'or else'?"

He smiled at her. "There's no coercion here. You know the former captain's behavior as well as anyone. Do you, freely and of your own will, agree that his replacement was necessary? While you are thinking about that, I'll need Tony's answer to the same question. Perhaps he will set an example."

Choosing my words carefully, I said, "I know Captain Krull has his faults, but I don't know enough about this proceeding to validate it. There are a number of irregularities . . . "

Ellison cut me off. "Both of you fall far short of the standard of the complete support I need to run this ship. Wait outside."

"*Dag*," I asked aloud, "are Asimov's laws still in force?"

"Yes."

Ellison laughed. "No, I can't execute you. Now go to your quarters."

✳ ❋ ✳

Ellison gave us, and two other 'recalcitrant' crew, a choice. We could be confined to quarters until the *Dag* reached Samios and turned over to the authorities as, technically, mutineers, for failing to accede to Ellison's takeover. Or we could be put aground on Haumea, with supplies, to be picked up later. One of the crew, Commtech Jensen, chose confinement to quarters.

Besides myself and Kari, only Biotech Samuel Levi chose to stay with Captain Krull.

✹ ✸ ✹

They left us with Captain Krull at the derelict robot base on the north pole in the middle of a crater-pocked field of dusty ice as hard as rock. They took the lander, of course, and our personal comps, leaving us with no outgoing communications.

We had a standard emergency kit with a hemispherical six-person vacuum tent, a field printer-refiner, and a thirty-square-meter roll-up solar array rated at ten kilowatts—which out here would generate about five watts. At least, given Haumea's 287-year orbit, the arctic summer would last longer than any of us would live.

I looked up toward the departing lander, now a blue-violet pinprick with a ghostly tail against a jet-black sky. Distant as it was, sunlight reflecting off the surrounding ice field gave more light than would allow our eyes to see stars.

Sam started rummaging through our rations. "The schlemiel didn't leave us with enough to survive," he said. "Not in this place of no return, this land of darkness and the shadow of death."

I stared at him. The Sun wouldn't set at this latitude for years.

"It's a quote. Job. That guy came out of it okay."

"Well, we aren't effing intended to survive," Kari said. "Too inconvenient. There'll be some kind of exculpatory narrative, with doctored video."

"Kari, Tony, Sam," Captain Krull said, "We are going to do much more than survive. But we have much work to do."

We all turned to him. All kinds of questions went through my head. Was he still in charge? The spaceship was gone. He was captain of nothing.

"There's 200-watt radiothermal generator at the east pole data node. That was thirty years ago, of course, but it should still be good for 100 watts or so."

We stared.

"Yah, yah, I studied lots of stuff about Haumea before we came here."

"The east pole is about 1200km away," I said. Haumea may be a 'dwarf' planet, but as someone said about Pluto, a Chihuahua is still a dog. "And the east pole is 500 km higher than the north pole. We'd have to lift everything up five hundred kilometers!"

"Yah, yah. We have a big mountain to climb. Where I come from we have lots of mountains to climb. But Haumea gravity is only a few percent and it is smooth, yah? Two Charon-sized objects merged and the heat of that melted everything, drove off most of the water but not all. For a while there is an atmosphere and an ocean, which had time to freeze. So it is sea level all over, because of hydrostatic equilibrium."

Captain Krull continued. "So we build a sled. We build a platform for the vacuum tent, a mast and struts for the array. That," he pointed at the small robot base, "is our mine for stuff to build with. Then we move, while our bellies are still full from the ship. The gravity will get lower as we go."

On Earth, I weigh about a kilonewton. Here, I weighed a bit less than fifty Newtons, maybe sixty in my vacuum gear. The emergency gear was likely another twenty or thirty.

Sam perked up. "We do have to move. Except for the base, there's nothing but ice around here to feed the printer and not much power. We'd starve after the rations are gone."

That would be the big problem. Our skin-tight suits powered themselves from our motions moving fluid through their capillaries, as well as the temperature differential between our bodies and the 30 kelvins or so radiative temperature of the surface. But our bodies had to be fed to power our suits.

"Yah. There's some bare rock at the east pole. So you'll be able to feed the printer some real regolith."

"If that field printer eats regolith," Kari said. "Okay, I'll check it out."

In spite of myself, I started thinking about the engineering problems, too.

We explored. There was a generator; its hydrogen fuel supply was long gone, but maybe we could crank it by hand. Some of the batteries worked. There were some hollows and cracks in which some dust had collected, and the ice itself was slightly dusty.

That night, we slept in the vacuum tent, a hemispherical thing with a frame on the bottom to make it flat. One inflates the sides, goes in, seals the opening and pressurizes the rest at a quarter bar, mostly oxygen, and some nitrogen. To get out, you need to pump it down, but complete vacuum is hard to achieve with the field pump; we lost some air on every cycle. Modesty consisted of sleeping bags, or looking at the wall. We had a glorified chamber pot.

* ✸ *

The next day, Kari got the printer to eat dust. Its refining operation was partly exothermic, so it didn't use as much of our scarce power as it might have otherwise. But that power had to be split in a delicate balance of printing toilet paper and printing anything else. Speaking of the TP, I can tell you from personal experience that the difference between 5% and zero gravity does matter.

We built the *Ernest Shackleton* in six days. Its mast, yardarm and runners were salvaged from pallet supports. Haumea has one of the highest albedos in the solar system, and we doubled our effective collecting area by tilting the array down slightly. We salvaged some batteries. Every Earth day, we recycled oxygen, printed some sugar, protein, and some TP; supplies went down, but not too rapidly, Sam thought.

Captain Krull drove us hard, but there was a certain exhilaration to it. We made sixty or so kilometers every day.

Navigation was simple. The east and west pole stations had launched data tethers—strong fiber-optic lines—to the poles, which were out of view to the satellites. The data had flowed overland to the dishes on either end of Haumea. We followed the data tethers.

✳ ✳ ✳

Grunt, pull. One's mind drifts while man-hauling a sledge. A few hundred kilometers below me might be a lake. I thought of fish and swimming east.

After six hundred kilometers south, we got short nights every four hours.

We came up against an exception to flatness. Pressure, apparently, tipped a huge hunk of the ice crust up about four meters, creating a wall that ran east and west to Haumea's horizon.

Captain Krull nodded. "That big impact near the east pole broke off the moons. That all happened, what, a billion years ago? Haumea continues to lose angular momentum to its moons, and the ice slips toward its center faster than the rock. So we get pressure ridges, like this."

The *Ernest Shackleton* massed maybe twenty tons—but weighed only a couple of kilonewtons.

It was my bright idea to lever up the front end to the top of the ridge and just push it on up and over. That would save time, and we were all tired. Captain Krull frowned and looked at Kari. Kari frowned and looked at me.

"If it doesn't go, we can always unload and lift it that way."

"Yah, yah, okay."

We stood two on a side, a bit forward. If we got the center up and dipped the back, the front runners ought to just clear the wall.

It worked just like that, and we were congratulating ourselves when

Kari simply went limp and slid slowly to the ice, under the runner. The sled started to slip back. Captain Krull and I were on the other side of the sled and Sam was looking in the other direction at the lip of ice beginning to give way.

"Sam," Captain Krull said, calmly but urgently, "Kari has fallen. Get her out from under the runner."

Sam turned, and it was a race. I moved as fast as I could to the back of the sled and tried to halt its slide, while Captain Krull ducked under the runners and tried to lift from below. Sam got Kari out while, in slow motion, the sled made a mockery of the captain's effort to clear two kilonewtons overhead.

The runners had some clearance, but I could not remember how much.

"I am okay, Tony," the captain said. "It's tight and you will probably have to dig me out. But see to Kari first."

She was non-responsive. By virtue of his biological training, Sam was our doctor, but this was way out of his comfort zone. He stood frozen.

As a ship's officer, I had some EMT training, but in this era of robots, hand comps, and so on, I hadn't taken any of it too seriously.

"Where's the med kit?" I asked, thinking that a place to start.

"Is she breathing?" Captain Krull asked, in gasps, from under the sled.

I couldn't see any evidence that she was. Maybe . . . some slight fogging on her faceplate. Not enough, I thought.

CPR? I could do the 'C' part from outside the space suit. Then my eye caught her suit air controls. Maybe that could take care of the 'P' part; I turned the oxygen up to max. I spread her out and pushed down hard on her chest, I hoped not too hard, where I thought her heart was. A bit faster than once a second, I remembered. I did this for about twenty seconds and was rewarded by more fogging of the faceplate. Her eyes opened, but she didn't look good.

"My gut, I want to puke. My back is killing me."

In 5% gravity? Sam showed up with the med kit. It wasn't sealed and its comp had been removed. Among other things, it was a long-range communications device, of course. But it was also the brains of the kit. I looked at its contents; right near the top were smart caps of aspirin and cardiol.

Heart attack? She didn't complain about chest pain, but when all you have is a hammer, everything looks like a nail. The space suits have a passive oral lock built into them. I put the cardiol and aspirin in, closed the cover, and continued compressing as the tube found its way into her mouth.

That was everything I could think of or remember to treat a heart attack.

For whatever reason, after a few anxious minutes, she began to breathe easier.

"Hang in there, kid," I said. "I'll be right back. Sam?"

Sam came alive and followed me to the back end of the sled.

"Captain, if we lift up the back, can you wriggle out?"

"You'll need to hold it up about five seconds, Lieutenant," he said.

I looked at Sam. He seemed puzzled for a moment, then nodded.

"Okay. One . . . two . . . three." Up the back end went. Easily at first and then my muscles started to burn.

Captain Krull shot out from under the rear in much less than five seconds.

We all got back to Kari, now sitting up.

"Geeze, what hit me?"

"We don't know," Sam said, "but we treated you for a heart attack, and you're still with us."

"Heart attack?"

"We're guessing. They vanished the kit's med comp. What did they think they were doing?"

Captain Krull interrupted. "To the problem at hand. Women having different symptoms for heart attacks, yes?"

"Oh, of course. How old are you, Kari?"

"I'm sixty-three. I know . . . I guess I can't fool Mother Nature forever."

Sixty-three, and she'd been through three weeks of backbreaking labor on short rations with inadequate sleep in not enough gravity for circulatory health.

"My sincere apologies, Lieutenant," Captain Krull said. But, in contrast to the formal words, he knelt down by her and took her hand and held his helmet next to hers. What he said, off radio, I will never know.

The captain stood and gestured to the *Ernest Shackleton* with its nose against the four-meter ice wall. "The three of us will have to take care of this the hard way. In an hour, it will be night. We should have all the cargo above the wall by then. Then we rest, then heave the frame over when again it is light."

We managed, just barely. The pinprick sun vanished from the near airless sky as if cut off by a shutter. Then, more slowly, our eyes let us see the stars.

★ ✳ ★

The ice wall was but the first hint of the much rougher terrain leading to the meridional pole. But the gravity was much lower. After another day of sledging, we discarded all the ballast, rails, mast and solar yardarm. That left about a ton of mass—two hundred newtons of weight. We simply lifted the remaining framework, with Kari on it, and carried it the remaining hundred and twenty kilometers to the pole.

The last fifty kilometers were more rock than ice, and jagged, fractured rock at that, showing little of the expected space weathering.

"It's been uncovered in the last million years, maybe," Captain Krull said. "Maybe our time scale is wrong. Or the moons have found new games to play. Chaos is like that."

"Life is like that," Sam said. "Long periods of steady, sane, stability, and then it all goes to hell."

Later, when by chance we were alone in the tent making a minor repair, Captain Krull touched my arm. "I do not pry into crew files. I know their qualifications and assignments. The rest I left to others whose job that is. I now regret that I had not looked deeply into Lieutenant Ellison's file; there may be nothing there, but I did not look. And I did not look into Lieutenant deWalt's file."

"You had visions of a relationship?"

"Yah, yah, something like that. I am forty-eight years old. She is sixty-three. God laughs at our visions."

I did not share my own visions of Kari, and I was thirty-two.

★ ✹ ★

The next day we reached the east pole station and found it had been vandalized. That wasn't totally unexpected; the lack of communications meant that some thought had gone toward our demise, and there was a bright new crater next to where the big telemetry dish had been. There was another impact near the site of the radio thermal generator, which was also missing.

Two storage sheds at the south end of the facility seemed intact, however.

Captain Krull pointed to them. "Let us see what we find. Since this base had no people to maintain it, and robots were primitive, they relied much on simple redundancy."

The result brought the first grin I ever remember seeing on Captain Krull's face. "My enemies do not research well. We have an intact backup radiothermal generator—150 watts. We can stay here a while."

★ ✹ ★

Sam enlisted my help in collecting regolith and organic salvage for the printer. It drew about a kilowatt. With a lash-up of batteries and power conditioning, he could run an hour for every ten that the RTG was on, with an allowance for other power needs.

Keeping us warm was not one of them. There was only a trace of nitrogen and argon around us.

"Think of living in the world's biggest thermos bottle. As long as we keep our floor above the rock or ice, our problem is not getting warm, it is in losing warmth by radiation at the same rate we generate it," Sam said. "But, we're still in trouble. 150 watts still isn't enough and I can't print all the food we need."

"How much power do we need?"

"We burn about 100 watts each from food and air. Even with the most efficient technology, we'd have to gather about twice that from the Sun or nuclear sources. We need better than a kilowatt, probably two. And that doesn't even address the nutrition problems. I can do sugars, simple proteins, some vitamins . . . but in a year we'll start falling apart. We're toast"

"So we just give up? We're toast so why bother?"

Sam shrugged. "Eh? Not yet. I just need to kvetch a bit."

Tiredness and fatigue kicked in for me. "Sam, I am getting a little tired of being everybody's kvetching board! Do I have a sign on my head that says 'tell me all your troubles?' Do I look like a shrink?"

"Actually, you and my uncle Benjamin could . . . " He must have seen my face. "Sorry."

"It's okay, Sam. Just not now."

✱ ❀ ✱

A week later, we all met in the pressure tent. It stank, but it was good to be out of our airtight space underwear.

"We can't survive on 160 watts," Captain Krull said.

Kari nodded. "But how about 310 watts? I'll bet there's another one of these on the west pole."

Kari was returning to her old spunky self, as long as she didn't push herself. Back in civilization, she'd be fixed up good as new in a fortnight. Here, she might drop dead tomorrow.

Sam shrugged his shoulders. "It wouldn't do it."

Captain Krull nodded. "We need to call for help. There's enough metal around that we can build a big dish, and we can use the batteries to provide the power for a brief burst."

That sounded good to me, but Kari spoke up. "Sir, Ellison thinks he's finished us off. As soon as he finds out otherwise, he'll come back to finish the job. He has to. Either that or try to leave the solar system."

"His hatred is that much?" Captain Krull asked, softly, with what seemed a sense of wonder in his voice.

"It's beyond hatred now, Captain," Kari said. "He's burned the bridges, he's staked himself out, he's painted himself into a corner, crossed the Republican."

"Rubicon," Sam said.

"Rubicon, okay, whatever. If he's found out now, he'll go to prison forever. They all will. So they will come back first and make sure we aren't talking."

"Yah, yah. So, we need to be elsewhere. For that we need more power."

"Can we convert the RTG's to actual reactors?" Sam asked.

I shook my head. "They use the wrong kind of fuel, plutonium 238. It won't sustain a chain reaction."

There was a long silence. "Maybe we have enough for one or two of us to make it," Kari said. "I've had a long life . . . "

"Quiet, Lieutenant!" Captain Krull snapped.

"Captain, we have to face . . . "

"I SAID QUIET!"

We sat in shocked silence. Kari's heart! I thought.

Captain Krull was oblivious; he had gotten his silence. "Now, we *all* make it through this or we all die. So, unless you propose a mutiny within a mutiny, that is the way it will be. My will is that we make it. Is that understood?"

There were tears in Kari's eyes, the one person in all my experience who had actually liked Captain Krull, or perhaps more than that. He had struck at her like a snake with perhaps as much forethought.

"Very good. Now, I know where there's a two-megawatt reactor," Captain Krull said.

"Huh?" we all said.

"Where?" I asked.

"Namaka."

Namaka was the inner satellite of Haumea.

"That is where the mother ship for everything on Haumea ended. It disassembled itself, of course, but its propulsion reactor should still be there."

"It may as well be on Earth's moon," Sam said.

Captain Krull frowned coldly. "Not your field, is it, Sam?"

"No, uh, sir, but I know we'd need a rocket to get there."

"Oh?" Captain Krull stared at him in a way that made me very glad he was not staring at me. That would only be a matter of a minute or so, I realized, and I was thinking furiously.

"Oy vey. Captain, it would take months to make enough rocket fuel from the power we have, and by then we would be all dead. So unless you have some kind of Indian rope trick up your sleeve . . . "

"In a way," Captain Krull said with a glimmer of a smile. "That is very much what I have in mind."

Of course! The rope trick! Our position was ideal for an orbital elevator. Haumea rotated so rapidly that its synchronous orbit was only a little ways above the elongated poles. But how would we get something even a couple hundred kilometers up?

"The mission is very redundant. For almost everything, there is an unused backup. Look for spare data tether launchers."

★ ✹ ★

A days search found two unexpended launchers. I pointed them straight up, and got one of them to work, giving us a twelve-hundred-kilometer orbital tower under tension. We printed out a tether climber—well, actually, a clothes wringer, from the emergency printer-refiner's eclectic library; the same machine might have ended up in an emergency somewhere in Earth's tropics.

"Remember always," Captain Krull said at being shown the device. "Once it is built, what a piece of equipment was *designed* to do matters not. What matters is what it can do."

We modified the *Ernest Shackleton* by adding pressure tanks to the frame, for crude cold gas maneuvering rockets.

All of an orbital tower, of course, rotates at the same rate as the planet to which it is attached. Beyond synchronous orbit, everything on the tower moves faster than orbital velocity for that altitude. It took three excruciating days in shifts to crank ourselves by hand up out to where our velocity would get us to Namaka. That was at 394,661.42 meters above Haumea's east pole. I think I will remember that number the rest of my life. I had to work it out five times on my suit calculator before Captain Krull was satisfied.

We spent several days hanging at 1.3% of an Earth gravity, with Haumea overhead, getting our position on the tether exactly right and waiting for Namaka to be in just the right place to let go.

★ ✹ ★

This leap of faith resulted, five days later, in a half-meter-per-second crash landing with dry gas tanks—but the harpoon on our underside stuck into Namaka's ice and caught us up before we bounced away.

We found the main reactor, pretty well exhausted.

We found its backup, essentially untapped.

Our last ration bars were consumed as a feast when we got it on line. The robot base station had a printer-refiner as well, much more capable than our emergency version. With Sam's help, it could print vitamins.

Kari, bless her, found a way to 'talk' to the base computer through our suit helmet displays. It was dumb in the ways of humans, but she could teach it some tricks.

I found the discarded base ship's engines. They were useless junk.

Sam found some plasma ice boring tools still attached to defunct construction robots. He thought they'd greatly reduce our ice-chopping labor.

"Those shoot out hot hydrogen plasma, with magnetic fields

focusing it into a tight stream, right?" Captain Krull asked when shown the borers.

"Yes, sir, that's how they work."

"How fast is this plasma they shoot out?"

Nobody even thought to suggest to Captain Krull that they weren't designed to be rockets. At this point, we were following him on faith and the force of his bullying personality.

After a couple of days of clever testing, we found their plasma exited at six to sixteen kilometers per second, depending on how fast we fed them water. They didn't make really great electric rockets; their efficiency was low. But they were much better than cold gas, and could get us to Samios in about six months, if we took enough ice.

So the *Ernest Shackleton* was reborn as an interplanetary spacecraft. Imagine a ladder spinning about its middle with its rungs parallel to its intended direction of motion. I lashed the reactor and generator from Namaka to one end of the ladder and our vacuum tent to the other and stuck a ball of ice, ice mining machine, and the torches in the middle. Radiator panels covered the ladder from the center to the reactor, and the solar array, all ten watts of it, filled in the rungs on the other side.

We could conceivably make Samios on short rations, but our plan was to fabricate a communications system and call for help once we were well away from Haumea.

None of us had ever made a radio, but we all knew how it worked in principle and had several low-power systems to cannibalize. We mainly needed an amplifier.

"There's probably a robot comm unit in the printing file, if I could find it," Kari said. "But the printer memory isn't designed to be searched . . . "

Captain Krull's head spun instantly.

"Maybe something else will work," Kari finished softly.

We could print Sam's organic molecules, because he knew where every atom in one of those things belonged. A radio amplifier was different.

I told them what I remembered of the subject, which wasn't much. The earliest such things used something called vacuum tubes.

"Okay, that sounds good," Captain Krull said. "We can print the parts. We'll have weeks in which to experiment. At least the vacuum part of a vacuum tube wouldn't be a problem."

Captain Krull laughed at his joke.

Sam and I laughed nervously too. Kari kind of smiled, but there was a tear in her eye.

Then something quite unlikely happened. Captain Krull apparently noticed the tear, and said very softly, "Yah, yah. Sometimes things, they get so tense one must laugh or cry. For me, I had better laugh." He looked around at all of us. "You must not see me cry, yah?"

✶ ✷ ✶

We didn't quite have enough thrust to lift off of Namaka. With Kari handling the cold gas thruster valves, the three of us men got upside down below the ship and with our feet securely gecro'd to the girders, we pushed the little moon away from the *Ernest Shackleton* as hard as we could. That, we figured, should give us about ten meters per second up to start with.

Without radar or anything like it, it was hard to tell how successful our maneuver was and Kari kept her hand on the gas thruster controls. But once we were about four kilometers up, we seemed to draw away. At about three and a half hours, Captain Krull figured that we'd reached escape velocity, judging by the change in size of a crater below.

Navigation was simple. We found Ice Chip, blinking brightly every three hours, with a salvaged robot's camera. This far out from the Sun, any interplanetary trajectory is close to a straight line, so we just pointed at it.

Which was almost our undoing.

"Up! Everyone! Keep the lights off!"

I groaned and opened my eyes. A few red equipment diodes provided enough light for my dark-adapted eyes to see Kari rapidly shove herself into her dirty spacesuit.

"What is this?" Captain Krull asked.

"They are coming to kill us, I think," Kari said, as if reporting the unchanging outside temperature.

Captain Krull abandoned the modesty of his sleepsack for the tent window.

"Toward Samios," Kari said, handing him the camera, "it's very, very faint, but it's blinking every forty-five seconds."

I sat up. The *Dag* normally rotated every ninety seconds, but it had two outboard hulls.

"Suits, everyone," Captain Krull said. He said it unhurriedly, but there was tension in his voice. "Tony, you will have to take down the reactor. Kari, kill the plasma thrusters, god help us they will start again. Then kill our spin and keep us pointed at that blinking thing, wings edge on. Sam, start pumping the tent down, then get your suit on."

"Oy vey, first things first," he complained but moved quickly to the tent controls.

Pumps soon started whirring. It would take about ten minutes to get the tent down to a millibar; we'd dump the rest of the air. I concentrated on getting into my suit; I can't breathe a millibar.

I didn't have to ask why to take down the reactor. The radiator was an infrared beacon. But it would take an hour or more to get everything down to merely room temperature. It would still be noticeable at 300 kelvins, but not a beacon. Our only real hope was that they wouldn't look in our direction, or at least wouldn't be expecting to see anything.

"You all know what you have to do," Captain Krull said. "Radio silence from now on." His voice was starting to get a bit tinny. He put his helmet on.

The reactor take-down required turning valves on the center end of the radiator. We hadn't taken time to automate that; except for Kari, we hadn't expected to have to go non-critical. One would not normally go outside alone, but this was decidedly un-normal. Despite the rush, I took extra care to keep my carabiners on the frame as I moved up to the center.

The ice-mining bots had done a pretty good job of hollowing out our fuel iceberg; we were very near the turnaround, with only a third of the ice left.

The engines and the radiator controls and the power supplies all sat bolted to a metal grid salvaged from the floor of the utility shed on the east pole. The spin gravity was almost negligible this near the spin center. I brachiated over to the reactor controls and hit the scram button. At the end of the other wing, drums rotated, neutrons were absorbed, and the reaction went subcritical.

Now I had to cut the radiator flow off at just the right speed. Too fast and the reactor core would melt. Too slow and the working fluid would freeze up in the radiator pipes. There was no manual on this, but I knew it would take one point five rotations to close each valve. I settled for a quarter rotation every five minutes, and hoped.

Kari kept our 'nose' pointed at the *Dag*, minimizing the radiator exposure. This put me on the other side, unable to see our adversary for all the ice in between us. Turn the wheel.

Not moving, I started to get a bit chilly. I touched my toes about twenty times to build up some heat.

Turn the wheel.

The plasma torch . . . it would run for a few minutes on batteries. Long enough to cut the old *Dag* to shreds. It would take just a few minutes to unbolt them.

Turn the wheel.

The men and women aboard her had been coworkers, friends, and in a couple of cases lovers. All their lives, for mine? Could I do that?

I looked at the beast. It microwaved water into atomic ions and directed the exhaust with magnetic fields.

I nearly broke radio silence then and there.

Instead, I turned the wheel. Nuclear gods must be served.

In reality, I did not have to wait long. Captain Krull and the others joined me; we would all wait out the closest approach in the ice shell. We would not be able to see them, but they would not be able to see us. The deflated tent might make them think the best (for them) had happened.

I put my helmet against Captain Krull's. "The plasma is heated by microwaves . . . "

\* ✹ \*

The *Dag Hammarskjold* missed us by no more than two hundred kilometers on its return to Haumea. For all we could tell, its crew remained blissfully unaware of our existence.

We cobbled together a radio, modulating one of the torch microwave heaters and, about a hundred days out from Namaka, I called Thera.

"You get to call your girlfriend," Sam said. "I should be so lucky, I should be so lucky."

Captain Krull laughed for the first time that I remembered since his 'trial.'

"Sam," I said, "she's a cop."

Then Captain Krull reached over to touch Kari. "We will make it now, I think," he said.

After a long time, without smiling, but relaxing ever so slightly, Kari put her hand over his.

"Yah, yah, we will make it."

\* ✹ \*

The relatively huge, beam-boosted Cislunar Republic Spaceship, CLRSS *Elizabeth Reynolds* came up behind our ramshackle vehicle. It was a sleek, tri—hulled, ring-winged construction, obviously able to use an atmosphere, if available. My mouth watered to see it.

"So, we are rescued by our enemies," Kari said. "We could have made it to Samios."

"Yah, yah. But this situation has its own definition of friends and enemies," Captain Krull said. "Politics aside, we are all spacefarers. We live by doing things right. Stow everything properly, as if we are to come back."

"I should live so long," Sam said. "I should live so long."

But he tidied up, tethered down, shut lids and closed valves just like the rest of us. Someone, Captain Krull must have thought, would come back to the *Ernest Shackleton* and judge him by what they saw. Whatever his faults, they would see Captain Karl Krull's determination in this ramshackle ship. They would see the discipline that held us together and alive for two months. I had no problem with that, but I hoped that a few years in vacuum would ensure that in some distant future, they would not judge us by what they smelled.

I powered the reactor down again, but our rescuers were still very careful. They came in from the front along our spin axis, matched our one-sixth-g spin rate and grabbed our 'ladders' with a couple of robot arms. Thus secured, they sent a pinnace, which dropped lines down to our tent. We deflated, emerged, and allowed ourselves to be drawn up and aboard the small tubular craft.

Once aboard the *Lisa*, we made use of the facilities in the locker room immediately next to the airlock. The joy on Kari's face lit up the whole room. There we found that Captain Krull had somehow managed to keep a clean, lightweight ISA coverall with him throughout the entire ordeal. The rest of us made do with ill-fitting CLR utility coveralls. Only then did we accede to meeting our rescuers.

Captain Duluth, a short, muscular woman of about seventy years, received us with full honors. Then she had a private meeting with Captain Krull while the rest of us enjoyed recounting our tale to the crew of the *Lisa* and getting caught up on the fate of the mutineers.

Which, to this day, is unknown. Their stay at Samios was brief; Thera hadn't been fooled by Krull's trial and scheduled their big interferometer to check out the site of the 'crash' that had supposedly killed us. Before she could, Ellison had dumped the documentary crew and headed out again on a 'rescue' mission. The *Dag* is still out there, somewhere.

And needs to stay there for the rest of the mutineers' lives. Tech Jensen was not on the ship when it arrived at Samios.

Captain Krull asked Captain Duluth if he and Kari could take the *Ernest Shackleton* on into Samios, after suitable repairs. Saner heads prevailed, however; fix it up as one might, the *Ernie* was not to be considered spaceworthy by any reasonable standard. Kari actually seemed more disappointed than Captain Krull.

We had our final meeting on Samios, after all the interviews, the trial—some of the documentary crew had participated in the mutiny—and the wedding. I kissed the bride, for the first and only time in our two-year- long and occasionally all too intimate relationship. We had shared a chamber pot in a vacuum tent, a circumstance that did not encourage any other kind of nether sharing.

Unless, of course, one is hopelessly smitten. In a rare example of diplomatic ice-thawing, Captain Duluth married Kari deWalt and Karl Krull. They headed inward, him to take charge of a prison in the Earth-Sun L1 orbit, she to be its chief engineer. Media hero or not, Karl Krull had lost a very expensive spaceship, and the ISA did not want any unlucky captains. He would never command an ISA spaceship again. But no terrestrial before the merger of the CLRSS and the ISA into the Interplanetary Administration would ever come close to his legendary career.

I stayed on Samios, recording this, and waiting for an opportunity, perchance, to salvage the *Ernest Shackleton* when it bullets by the big space colony.

Sam decided to stay with me a while. He dreams about building an even more remote space colony around Proxima Centauri, a new promised land too far from terrorists and tourists to worry anybody. At a tavern on a river leading to the equatorial sea of Samios, he hoisted a glass to Thera and me.

"To Captain Krull, who saved our lives and our honor. Nobody else could have got us off that planet, made us make that spaceship, and gotten us back to civilization alive. And I should live so long as to ever be within an astronomical unit of him again!"

I had to laugh and raise my glass to that.

# STORY NOTES

Haumea (Ha-oo-meh-a) is the next very real and bizarre "dwarf" planet beyond Pluto. It is shaped like a rugby ball, or Aussie rules football and spins on its side. It has (at least) two moons as described. The story has its roots in reality as well: the infamous "Mutiny on the Bounty" and the epic open-boat voyage of Captain Bligh and the loyal crew members to Timor. But this is not Bligh's story; Captain Krull has some similarities of character but is his own person in many other ways, and we meet him toward the end rather than the beginning of his career. And, of course, a woman is involved.

. The large space colony, only (!) an astronomical unit or so away, is a stretch, but serves notice that solar energy can still be a player 40 AU from the Sun, if you have enough aluminized Mylar, or the equivalent. It needs to be near a small kuiperoid because, regardless of how good one's engineering, there will always be some leakage.

Some of the details in this story will seem quaint to readers eighty years from now, and others may not have happened yet. As with realistic science fiction in general, the background of this story is something that plausibly could happen, not necessarily something the author believes *will* happen. Events here may be more dramatic than what one normally encounters in real life, but that is true of fiction in general; we want you to read this stuff! We select from a generally plausible future the stories and events that are most dramatic and entertaining, confident that the real future will provide events that are just as exciting, though not those described here. Apollo 11 was not Verne's *From the Earth to the Moon*, nor Heinlein's *Destination Moon* script. But similarities abound because both were built on a foundation of natural science and not magic.

Like any fiction, these stories are tales of people with faults and courage, bad luck and determination, struggling with their inner and outer environments. But Haumea and all of these stories are also thought experiments about the future. We are constantly asking: Where do we want to go? Where do we *not* want to go? and Where do we think we *might* go? The number of answers is incalculable, but I hope that these stories, at least in some approximation, can be counted among them.

G. David Nordley, January 2015

www.ingramcontent.com/pod-product-compliance
Lightning Source LLC
Chambersburg PA
CBHW032138170626
46808CB00006B/2287